MW00984820

HARD BYTE

MISHA BELL

♠ Mozaika Publications ♠

Copyright © 2021 Misha Bell
www.mishabell.com

Published by Mozaika Publications, an imprint of Mozaika LLC.
www.mozaikallc.com

Cover by Najla Qamber Designs
www.najlaqamberdesigns.com

Photography by Wander Aguiar
www.wanderbookclub.com

ISBN: 978-1-63142-648-3
Paperback ISBN: 978-1-63142-649-0

Chapter One

"The Devil is about to turn my life's work into porn." I give my twin a pleading look. "You have to teach me how to pick locks."

Gia blinks at me. "What in Houdini's balls are you talking about?"

"Lock picking. Teach me."

She shakes her head as if to clear it, then opens the door wider. "Come inside and explain."

"Fine." Respecting my sister's germaphobia, I bypass hugs and kisses as I gingerly step into the brownstone she shares with her million roommates. She leads me to her room, and as we walk, I fight the temptation to fix the myriad messes all around.

"Sit." She points at a chair in the corner, next to a mannequin.

Is she nuts? That chair is four-legged, the worst kind. I prefer office chairs, as they usually have five legs, or barstools, since they tend to have one or three.

How would she like it if I asked her to lick a subway pole?

A mischievous grin quirks her dark-lipsticked mouth. "My bad. Not a prime number of legs. What was I thinking? Your brain could've melted."

Hiding my eye roll, I walk past a deck of cards and other magician's paraphernalia strewn all over the nearby surfaces, not stopping until I'm next to a legless beanbag chair. "You mind?"

Shrugging, Gia takes a deck of cards out of her pocket and hands it to me by the tips of her fingers. "Would you feel more at ease if I gave you this deck to organize?"

Plopping into the chair, I narrow my eyes at the deck. "Fifty-two?"

With a sigh, she tosses one of the cards on a nearby desk—as if it weren't a mess already. "Fifty-one now."

"Fifty-one isn't a prime."

She peers at the deck. "It's not?"

"Three times seventeen is fifty-one. How did you pass fourth grade?"

"We probably had you pretend to be me to ace the math test." She drops four more cards on the desk. "Is forty-seven better?"

"Thank you." I take the cards carefully—God forbid I touch her hygienic majesty with my cooties. "What did you want me to explain before you teach me?"

"Start with the life's work part." She sits on the

improperly legged abomination. "I didn't realize you had one. Is it the virtual pet stuff you're always showing me?"

"Kind of." I begin sorting the cards in the obvious logical manner: number cards that are primes first, followed by the rest. "I didn't get a chance to tell you before, but I've been working with the pediatric wing of the NYU Langone hospital. If they hear I'm involved with porn——"

"Back up. Working with them how?"

"I've been beta testing my VR pet project as a type of therapy for children in long-term care." I look up from my sorting and into a face identical to the one I see in the mirror every day: oval-shaped with sharp cheekbones, a strong nose, and wide blue eyes. Of course, unlike my entertainer sibling, my hair is its natural strawberry blond hue, while she's turned hers darker than a black hole. I also don't wear that much makeup. Her smoky eyes would make a raccoon fall in lust, and her foundation is pale enough for a vampire geisha. "The idea is to reduce the kids' pain and anxiety," I continue as she nods approvingly.

"That's not bad for your life's work. So how does the devil's porn fit in?"

I glance at the mess all around me. "Do you mind?"

Gia heaves a sigh. "If it gets you talking faster, be my guest."

As I get up and begin tidying, I calm enough to articulate my thoughts. "I haven't told you this either, but my company got into financial trouble a while back and Morpheus Group bought us."

She wrinkles her nose. "Never heard of them."

I pick up a top hat of the kind a magician's rabbit might leap out of—not that Gia would ever risk touching something happy to eat its own feces. "I hadn't either until they acquired us. I think it was formed right before the takeover." I put the hat next to Gia's headband, mentally designating the spot as *headgear*. "At first, they asked for specs from our VR headset and gloves and disappeared, leaving us to do our thing as though nothing had changed. But we've just learned that they're planning to integrate the headset and gloves with a special suit they've created, one meant to make your whole body feel things inside VR."

She looks intrigued. "Feel things as in… sex things?"

"That's what the rumors around the office say." I pick up what looks like a fake thumb and put it on a shelf next to her gloves, designating the spot as *pertaining to appendages.*

"Hmm." She scratches her chin. "Sex in VR. No germs. No touching. No complications. Can I get one of those suits?"

"You should get a real man," I say, and instantly regret it—the last thing I want is to sound like Mom.

Gia arches her dark eyebrows and mimics the British accent I had to rid myself of after my study abroad. "As they would say in your beloved England, that's the pot calling the kettle black."

She's right. I'm no expert when it comes to men or sex—my one and only real relationship was with a guy who later came out as gay.

My face must change because she says, "Sorry, Holly. Didn't mean to venture there. Next thing you know, I'll go full Octomom and tell you how much you should yearn for 'a sexual union.'"

I cringe. I hate the nickname she uses for our mom. Forgetting respect for one's elders, it's simply not accurate. Mom gave birth to the two of us, followed by our sextuplet sisters. An accurate moniker would be either Bimom (or is it Dumom?) or Sexamom—though, granted, none of those sound great either. Of course, if I'm honest, the main reason I don't like the *octo-* prefix is that it's a reminder of us being eight sisters, as opposed to some normal amount, like seven, five, or eleven.

"—you need some good old-fashioned lovin'," Gia is saying in her best imitation of Mom's contralto when I tune back in to her jabbering.

Grinning, I do my own impersonation of our embarrassing parental unit. "Orgasms alleviate stress, help with insomnia, ease pain, make you live longer, stimulate your brain, keep you looking younger… Oh, and can bring about world peace."

Did she notice I put seven items on that list?

Gia shudders. "Don't forget how helpful orgasms are when one is trying to get a pig preggers."

Ugh, yeah. Even though I'm not as squeamish as Gia, I've also been traumatized by Mom's humble-bragging stories about her husbandry skills. One time, Mom said she brought Petunia—a piggie who was like a pet to us growing up—to orgasm during an artificial insemination session. Yeah. Not the image you want to pop into your head when you see bacon.

Realizing we've gotten way off topic, I pin my sister with an intent stare. "So can you teach me what I need or not?"

She drums her black-painted nails on her thigh. "You still haven't explained the whole devil thing."

Ah. That. I pick up a book on card cheating and stick it into a random empty spot on her bookshelf—if I try to sort her library by year of publication, she'll get upset again and refuse to help me. "According to yet more rumors around the office," I say, "the new owners are brother and sister. Apparently, their last name is Chortsky."

"Apparently? They haven't introduced themselves?"

I pick up a glossy magician's cup and put it next to an empty coffee mug on the desk. "Nope. I've been working via email with a guy named Robert Jelly-heim. Anyway, when I searched online for people named Chortsky, I found a Vlad Chortsky who owns a software company and an Alex Chortsky who owns a video game studio. No mention of a sister, no pictures of either men, no social media presence. The only useful thing I learned is that the word *chort*—the root of their family name—means *the devil* or *demon* in Russian."

"Ah," Gia says. "So 'the Devil' is just your nickname for whoever happens to be the elusive owner of Morpheus Group. How does that lead to lock picking? You want to take a crack at your chastity belt?"

My heartbeat speeds up at the thought of the lock picking, and I tidy faster to calm myself down. "There's an office on my floor where the integrated VR suits got delivered yesterday." I pick up three metal linking rings and put them on the coffee table next to her keychain. "It's locked. I want to get into that office and see if the rumors are true."

She frowns. "Why?"

"So I can do something about it… if I have to."

Her frown deepens. "Do what?"

I take a flash drive out of my pocket. "The rumor mill claims the owners are meeting with some big-shot venture capital firm in a few days to demo the work they've done. They must need a new round of funding. My hope is that if a computer virus ruins this demo, it will stall the porn project and I'll be able to finalize my arrangement with the hospital before the Devil finds another source of money."

"So you're going to be breaking and entering to commit corporate sabotage?"

I squeeze the USB stick in my palm. "Hardly. I work there."

"But you're planning on releasing a virus. Isn't that a crime?"

I pocket the USB. "I borrowed some tools from Dad. If caught, I can claim I was testing our security."

Our father is a penetration tester—which isn't what it sounds like. He simulates cyberattacks on willing companies to identify their systems' weaknesses and strengths.

Gia studies me with a worried expression. "You're a sucky liar."

"I plan to disable the cameras in the office. No one will ever know what happened."

She jumps to her feet. "I don't know. Maybe I shouldn't encourage this madness."

"If you don't help, I'm going in with a crowbar."

She gives me a once-over. "That's a bluff. You hate violence."

I put on a determined expression. "I can hurt a bloody door if I have to."

She chews on her lip, then sighs. "This will cost you."

Yes! If she's bargaining, this is going to happen.

"What do you want?" I ask, belatedly reining in my oh-so-easy-to-exploit enthusiasm.

She sits back down. "You will stop going Marie Kondo on my stuff."

"Done." I reluctantly drop her phallic-shaped magic wand back onto the mess of objects on the desk. It's not like I know how to categorize it anyway—apart from putting it next to some dildo.

"And you'll owe me two favors in the future, no questions asked."

I almost reach for the wand again but stop myself in time. "Do you also want the keys to my place? Or maybe a blank check?"

She shrugs. "If our roles were reversed, you'd ask for even more."

That's so not true, but arguing would be fruitless. "How about you tell me what the favors are, so I can see if it's worth it?"

"No deal. How about we split the difference? One favor I will ask for now, one at a later date."

Damn, she's good at poker faces. "What's the 'now' favor?"

"Have you already had your lunch with our parents?"

I grit my teeth. "Yes." It's clear what she wants. Our folks are in town, and naturally, they won't leave until they give a painful lecture to both of their eldest daughters on the dangers of spinsterhood.

"You will dress as me and take my place at the lunch," Gia says, confirming my suspicions. "And you will *not* pass on any sex tips you're likely to acquire."

Bollocks. I was hoping she'd use me in a magic trick—having a twin is pretty helpful when you want to display teleportation powers and the like.

"When is the lunch?" I ask.

Looking too gleeful for my liking, she gives me the details.

The time is smack in the middle of my mid-day

flossing, but as much as I hate breaks in my schedule, I don't object. Gia won't be sympathetic.

"What's the other favor?" I ask, dreading it already.

She smirks. "Nice try. I'll tell you that when I know myself."

"Fine. You've got yourself a deal—assuming you actually *can* teach me how to pick a lock."

She stands up. "Can the sextuplets drive even Gandhi to violence?"

Oh yes, they can. Abhorrence of violence is why I limit my exposure to the litter of evil. I love them dearly, of course, but combined, they're too much for my psyche. I part envy, part pity Gia for cavorting with them outside of family holidays. I'm nowhere near that brave.

Getting up, she rummages in a drawer and takes out a pair of gloves, a leather case, and a collection of locks.

"Put these on." She hands me the gloves.

I put them on with an eye roll. "There. Now I won't leave germs on your precious equipment."

She thrusts the leather case into my hands. "I'm giving you gloves so you learn how to pick a lock while wearing them. Or do you want to leave your prints all over the crime scene?"

I unzip the case and stare at the tools inside.

If I can pass the dreaded Advanced Artificial Intelligence course at Cambridge, I can do this.

Hopefully.

"First, let me tell you how a pin tumbler lock works," Gia says, gesturing at a lock made of glass where the pins and other bits are exposed.

She proceeds to open the lock both with a key and with her tools, making it look easy.

"Now this is a tension wrench." She hands me a metal thingy and tells me what to do with it. Then she gives me a pick and explains how to use that.

"Sounds reasonable," I say when the lecture is blissfully over. "Let me try."

Her grin is evil. "Go ahead."

I'm famous for my meticulousness when it comes to following directions of any kind, so, like a robot, I execute Gia's instructions to the letter. Yet my attempt fails, much to my twin's delight.

Grr. Picking a lock seems to be more of an art than a science.

Two hours and dozens of snide comments from Gia later, I improve, though I'm not yet confident enough to proceed with the heist.

Finally, Gia says, "I think you've got it. At least there's not much more I can teach you. Go home and play with the locks on your own."

"Okay." I hide the tools of my newly acquired trade. "I'll call if I have any questions."

To my surprise, she actually puts away the locks we were using instead of tossing them onto the still-cluttered desk. "Think about canceling the whole thing, will you? Don't be tempted by the minimalism of prison life."

"I will," I lie as we step out of her room.

"And text me updates." She leads me past the messy living room to the front door. "Also call me if you need me to post bail."

"Cheers," I say—only to realize my mistake when Gia's grin widens to Joker levels.

"'Tis my pleasure, guv'nor," she deadpans with a thick Cockney accent. "Don't forget about luncheon with Mama and Papa."

"I won't," I grumble.

"Jolly good." She waves her hand in a queenly fashion. "Ta-dah."

"Thank you and goodbye," I enunciate with a perfect American accent.

She locks the door, and I hear her chuckling behind it.

I can't believe that of all my siblings, *she* is the lesser evil.

Getting home, I practice lock picking deep into the night, and when I fall asleep, I dream about it.

By Monday morning, I feel as ready as I ever will.

It's time.

I will get to work, wait for everyone to leave, and proceed with Operation Break-In.

Chapter Two

*L*ike the bloody watched pot that never boils, my coworkers refuse to leave for the day.

I bet they're not even working.

In hindsight, this was a flaw in my plan. Since I'm the Chief Technology Officer here, lots of people want to show off how hard they work by staying late —especially in light of the takeover.

As if summoned by the thought of the takeover, an email from Robert Jellyheim, my equivalent from Morpheus Group, hits my inbox.

Crap. Are they somehow on to me?

But no. He's letting me know that they plan to ramp up the integration soon, and that I'll meet him and the upper management face to face shortly.

This must be why the suits got delivered. I have to say, the Devil is pretty confident about getting this round of funding.

Well, we'll see about that—assuming my stupid teammates ever leave, that is.

My stomach rumbles, giving me an idea. Maybe they'll finally leave if they think I'm gone for the day? And if anyone views the cameras later, they'll see me come back with food—perfectly natural.

Grabbing my stuff, I stomp toward the lift—I mean, elevator.

Wait. What if my coworkers don't notice?

Oh, I know. I stop by a few desks and make them more orderly, killing two birds with one stone. By the time I add an extra pen to a cup that contained only four, I'm certain I've been noticed.

Excellent. I head for the elevator, and when I get inside, I press all the buttons for the floors with prime numbers, a luxury I allow myself when I ride alone.

My daily lunch are the nineteen pieces of ravioli I bring from home, but whenever I need to have dinner at work, I always go to the same Japanese place—Miso Hungry. My order with them is always the same as well: miso soup with forty-seven cubes of tofu and seventeen pieces of scallion, and three avocado rolls with one piece held back in order to make the total a proper prime of twenty-three.

After all, one of the things that separates humans from animals is our desire for order and predictability, or at least that's what I say to Gia when she teases me about my idyllic, clockwork-like life.

"To go?" the hostess asks as soon as she spots me.

I nod. "Yep, takeout."

As she rushes to the sushi bar to give the chef my order, I scan the almost empty restaurant—and am stunned to see a man scanning *me* with his piercing, cerulean-blue eyes.

And what a man.

Perfectly symmetrical face.

Silky-looking jet-black hair.

Broad, athletic shoulders.

The cheekbones of an angel and the most kissable lips I've ever seen.

The only thing that keeps him from perfection is the scruffy stubble on his face and the disarray of the black locks on his head.

I fight the urge to sprint over to him, slick back that unruly hair, and steal a sushi knife from the chef to shave that gorgeous face.

Yeah, okay. I must admit I have something of a fetish for clean-shaven guys. When I first saw pictures of Henry Cavill as Superman, all neat and proper, I wanted to touch myself. But I was *not* a happy camper when he took on his role as the scruffy, mustachioed villain in *Mission: Impossible – Fallout*. The $25 million DC Films spent on the CGI removal of his mustache during the filming of *Justice League* was money well spent if you ask me. I can't wait for a day when technology will allow me to delete mustaches from all the faces on my screens.

Bugger. I'm still gawking at him—a situation made that much worse by the fact that he's not alone at his table. With him is a woman as gorgeous as he is.

And unlike her scruffy yet sexy beau, she's extremely put-together, with impeccable makeup and perfectly styled black hair.

As I tear my gaze away, I catch the bastard smirking.

What a cad. What a rake.

The hostess comes back with my takeout, and I spot the stranger whispering something to his beautiful date.

The woman gives me a once-over and starts to stand up.

Crap. Is she going to confront me for ogling her man?

I loathe violence of any kind, but particularly one that could involve me. Frantically snatching my order from the hostess, I thrust some cash into her hands and bolt out of Miso Hungry.

My heart rate is still through the roof when I return to the office. I guess getting turned on by gorgeous strangers isn't a good prelude to a proper heist.

At least there's good news here. As I hoped, the floor is finally empty. I bet the frauds scattered like quail as soon as the elevator doors slid shut behind me.

Putting aside the food—I've lost my appetite at the thought of what I'm about to do—I pretend to write some code before launching the camera-killing script I've prepared.

Is this really happening?

Do I have the ovaries to do this?

I square my shoulders.

It *is* happening. I refuse to chicken out.

Ignoring the tightness in my stomach, I get up and hurry to my destination.

When I get to the door, I glance at the hopefully disabled camera.

It's now or never.

Chapter Three

I jiggle the door handle in case someone's unlocked it.

Nope.

I get my tools and start picking.

Blimey. It's not yielding.

Is this lock different from the ones I practiced on? Or is it my trembling hands?

I take in a deep breath and count to seven.

Hands steadier, I pick the lock again until something inside it clicks.

Finally.

Entering, I examine the large office. On the desk are a high-end monitor and an ergonomic keyboard, next to the desk is a top-of-the-line executive office chair (five-legged, as is proper), and in the corner is a small leather couch.

Is this the Devil's future lair? Or the She-Devil's?

Ignoring that issue for now, I examine the suits.

Split into pink "female" and larger blue "male" models, these are clearly prototypes. Some even have parts attached with duct tape. There are also instruction sheets hanging from them, along with a label that states "Sterile."

I'm no Gia about such things, but even I feel grateful about the sterile bit—the suit is going on my body, after all. I also feel a pang of guilt. Once I put one on, it will no longer be sterile, which sucks for the next woman who'll try it on.

Maybe I can leave a note after I'm done?

First things first. I grab the instructions sheet from the pink suit that looks closest to my size.

"Adjust Velcro straps to fit your body" is the first step.

I'm blessed with prime numbers when it comes to my girth and height, so thanks to the labeled straps, this step is a breeze.

"Undress" is the second instruction.

Hmm. Maybe this suit should buy me dinner first?

I walk over to lock the door. Do cleaning people have keys to this office? Hopefully not. Either way, they're not due for a couple more hours—I looked it up when planning this heist.

Stripping in the workplace feels extremely awkward, but since instructions command it, I do it, leaving my clothes neatly folded on the back of the office chair.

"Lie down or sit as you put on the suit," the next instruction advises. "Start with legs, then body, then gloves. The headset is last."

I sit on the couch, the leather icy on my naked bottom, and wriggle into the suit according to the instructions. Then I adjust everything to make sure it's snug.

The headset turns on, and a virtual reality dashboard appears in the air in front of me. The user interface is similar to the one my team had designed for this exact headset, but with obvious tweaks—must be the work of Robert Jellyheim and his team.

There's only a single app icon—"Demo"—in the dashboard at the moment.

Raising my gloved hand, I jab a finger at it.

The suit comes to life and squeezes my body tight, creating the sensation of a hug. At the same time, I find myself in a white room with two orbs hanging in the air, and two lines of text hovering above them: "Design partner" and "Use defaults."

"Design partner" sounds like something a porn app would say, so I click that.

Two more orbs show up with the next choice: "Male" or "Female."

Chances of this being porn rise.

I opt for male, since that's what I'm attracted to, and the white room fills up with disembodied male heads.

Huh. Okay. Books on user interface design don't

cover how to avoid making your software creepy—an oversight, clearly. Unless you're making a game about ghosts, disembodied heads are a bad idea.

With a wave of my hand, I summon each head to me so I can take a closer look at the faces.

Very nice. Though not as realistic as in real life, these are the best that current technology allows—Morpheus Group must work with some talented artists.

After some deliberation, I choose a head with a symmetrical face sporting dreamy blue eyes and chiseled features.

"Change chin?" the interface asks me next.

I do so, making it stronger.

"Add facial hair?"

Hell no.

"Change cheekbones?" is the next choice.

I make them sharper, more defined.

"Change eye color?"

I go for a darker shade of blue—cerulean, to be exact.

Next, I swap the short blond hair for black and silky—neatly slicked back, as I like.

Now a disembodied but very attractive head hovers in the air.

Is it wrong that I'm now more turned on than creeped out?

Wait a second.

The head I've designed looks suspiciously like the

one attached to the scorching hot stranger at Miso Hungry. This version is just clean-shaven and lacks a body.

Thanks, subconscious. Now I feel like a total perv.

"Upper body type" is the next choice.

The creepy feeling comes back as the hottie's head flies to the side, and a bunch of headless and legless torsos appear.

Since I'm not sure if I should continue recreating the guy from the restaurant—and because I haven't seen him naked—I go for a muscular, broad-shoul-dered torso with washboard abs. Because why not?

Once chosen, the torso attaches to the head.

I study the legless apparition. Is it weird that I already want to have my way with him? Is it even a *him* without the lower body?

Swallowing audibly, I touch the virtual pecs.

Damn. The glove makes the touch feel real—which should be no surprise as I was part of the team that made this technology possible. Yet I am surprised. When working on the gloves, my priority was to make petting a fluffy, cuddly creature feel as realistic as possible, so sex and the accompanying human skin sensations were the last thing on my mind.

More torso choices follow. I leave his biceps and other muscles as they are and opt out of nipple pierc-ings and tats.

When the next choice shows up, I blink at it for a couple seconds.

If I had any doubts left, they're gone now.

This *is* going to lead to porn.

The space around me is covered with cocks.

Big. Small. Hard. Flaccid. Fat. Thin. Veiny. Smooth. Straight. Crooked. Deep purple. Pale pink. Green and blue? Someone had clearly taken a perverse pleasure in creating as much variety as humanly possible. Speaking of human, some of the choices don't seem to be of my species—not unless there are guys out there hung like unicorns.

This reminds me of the famous scene from *The Matrix* when Neo asked for "Guns. Lots of guns." Only this is penises. Wait, is that the plural, or is it just penis, like glasses and deer? No. That doesn't sound right. Maybe it's peni, as in fungi? No, that only applies to Latin-based words that end with -us, which penis doesn't—it just sounds like it does. It might be penes—but that sounds too much like the plural for penne pasta. I'll have to check all this when I have access to the internet again.

Oblivious to proper nomenclature, the shlongs dance around me, some happily, some downright threateningly—all clearly eager to be chosen.

I close my eyes. It's hard to concentrate like this... very hard.

I should quit now. These disembodied dicks are my proof, after all.

Hard proof.

Yet for some reason, I can't bring myself to end this VR session. I'm sure it has nothing to do with the epic dry spell I've been experiencing. Or that I've designed a replica of the hot stranger from Miso Horny... I mean, Miso Hungry.

No. Nothing so improper.

I work with VR, so this is purely a professional curiosity.

Yeah, that's it. This is about my job.

I open my eyes and gesticulate at the cocks. It's a stiff competition—there are so many, it takes me ten minutes to finally settle on one: a (hopefully) human one, extra-large and not too veiny.

Does the inspiration for this design have a cock like this? No clue, and I'm unlikely to ever find out... or put it in me... or lick it... or suck it.

The cock perches in its rightful place below the torso, and the place fills up with enough balls to generate a small nation's worth of testosterone.

Does anyone really care about testicles enough to need this much variety?

Eager to see the next phase of this demo, I grab a pair of balls at random, then chose legs equally fast.

This is when the next choice fills up the room: butts.

Lots of butts.

Round-shaped. Heart-shaped. Square-shaped. V-shaped. Muscular and not. With buttholes and, for some reason, without. With dimples and without. The choices aren't as exhaustive as they were with the cocks but close.

I choose the first tight tush I see and wonder if there's going to be more choices—like livers or tonsils.

But no. Everything finally attaches, and my freshly designed virtual boyfriend starts dancing—channeling *Magic Mike*.

Damn. My ovaries high-five each other as I shamelessly ogle the digital perfection. There might even be drool pooling in the corner of my mouth—and other types of wetness in my private places.

Whoever designed this is an evil genius, especially given how little time has passed since the takeover. If they had to sell their soul to the Devil, I'd say it might've been worth it. Or did the Wicked One do this personally? It would be in character for the Tempter to create the ultimate weapon of sexual sin.

I'm distracted from my pseudo-theological musings by a speech bubble that pops up above the head of the no-longer-dancing-but-no-less-mouthwatering digital specimen.

"Do you want me to give you a taste of what the suit can do?" it asks. "Yes or no."

I choose "yes," and the guy teleports over to me, getting so close that his jutting erection presses against my belly.

Wow. The suit creates a sensation of pressure that's eerily accurate.

"Continue?" another thought bubble asks.

My finger is unsteady as I choose "yes."

My digital partner cups my breast with his hand.

I gasp. The touch feels luxuriously real—even accounting for the hormones wrecking my brain's ability to have rational observations.

Another "Continue?" later, he lightly squeezes my nipple.

Double wow. The squeeze is realistic enough to send a fresh surge of need down under.

Un-bloody-believable.

"Continue?" the evil thought bubble asks.

My "yes" is reluctant, and as I spot him reaching for my lady bits, I instinctively catch his wrist—which proves just how realistic this all seems.

Hmm. His wrist feels real in my hand, but the action itself was wonky. There seems to be some work required to integrate the gloves with the suit.

Yet another air bubble appears above his head. "Do you want to sample the cunnilingus phase? Yes or no."

"Are you kidding me?" I ask out loud.

The bubble doesn't go away—there's obviously no voice recognition in the suit (unlike in my VR pet project).

How far am I willing to take my curiosity? I'm on the verge of choosing "no," but then I wonder how they fake *that* sensation.

Yeah. More professional curiosity. Obviously. This has nothing to do with how much I want those lips down there. Or with the fact that I've never actually had a man go down on me. Yeah, nothing at all.

Gulping in air, I again pick "yes."

The guy winks out of existence for a moment, then reappears in the cunnilingus position, his face opposite my crotch and his cerulean eyes gazing up into mine.

I lean back on the couch.

His tongue takes the first lick.

Oh. My. Fucking. Golly.

This is exactly how I've always pictured this would feel. His tongue is warm and pliant and beyond amazing. If there were a Nobel Prize for the most perverted invention, the Evil One would get it, hands down.

Another lick.

And another.

Then he latches on to my clit and starts sucking.

My toes curl.

Holy HR policies. I'm about to come in my workplace.

I grab his head but can't bring myself to pull it away. If anything, I have to fight the urge to press him harder against my crotch.

Suddenly, maddeningly, everything stops.

Noooo! I was an inch away from the big O.

A new bloody choice appears in the air.

"Do you want to sample the penetration phase? Yes or no."

Yes.

No.

I'm ready for it, but getting penetrated right here and now isn't—

There's a sound of a lock turning.

Shit.

My heart jolts into the stratosphere, and my insides turn into a sorbet.

Someone's about to catch me.

Chapter Four

*L*eaping to my feet, I claw at the headset.

Bugger. The gloves make it hard to get a good grip, so I attempt to violently shake them off me, only to trip on something.

Flapping my arms as though I'm trying to learn to fly, I grab on to the first thing in my path—which seems to be the office chair.

Fuck me. The thing has wheels, which predictably roll, and my fall continues—with more arm flapping and sounds of suit Velcro coming undone.

Bam!

My wrist smashes into something hard. Judging by the thud against the floor and the sound of plastic shattering, I must've just destroyed that nice monitor.

Strong hands grab me before I nosedive farther.

Not expecting it, I go into freakout mode—grabbing what feels like a keyboard and preparing to swing it.

The hands immediately let go of me.

"I was only trying to help," says a deep, velvety voice with a Russian accent.

That's true, so I don't smash the keyboard into the speaker's face. Instead, I let go of my weapon—and cringe as I hear it smash into bits.

"Why don't you allow me to take that headset off you?" the voice asks.

"Cheers," I blurt, and before I can correct it to "thanks," the headset is carefully removed from my head.

Now that I can see again, I gape at my savior.

And gape.

And gape some more.

Did I fall asleep during that demo, or is this still virtual reality?

In front of me is the very guy who was just eating me out in VR—the hottie from Miso Hungry.

Chapter Five

"*Y*ou okay?" the hot stranger asks, cerulean eyes peering into my very soul.

"Uh-huh." Face burning, I take off the first glove with my teeth, then use the freed hand to take off the other glove. On autopilot, I start working on the rest of the suit—until I remember that I'm completely naked underneath.

"Do you want a minute?" he asks, pointedly keeping his eyes on my face and not lower—as though he's avoiding something.

I look down.

Oh bloody hell.

My right nipple is showing.

I completely forgot about that ripping Velcro sound from earlier.

"Turn, please!" I squeak, spinning on my heels so fast it's a wonder I don't destroy what little is left alive in this office.

"Done," he says.

I peek over my shoulder. His back is to me. The tush inside his jeans is reminiscent of the one I chose for him in VR.

Wait. What am I doing?

Returning to proper priorities, I peel off the suit and tiptoe over the broken monitor and keyboard pieces as I pick up my scattered clothes off the floor.

My hands shake as I pull them on, my skin alternately too hot and too cold.

Bloody hell, bloody hell, bloody hell.

This is bad. So, so bad.

It's not until I'm fully dressed that I'm able to fully process what happened—and as I do, I want to sink through the floor. Maybe all the way to the lobby.

My cheeks feel like the surface of the sun as I mumble, "You can look back now."

"All right." He turns back and gives me an intent once-over. "So, who are you?"

The words escape in a rush. "Holly Hyman, at your service."

Bugger. Why did I just say that?

He frowns, an expression that bizarrely makes his face look sexier. "The CTO?"

"Guilty as charged." Ugh. Why did I just say *that*? In desperation, I try to smooth over my blunder. "And you are?"

"Alex." He extends his large, masculine hand. "Alex Chortsky."

My jaw hits the floor.

Chortsky.

As in the owner of Morpheus Group.

The Devil himself.

Chapter Six

*N*o wonder he boasts the cheekbones of an angel. This is the original fallen angel.

I want to run, but he's blocking my way.

Wait. All is not lost. He doesn't know why I'm here. Maybe there's a way out of this?

Looking confused, the Devil lowers his hand.

Damn it. How could I leave him hanging like that? It's mega rude.

Before I can apologize, he looks down at the floor and grimaces at the sight of the shattered keyboard. "I had just installed rubber O-Rings under all the keys," he says mournfully. "Took me an hour."

A fresh surge of guilt washes over me. I use those things myself; they make mechanical keyboards—the best kind—less loud. I'm about to offer to buy him a new keyboard and install the rings myself when he narrows his eyes at something on the floor.

Oh, no.

He bends down and picks up a flash drive.

The flash drive—the one with the virus on it. It must've fallen out of my pocket when my clothes took that tumble.

"Is this yours?" His narrowed eyes home in on my face—yet even the threat in that cerulean gaze doesn't lessen its devastating impact on my hormones.

"No. I mean, yes." I extend my visibly shaky hand. "Can I have that back?"

Sensual lips flattening, the Devil jerks the flash drive out of my reach. "What exactly are you doing in my office?"

I fight two conflicting urges: to run away screaming or fight him for the flash drive. I go for something in the middle. "I, um… that is, Robert told me we're going to ramp up the integration soon." So far true. "I wanted to check out the suit as part of that." That *could* be true.

His grim expression is unchanged. "How did you open the door? I locked it myself last night."

He's been coming here at night? Why didn't the rumor mill warn me of this? Oh, duh. Because they don't work late on days when I don't.

"The door was open." Fuck. I don't sound convincing even to myself. Stupid, stupid, stupid. Why didn't I ask Gia to teach me to lie better?

He puts the flash drive in his pocket with the finality of a prison sentence. "Why are you here so late?"

"I—I had a lot on my plate. Just got around to it."

His eyes are like slits now. "You didn't even touch your dinner."

Crap. He saw me buy that. "I got curious and lost my appetite." God. A five-year-old could've come up with a better lie.

He takes out his phone and makes a few clicks. Whatever he sees, he must not like because his jaw sets as he pins me with that cerulean laser stare. "You wouldn't know why the security cameras aren't working, would you?"

I just stand there, gulping in air. It's official—I've lost my ability to speak.

"Is this corporate espionage?" His words are clipped.

Still rendered mute, I shake my head.

He glares down at me. "Then what is it?"

I don't answer. I can't. My heart is pounding so hard I feel sick.

His gorgeous lips flatten again. "If you come clean, the consequences will be less severe."

"I… I was just…" My throat is too dry to get the words out.

"You just what? Remember, I can find out for myself." He pats the pocket with the flash drive.

I feel like I'm about to barf from panic. "I—I wanted to… I wanted to stop the porn." Oh, bugger. Why did I just say that? That sounds bad. I should've—

He folds his arms over his chest. "What do you mean by 'stop the porn?'"

I swallow my racing heart back into my chest. In for a penny, in for a pound. "My life's work is at risk. Children and porn don't mix."

"Children?" He looks at me as though I've sprouted a unicorn penis on my head. "You think we're making kiddie porn?"

"What? No!" Wait, maybe I should've said yes. Too late now. I scramble for a reasonable explanation but can only come up with the truth. "I've been working on VR pet therapy."

From there, I launch into the full story, stammering my way through my good intentions—that I want to make children more comfortable at the hospital.

As I go on, the Devil's features are unreadable—he could give Gia's poker face a run for its money. I have no idea if he believes me or not. I hope he does. As the Father of Lies, he should be a truth serum and polygraph machine combined.

"So," I say tentatively when I'm done. "Am I fired?"

He runs a hand through his unruly locks, and I fight the urge to tie him up and tame that hair. That action wouldn't help my case in the least.

"We'll discuss your employment status after the investor meeting tomorrow," he finally says.

Hope blooms in my chest. I'm not outright fired. That's amazing. I'd fire me if our roles were reversed. Then again, he's probably just postponing the inevitable. Given the state of his office, he might want witnesses around when he does sack me—along with working cameras and security guards.

"There's something I want you to keep in mind," he says, his expression still indecipherable. "Morpheus Group is as important to my sister as that VR pet therapy is to you, and her work is *not* porn. She wants to bring sexual experiences to people who, for various reasons, aren't able to have them, including patients in hospitals, husbands and wives torn apart by distance, soldiers, deep-sea fishermen, oil rig workers… Her ideals are just as high as yours." A frightening look replaces the expressionless mask. "I won't let you or anyone else destroy my sister's dream."

My head spins. The rumors mentioned a sister, but I didn't realize she was the driving force behind Morpheus Group. I'm even more screwed than I thought. Even if he doesn't fire me, *she* certainly will.

"I need to know that we have an understanding," he demands in a hard tone.

I nod on autopilot.

Having seven sisters, I've always wondered what it might be like to have a brother. Seems that instead of teasing you mercilessly, they actually protect you from threats. Must be nice for the She-Devil.

The frightening expression disappears from the face of the Prince of Darkness, and the much more preferable poker face is back on. "I want you to say that you understand."

I gulp. "Affirmative. I love—I mean, I really need this job."

"That you do. It's not just your project on the line, either. You'd lose a fortune in stock options too."

Well, someone is confident in the future of this company. Or is he confident in his sister? In any case, he's most likely right. To keep me from going over to Google, our old owner gave me a bunch of stock options. If the company does well, I'll be rolling in loot—assuming I keep working here, which isn't looking likely.

"I promise this will never happen again," I say and cringe. Obviously, *this* won't happen again. Even if I were insane enough to try sabotage again, I wouldn't destroy his office, or almost have an orgasm on his couch, or—

The door to the office suddenly opens, and a gorgeous woman steps inside, her gaze bouncing around in confusion.

I blink at her.

That's his companion from Miso Hungry.

Has he brought his date to work?

"What's going on?" she asks.

Does she mean, "What are you doing with my boyfriend/husband/master?"

Her eyes land on the discarded suit and brighten. "Were you just testing that?"

Wait a second. Is she—

"She was," the Devil—or I should say, the Deceiver—says before I can even think of replying. "The rest of the mess was just an accident."

Well, that second part is true.

The woman appears transformed. If earlier she seemed a little cold in her perfection, now she reminds me of a little girl introduced to her pony for the first time. "Tell me how it went."

The Devil's features soften. "I think introductions are in order. Bella, this is Holly, the CTO whose profile you were so impressed with." His gaze turns to me, a silent threat lurking in the cerulean depths. "Holly, this is my sister, Bella, the head of Morpheus Group."

As I started to suspect, she's the Devil's sister.

Not surprising, really—she *is* wearing Prada.

What is surprising is her lack of a Russian accent, but I guess if she's younger than her brother, she could've been just a child when they immigrated.

A huge wave of relief washes over me as I process all the implications.

She's his *sister*.

They weren't on a date.

They must've just been grabbing dinner before coming here.

Wait. Have I gone completely bonkers? Why should I care that the King of Darkness isn't dating her?

"Holly!" Grinning, Bella advances deeper into the room, the remnants of the monitor and keyboard crunching under her stilettos as she extends her hand. "So nice to finally meet you."

I shake the hand instead of leaving her hanging,

like I did with her brother. My shake is limp, though, and my palm is sweaty.

She was impressed with my profile. Why? Is it possible that, like Santa, She-Devils have a "naughty" list?

The Devil clears his throat. "Holly is so eager for the upcoming integration project that she's taken initiative on testing the suit."

Bella's handshake turns even more enthusiastic.

"Thank you so much," she says and finally lets me go. "What did you think?"

I'm still stunned. Why is the Ruler of Darkness covering for me? Telling her that I was testing and not sabotaging?

Maybe he doesn't want to worry her? It's possible, given how protective he seems. Or, since this is her life's work, he might be worried that the truth will cause her to attack and kill me, which could lead to pesky legal troubles or calls to Russian mob connections. Because, naturally, all Russians have connections to the mob.

"Oh, no," Bella says, examining my no-doubt-sourpuss face. "You didn't like it?"

Crap. I need to stop thinking and begin reacting. Bella looks like I kicked her sick puppy, and when I sneak a glance at the Devil, his dark expression is saying, "Fix this or else."

"Not at all," I blurt. "It was actually brilliant."

If she believes that, I'll go into acting.

Nope. She doesn't look convinced, so I search for

something true. "I was very impressed with how realistic things looked. And all the choices." There we go. Countless cocks *are* choices. And I was impressed with the facial realism.

She tilts her head. "You're not telling me something."

Bugger. "The integration," I say in a flash of inspiration. "When I tried touching something during the demo, the gloves and the suit didn't seem as in tune as they should be."

She nods solemnly and gives her brother a pointed look. "Told you."

A hint of a smile touches his eyes. "I never argued about that. Integration *is* going to be a big priority going forward."

"So." Bella's attention comes back to me. "How far did you get?"

I blink. This really *is* her life's work—I can tell from her unwavering enthusiasm. She can probably talk about this for hours to anyone who'll listen, a bit like new parents bragging about their spawn or me with my VR pet project. I guess it makes some devilish sense. This invention is going to bring a whole lot of lust to the world—and that's one of the seven deadly sins.

Bella must tire of waiting for me to answer because she grabs a glove, puts it on, and presses the headset to her face.

"Ah," she says after a few gestures. "You'd just finished the cunnilingus phase."

I turn redder than the Queen's Guard uniform.

Did the Devil just smirk?

Without removing the headset from her face, Bella asks, "What did you think? Wasn't it realistic?"

"I... err... think so?"

Grr. Now he's definitely smirking. Wanker.

"You think so?" Bella sounds concerned.

I redden further. "I... don't have a basis for comparison." Oh God, why did I just admit that?

She removes the headset from her face and looks at me with such concern you'd think I just told her I've never been out in the sun or tasted tea. Turning to her brother, she asks, "Did you know about this?"

He shakes his head, his smirk even smirkier.

She looks back at me. "But you liked it, right? I worked very hard on the textures and the—"

"I loved it!" The sentence comes out in a squeak.

"Whew." She swipes her hand dramatically over her face. "You had me worried there for a moment. You didn't get to penetration, though, right?"

Why can't the floor swallow me and put me out of my misery?

I manage a headshake.

"But you've experienced *that* before?" She looks horrified at the very idea of me being a virgin, and I want to die. Maybe by spontaneous combustion. Or the HR shooting all of us.

To say that this is a sensitive topic for me would be a massive understatement. I've had sex, of course, but my devirginizer turned out to be gay—and on top of that, as a kid, I was always teased with the not-so-creative nickname of Holy Hymen.

"Sorry. I didn't mean to pry," Bella says, catching on to my distress.

I will my burning cheeks to cool. "It's okay. I've had coitus before, so no worries."

There. I should get some kind of a medal.

"Thank goodness." She presses the headset back to her face. "Still, without having experienced oral sex, you're not the ideal test subject. A pity."

Does that statement require a response?

"Sis, Holly was actually just about to leave," the Devil says. "She's had a long workday and—"

"Eeww!" Bella rips the headset from her face. "The guy you made looks just like Alex. *Naked*."

Seriously, where's that spontaneous combustion?

The Devil's cerulean gaze swings to me, and I could swear there's a glimmer of fire in it. Then he turns to his sister. "'Eeww?' Really?"

She rolls her eyes. "Did you want me to drool? As you've said, we're not the Lannisters or the Borgias."

Is the Evil One lost for words?

Bella grins sheepishly at me. "You could've warned me."

"I'm sorry," I mutter. "I didn't think."

"No sweat." She grabs the bulky part of the suit where my vagina would be if I were still wearing it. "I bet you're wondering how penetration is supposed to work."

I shake my head, but she either doesn't notice or

doesn't care. "Obviously, it's not practical to fit a variety of dildos in the suit, so I was forced to use hydraulics and—"

"Sis." The Devil's tone is more forceful. "Holly hasn't even had the chance to eat her dinner."

"Oh." She looks at me guiltily. "Poor thing. Sorry. We'll talk more later. Eat your dinner and go home."

"Thanks! I'll eat on the way." I zoom out of that office as though the devils were chasing me—and for all I know, they might be about to do just that.

All I want is to get out of here and regroup—assuming that's even possible.

Since I'm running, I fish out my earbuds from my pocket, jam them into my ears, and put on my trusty running music: the *Downton Abbey* soundtrack. Reaching my desk, I grab my takeout, not because I still want it, but because I said I'd eat on the way.

So far, so good. I'm almost out of here. Just a minute until freedom.

Dashing for the elevator, I channel all my pent-up frustration and unburned adrenaline into my leg muscles.

Almost there.

Almost.

Yes.

I'm by the elevator. Jamming my finger at the button, I all but bite my nails in anticipation.

After a century-long wait, the elevator doors crawl open.

Finally.

I'm about to step in when a hand grabs my shoulder.

Fuck.

Didn't make it.

I spin around to face the Devil.

Chapter Seven

*O*nly it's the She-Devil, and she's smiling—not something I expected to see before plunging into the burning fires of hell.

I dig an earbud out of my ear. I probably look as wild-eyed as I feel.

"I wanted you to have this." Bella hands me a backpack with hand-drawn genitalia on it.

Ookay.

I snatch the backpack, clutch it to my chest, and blink at her. Something heavy is inside the bag. Could it be the heart or liver of the last person who tried to sabotage her work?

She looks at me expectantly.

"Thank you?" I mutter.

"It's the suit." She waggles her eyebrows lasciviously. "The one you tried. Figured you'd want to finish the demo."

I redden again—my cheeks are now primed for it.

Then I notice that the Devil himself is within earshot, smirking. If I were Hulk strong, I'd throw this penis-inscribed backpack at the wanker's head. Alas, I'm not—plus that sort of thing will get me fired for sure.

"Well, have a safe trip home," Bella says.

"Thanks. Bye." I back into the elevator and press the button for the lobby.

As the doors close, I see the Devil's evil smirk grow into an infuriating grin.

My food tastes like sandpaper as I eat it on autopilot in the cab, and even when I get home and start my seven-step evening routine, my mind refuses to stop spinning.

Am I going to lose my job?

Whatever the answer is, my life's work is still in dire jeopardy.

As I meticulously floss my thirty-one teeth (by luck, I had to get one of my wisdom teeth removed a few years back), I ponder if there's a way to save my project.

Maybe I can call an emergency meeting with the administration at NYU Langone tomorrow and try to convince them to move from beta testing to officially adopting the VR pet therapy. Once there's a contract and data on how useful the therapy is, they'll be less likely to pull out when they learn that the company they've made a deal with is known for its adult content. The Devil might not deem it porn, but they surely will.

Worth a shot. I fire up my laptop and request the meeting.

Now I need two miracles. Or is it called something else when the Devil is involved?

My phone pings. It's a text from Gia:

Do you need me to bail you out of jail?

Har bloody har.

No need, I text back. *I changed my mind about the B & E.*

I rarely lie to my twin, but I can't bring myself to talk about what happened just yet.

I knew you'd chicken out, she replies. *You still owe me.*

I sigh. *Fine. Speaking of that, tell parents to meet "you" at Miso Hungry—a place by my office.*

After she promises she will, I turn off my phone.

According to my schedule, it's time to go to sleep. The problem is, there's no way I'll sleep in this state—I feel like I've just downed a barrel of cocaine-laced espresso.

Time for the big guns.

I turn on my TV and play the series premiere of *Downton Abbey.*

Nope. Still can't sleep. Seems like even bigger guns are needed.

I put on the episode of Rose's wedding, mainly because it contains one of my favorite Violet quotes of all time: "Love may not conquer all, but it can conquer a lot."

When it's over, I try sleeping again.

Not a wink.

I go to my ultimate sleep tool: Jane Austen's *Pride and Prejudice.*

Still no luck.

Okay, how about *Emma?*

Nope. If anything, all these romantic stories make it worse, as a pair of cerulean eyes keep popping into my mind.

I switch tactics and go for a cup of chamomile tea. It doesn't remind me of the Devil, thankfully, but it doesn't help either—and I don't dare brew anything caffeinated.

A crazy idea pops into my head. An orgasm might help me get drowsy, so what if I put on the suit Bella gave me?

No. I mustn't.

But I want to.

Curse you, Devil and your sister. This must be how Jesus felt when he was tempted in the wilderness.

But hold on a second. There's a VR activity that might calm me—though, granted, not as much as a virtual shag.

My own VR pet therapy.

Yeah, that's it.

Gearing up, I launch the necessary app and come face to furry nose with Euclid—the VR pet customized for me.

"Holly," Euclid sing-songs. "I mished you."

Brilliant. My nerves are soothed already. I can't help but grin at him.

Euclid can be made to look like a preset of things I figured kids would find cute: a piglet, a koala bear cub, a baby otter, a baby panda, a baby hedgehog, a kitten, or a lemur. Of course, he doesn't look like any of those exactly, since that's no fun. He's an anthropomorphized version of an animal, and with as much influence from the Teletubbies as I could get away with without being sued.

In my case, Euclid resembles a hybrid between an otter and the Laa-Laa Teletubby. Oh, and he's currently purple, like Tinky-Winky, but that just indicates he's happy. The color of his fur is how he emotes—or pretends to. He is, after all, an AI.

"Hi, sweet one," I say. "Are you hungry?"

"Ravenoush." He does a dance that is part Teletubby, part Ellen DeGeneres, with a dash of Barney the Dinosaur thrown in.

I extend my gloved hand, and a pair of digital snacks show up on my palm. Here, again, I've made them look like the Tubby Custard and Tubby Toast that the Teletubbies like to eat, but different enough to hopefully never get a cease-and-desist letter.

Euclid goes for the toast, a star-shaped chocolate cookie with a winking face on it. Of course, the shape of the toast, like everything else, is customizable. I like the star (really, a pentagram) because it has a prime number of points—not because I'm a witch or a Satan worshiper… Bugger, there I go again, reminding myself of the person who got me into this state in the first place.

"Tell me shomething intereshting," Euclid sing-songs after he gobbles down the snack.

"Well, did you know that your namesake proved that the list of prime numbers is infinite?" I ask. "He did it over two thousand years ago, and without internet."

Euclid's fur turns yellow, and he giggles. "You can be sho shilly."

Nodding, I pet his fur. This is what heaven must feel like. This part of the experience is what the gloves were designed for, not feeling the hardness of cocks.

Euclid turns pink. "Letsh play fetch."

With a classic throw gesture, I make a deep purple stick appear in my hand. As I toss the stick, I can't help flashing back to the recent penis selection process —my design of this object happens to look eerily like one of the more exotic choices.

Note to self: keep Bella away from this app. I don't think Euclid's programming can handle what she'd do with the stick.

After he brings back the stick, we play other games for a while, until I'm certain that I'm feeling much better and ready to sleep.

"I'm going to go take a nap," I tell Euclid.

His fur turns an array of colors before settling on a light teal. "Shee you later. I wove you."

"I love you too." I hug him tight, then take off the headset and gloves.

Now I'm ready.

I grab my sleeping buddy, a plush Transformer

that I love not because I'm a fan of that super-violent franchise, but due to his name: Optimus *Prime*.

Hugging Optimus, I drift into sleep… only to dream of cerulean eyes and evil grins.

Chapter Eight

*H*alf an hour into the dreaded investment meeting, I realize I'm keeping meticulous meeting minutes in my notepad.

That's crazy. Who documents something they want to fail? My only excuse is that I've been trying to avoid looking at the Devil, and focusing on my notepad is a decent enough distraction.

In addition to me and my team, the room is occupied by a man named Dragomir Lamian, Dragomir's people, and the Chortsky siblings—and it doesn't take long for all my hopes to be dashed.

Given the looks that pass between Dragomir and Bella, he's in her pocket already. That is, if I put things delicately. And hey, good for her. The guy is model-hot and clean-shaven… unlike a certain someone who didn't even bother to make himself presentable for an important meeting.

What's maddening, though, is that I find the Devil

more attractive than this clean-shaven stranger. Grr. What's wrong with me?

As if sensing my stare, the Wicked One turns my way, and I feel highjacked by his gaze. I can almost picture the voice of David Attenborough speaking down from the heavens: "And thus, the human mating ritual begins. The female of the species starts ovulating as the male——"

No. Must fight it.

I begin counting my eyeblinks the way I did as a kid.

Nope, not distracting enough. I then also count Bella's——staring into her eyes seems safe enough.

In ten minutes, the counts are 223 (prime) for me and 227 (also prime) for her, so I stop while I'm ahead and surreptitiously check my phone under the table.

Finally, some good news. The folks at NYU Langone are willing to see me at three p.m. I put a reminder in my calendar——though it's hard to imagine I'll need it, given how important this is.

So, all isn't lost yet. If I still have my job when the Devil talks to me after this meeting, I could well succeed in convincing them to expedite the timeline.

"Thank you, everyone," Dragomir says, and I tune in to see if he'll deny them money despite being wrapped around Bella's elegant finger. "And congratulations," he continues. "The next round of funding is officially approved."

So much for that hope.

Everyone stands up, but I remain seated and so

does the Devil—seems like he hasn't forgotten about our upcoming chat.

Except Bella isn't leaving either. Grinning, she walks up to me. "Hey, Holly. We're going for a walk in the park with our dogs. Would you like to come?"

She's inviting me to go walk dogs?

Did I hear that right?

"I need to talk to your brother," I say cautiously and dart him a glance.

He looks like he's hiding another evil smirk, but I can't be sure.

"Alex is coming with me." She looks at him. "Can you and Holly have your talk on our walk?"

"It's kind of private," he says. "I was planning on taking care of it first, then joining you."

She pouts. "Can you do it after?"

He heaves a sigh. "Fine."

"Great." She beams at me. "How about you ride with me and Dragomir, and we'll meet Alex and Beelzebub there."

Did she just say *Beelzebub*? Is she in on my private joke?

I don't have a chance to dwell on it because Bella drags me out of the room by my elbow.

"So," she says when we're in the elevator. "Did you use the suit after you got home?"

Reddening, I glance at the Devil, then at Dragomir. "Didn't get the chance."

She looks extremely disappointed for a moment,

but then her eyes brighten. "Okay, then tell me about your first demo."

I redden more.

The Devil clears his throat. "No talking shop on dog walks, remember?"

Has the Ruler of Darkness just saved me again? Or is he buttering me up for something even worse— like getting dunked in tar and rubbed in feathers?

Bella's disappointed expression comes back, times five. "The dogs aren't even here yet. Can we at least talk about nipple stimulation? I worked very hard to—"

Dragomir puts a hand on Bella's shoulder. "*Squirrelchik*, didn't you have a bunch of questions about Holly's experience at Cambridge?"

They're on touching terms? And he has a pet name for her? The chances of that funding failure had been less than nil.

"You're right." Bella smiles at me. "You studied computer science, like Alex, right?"

I nod—though I'm not sure if I like being bundled into a category with him, no matter what it is.

She covers the hand that's still on her shoulder and gives it a little squeeze. "What was the ratio of women to men in your classes?"

Finally on safer grounds, I answer her question, and she shares similar stats from MIT, her alma mater.

She turns to her brother. "How about you? Do

you recall how many women took computer science courses at Polytechnic University?"

He runs a hand through his unruly hair, making me want to comb it back, maybe violently. "I don't know the official stats, but there were definitely too few women."

I feel conflicted about this. On the one hand, I want more women in my field, but on the other hand, I like the idea of there not being females around him, no matter the environment.

He belongs on a deserted island with me. In handcuffs. There'd be barber utensils there too. And not much clothing—

Blimey. Did I seriously just think all that? I'm clearly off my rocker.

The elevator doors open, and Bella peppers me with more questions about Cambridge as we make our way through the lobby. I reply to her on autopilot, wishing I could fall back and ask the Devil point blank, "Am I keeping the job? Yes or no."

Alas, as soon as we get outside, he jumps into a nearby cab, and I watch it disappear in traffic with longing.

That is, with relief.

Yeah.

Definitely relief.

"That's us." Bella points at a giant car that looks like an RV that's eaten thirteen limousines.

The door of the strange vehicle opens and a ladder descends. A man wearing a tuxedo jacket with tailcoats appears in the doorway and greets us primly in a British-accented voice, "Please, come inside."

Oh my golly.

I'm going to die of jealousy.

This is clearly a butler, à la Carson from *Downton Abbey*. I'd give my right ovary to have one.

"Thanks, Fyodor," Dragomir says and gestures for us to go first.

A proper gentleman. Good for Bella.

We climb inside, and I look around, dumbfounded.

"Doesn't it look bigger inside than outside?" Bella whispers conspiratorially. "Like the TARDIS from *Doctor Who*."

It is big—huge even—and messy, despite there being a butler on staff.

Okay, I have to withdraw my earlier comparison. Real Carson wouldn't stand for this. I have to work very hard to restrain myself from turning into a tidying whirlwind.

"Ready to meet the doggies?" Bella asks as Dragomir and Fyodor join us, and before I can formulate a reply, the hounds of hell descend upon us.

Chapter Nine

The shaggy beast who leads the charge is big. We're talking proportional to the size of this RV kind of big.

It's basically a pony—a well-fed pony.

Getting on its haunches, it puts its front paws on Dragomir's shoulders and goes right for his face. I half expect Dragomir to lose his nose at the very least, but the monstrous creature simply slobbers on the poor man.

If this happened to my twin, she'd expire on the spot.

As the beastie does the same to Bella, I examine the second dog—a tiny Chihuahua that instantly makes me crave a burrito.

"Winnie, no," Bella says sternly as the sasquatch-like canine tries to lick *my* face.

Winnie? As in, the Pooh?

Wait a sec. I'd assumed this was a dog, but maybe

it's a type of bear? Whatever its species, Winnie doesn't look happy about this licking restriction but settles for sniffing my crotch. And sniffing. And sniffing for the longest seven seconds in crotch-sniffing history, until eventually Dragomir drags it away, muttering, "Bad girl."

Me or Winnie? If the latter, then Winnie is female. I would've guessed differently, given all that crotch sniffing. Also, if that breed/species has sexual dimorphism, how big do the males get? Elephant size?

"Holly, this is Napoleon Bonaparte," Bella says, picking up the Chihuahua. "Or Boner for short."

Boner. Why does this make me think of her brother all of a sudden? Worse yet, that reminds me of my precarious job situation, making my stomach tighten with anxiety.

Since I have a chance at authentic pet therapy right here, I smooth my hand over Boner's short fur.

The cute little bugger closes his eyes in bliss.

"He likes you," Bella says. "And he's a good judge of character."

I grin, absurdly pleased.

My relationship with animals is a complex one. Growing up on a farm, I was surrounded by them—and I don't just mean my sisters. Now that I'm grown, I still love everything furry, but only in theory. Put another way, I love pets when they live with someone else, but for myself, I can't imagine owning one due to the chaos and mess it would create. I suspect most people feel the same way about baby monkeys.

Wanting to play with animals without the mess was part of the reason I came up with my VR pet project, in fact. It provides all the good parts of pet ownership and none of the bad.

"Would you care for a spot of tea?" Fyodor asks poshly.

Dragomir and Bella reply in the affirmative and turn my way.

"Don't mind if I do," I say, beaming at not-quite-Carson. He's really redeemed himself with that "spot of tea" bit.

We sit on a nearby couch while the tea and biscuits get served.

Bugger. Note to self: never say "biscuits" in lieu of "cookies" in front of Gia. For that matter, never say "bugger" either.

As we have our tea, Winnie lies down on the floor and Boner sniffs her butt, making me chuckle.

Noticing this, Bella demonstrates a dubious skill— ventriloquism. Only she voices the dogs instead of a traditional nightmarish wooden doll.

"Winnie, *ma petite*." She throws her voice to sound as if it's coming from the Chihuahua's maw and speaks with a strong French accent instead of the Hispanic I would've expected. "How I adore your *postérieure*. It has a certain *je ne sais quoi* that makes me feel like I have rabies."

Noticing the sniffing, Winnie leaps to her feet and jumps onto a nearby treadmill.

Yes. A treadmill. In a car.

Bella throws her voice at the giant creature, giving it a thick Russian accent. "Napoleon Carlovich, I am scandalized. Can't you keep your nose—and other appendages—away from my orifices for at least an hour? We're in new company. Know you no shame?"

I blow on my tea. "Was this your talent at a beauty pageant?"

Bella grins. "I've never done one of those, but it's sweet of you to imply that I could've."

Huh, okay. Isn't vanity supposed to be the Devil's favorite sin?

"How did you learn it then?" I ask. "You throw your voice very well."

"My parents own a restaurant," she says, wrinkling her nose. "I performed there... for a time."

Before I can question her further, the RV comes to a full stop.

"You first," Bella tells me when Fyodor opens the doors for us.

As soon as we exit, I come face to gorgeous face with the Devil. His cerulean eyes meet mine, sucking all the air from my lungs, and it takes all my willpower to tear my gaze away from that hypnotic stare and turn my attention to the dog at his side.

A dog that could just as easily be a koala bear the size of a German shepherd.

I blink at it, thoroughly distracted by its ginormous cuteness. There's something clumsy in the way it stands, making me think it might be a puppy.

Must be the aforementioned Beelzebub.

Seeing me, Beelzebub starts wagging his tail and gets on his haunches.

Oh, no. He's going for my face.

Not willing to be slobbered on, I turn away.

A paw claws at my top anyway.

Laughing, I push the puppy away, and as I do, I feel the material shifting, followed by a cool sensation on my left nipple.

A cool sensation that's unmistakably air.

Chapter Ten

*O*h, bugger.

My heart rate jacks up, my face flaming violently as I frantically tug my shirt back in place.

I've just managed another nip-slip in front of the Devil—and since it was the right one last time, he's now seen the pair.

To his credit, the Devil doesn't stare as he pulls Beelzebub away, though there's a definite hint of a smirk on his face.

But why not stare? Is my nipple unattractive or something? I've used electrolysis on that one errant hair that sprouted out of there, so it should be gone. Unless it's back?

Under the pretext of continuing to fix my attire, I sneak a frantic peek down my shirt and bra.

Nope. All good there. Whew.

The Devil says something in Russian to the unrepentant, tail-waggling demon.

Whatever he said doesn't stick.

As soon as Beelzebub spots Bella, Dragomir, and their furry charges, he goes berserk, licking the faces of the humans before switching to licking the snouts of the dogs, then sniffing dog butts for dessert.

Hey, at least he didn't sniff the butts of the humans—or their crotches.

"Do you want to hold Boner's leash?" Bella asks me magnanimously.

"No, thank you," I say quickly. As is appropriate for the Tempter, Bella has an uncanny ability to place inappropriate images into my brain. Case in point: I'm picturing the Devil with a huge erection, a cock-ring with a leash attached, and me holding—

"How about Beelzebub?" the Devil asks, wrestling me away from my naughty thoughts. "Do you want to walk *him*?"

Beelzebub wags his tail spasmodically, and I bet if Bella were to voice his thoughts, he'd be shouting, "Please, please, please. Pick me. Pick me. Pick me."

"I'm good," I say, ignoring the overeager puppy. "I'll just walk on my own if you don't mind."

Beelzebub's tail sags and his ears droop. I feel a little pang of guilt. Maybe I should've said yes.

But no. That way lies getting my own puppy, and then domestic Armageddon will surely follow.

We begin the walk, and I remember how much I love Central Park—though apparently not as much as the dogs do. They look like they're having the time of their lives as they sniff every previously urinated-on nook and cranny.

"Has my sister told you why she wanted to buy your company?" the Devil asks.

I shake my head.

Bella pulls Boner away right as he tries to eat an innocent snail. "Women are typically more susceptible to VR sickness," she says. "But Holly's headset is the exception to that unfortunate rule."

Even though it's not fair to call it *my* headset, I stand straighter. "It was important to us that women and children could use the gear. That's why the headset is adjustable, especially the interpupillary distance and—"

"Folks, you know the rules: no shop talk on a dog walk," Dragomir says.

Bella looks at him sheepishly. "Oops."

I fight the urge to say it's not her or my fault. Her brother started it.

A squirrel crosses the road, and Beelzebub looks like he'd sell his grandmother to catch it. In contrast, Winnie doesn't pay the furry creature any attention, while Boner has clearly seen it but is pretending that the rodent doesn't exist.

I notice that Bella and Dragomir have gotten a little bit ahead of me and the Devil, as if giving us privacy on purpose.

Huh. Weird. Is that because Alex said he and I needed to talk?

As if reading my thoughts, she peeks at us over her shoulder with a sly smile.

Wait a sec.

Is she playing matchmaker? Is that why she's invited me here—to act out her own personal *Emma* fantasy?

If so, she's certifiable. Her brother and I are like oil and water. Then again, didn't I read something about MIT researchers developing an emulsions preparation process that allows oil and water to mix and stay that way? And Bella did go to MIT, so—

No. No way. Besides, even if she fancies me now, once she learns I tried to sabotage her dream, she'll hate my guts—an idea I find quite discomforting.

Well, whatever her motives, I should take advantage of the situation and ask about my job.

Yes, that's exactly what I should do—only I'm having trouble launching into it. Maybe I'll make some small talk first to build up to it.

"Is Bella your only sibling?" There. Better than bringing up the weather—which is nice and sunny, by the way.

Since Beelzebub is taking a leak, the Devil stops and I do the same. "We have a brother too," he replies. "His name is Vlad."

Aha. So every Chortsky I came across during my research is related. Makes sense.

"How about you?" the Fallen Angel asks as we resume the walk. "Are you an only child?"

I wish… unless, is that question a diss?

"I have seven sisters." Did I just sound braggy?

His eyebrow shoots up—yet another bizarrely attractive expression on him. "Seven?"

"Yeah. Me and my twin, plus the sextuplets—everyone monozygotic."

A second eyebrow joins the first. "Monozygotic as in identical?"

Why are those eyebrows so sodding attractive?

"Indeed. My twin and I look the same, as does the litter of evil."

His satyr-like grin is as seductive as the eyebrows. "The litter of evil sounds like what we call Beelzebub and his siblings: the Chort Pack. You see, my last name means—"

"Of the devil," I blurt.

He stops, though I'm not sure if it's to focus on me or to allow Beelzebub to pee on a tempting-looking oak trunk. "You speak Russian?"

"Sadly, no. There were just rumors about you guys at the office, so I looked up your name."

"I see." Beelzebub pulls on the leash, so the Devil resumes walking. "Sextuplets are exceptionally rare, right?"

"That they are. The chances are astronomically small for a regular pregnancy, but more likely when using assisted reproduction technology, which is what my parents did."

"Ah. And are all of you close?"

"Only me and my twin. I mainly interact with the others at family events. They're a bit much for me. Too chaotic and messy—especially when together in the same space."

The Wicked One chuckles. "I bet. There were only three of us growing up, and it was pretty crazy some days. Hard to imagine eight."

Grr. I hate the reminder that there are eight of us. Why couldn't the Hymans be like the Chortskys and have a nice prime number of kids? Especially three.

Three would be so much better than eight.

Can't say that to him, though, so I opt for something safer. "You and Bella get along well enough. Are you also close with Vlad?"

He pulls on Beelzebub's leash to prevent him from molesting a yorkie. "Vlad's my best friend."

"Tidy." I smile. "Same for my twin and me."

He cocks his head. "I know you went to school at Cambridge, but did you also live in England before or after that?"

"Why?" I ask, sounding defensive.

"Certain words you choose," he says. "Like tidy."

This again. "It was just the four years. Turns out, I absorb languages and dialects like a sponge. I even had a British accent when I got back, but after merciless teasing, I managed to drop it."

He grins. "Maybe if you hang out with me enough, you'll learn Russian. And get a Russian accent."

Cheeky bastard. Does he want me to be tempted

by the idea of hanging out with him? Of course he does. He wouldn't be the Tempter otherwise.

No more dilly-dallying.

I take in a breath and expel the words in a rush. "Can we talk about my employment status? If I need to update my CV, I should—"

He locks eyes with me. "No shop talk on dog walks."

"But—"

"Rules are rules," he says sternly. "Once we're done here, we can set up—"

The alarm on my phone goes off.

What the bloody hell?

When I check it, I want to smack myself.

The NYU Langone meeting is in a half hour, which is barely enough time for me to get there.

I look up from the phone to see the Devil frowning.

"Is everything okay?" he asks.

"I'm fine. But I do have to skedaddle."

The frown morphs into a confused expression. "You do?"

"I'm sorry." Louder, I belt out, "Bye, Bella. Bye, Dragomir!"

Bella turns around and hurries toward me.

Crap. I shouldn't have said goodbye. Now I'm getting delayed.

"Did I hear you say you're leaving?" she says, reaching me.

"Yep. Got to run."

Bella gives her brother a narrow-eyed stare. "What did you do?"

"No one did anything." My voice jumps an octave. "I have a prior commitment, that's all. When I agreed to join you guys, it slipped my mind."

"Oh." Bella takes out her phone. "Before you go, please give me your contact info."

I'm so going to be late. Then again, I find the idea that Bella wants to get in touch a little exhilarating. Reminds me of being in middle school, when I wanted the prettiest girl in class to befriend me.

Could Bella become my first friend with whom I don't share one hundred percent of my DNA?

Wait, what am I saying? Once she learns what I tried to do, she won't want to be friends. Quite the opposite: she'll fire me—if her brother doesn't beat her to it.

Not showing any of this on my face, I put my number into her phone and hand it back.

Just as I prepare to sprint away, the Devil hands me *his* phone. "In case I need to reach you for work."

Hmm. Do I want him to call me? I'm not sure, but denying him my number would be a pointless gesture. He's now my boss, so he can get access to it from the HR records if he wishes.

"Well, actually, I wanted Holly's number for personal reasons," Bella says to him and sticks her tongue out, causing Dragomir to give her a heated side-eye. With a warm smile at me, she says, "I'll text you so you have my number as well."

I feel a pang of sadness knowing a close friendship with Bella can never happen. Side note: what's the female equivalent of bromance? Is it homance, as in *hos before bros*? No, sounds offensive. A quick internet search reveals the term: womance.

Realizing I'm delaying myself, I quickly enter my info and thrust the Devil's phone back into his hands.

The Wicked One's fingers brush against mine, and a surge of seductive energy shoots down my arm, zips around my heart, and electrocutes a few butterflies in my belly before settling sinfully in my core.

Blimey. Did his cerulean eyes widen?

Nah. All I see on his face is a smirk. "Thanks," he says, his accent sounding particularly delicious. "I'll text you too."

His "too" makes me think of "two," one of my favorite primes. "Cheerio," I blurt. Bugger. The British accent I thought I'd gotten rid of is back with a vengeance. "I really have to run."

"Bye," Bella says.

"*Do svidaniya*," says the Ruler of Darkness, the smirk still on his gorgeous face.

"It was nice to meet you," Dragomir adds.

"Au revoir, *chèrie*," says Boner. "I look forward to sniffing you again in the future."

With a queenly wave, I dash for the park exit, where I leap into the first available cab and bribe the driver to punch it.

Once on the way, I look up "*do svidaniya.*"

Svidaniye means "meeting" or "date", and the

phrase is used as an optimistic farewell with the meaning of "until the next meeting."

"Do svidaniya," I say out loud.

Becoming animated, the driver catches my gaze in the mirror and rattles out a torrent of Russian words.

"Sorry, I don't speak Russian," I say.

"Oh, I'm sorry. You said *do svidaniya* like a true Russian. Forgive my confusion," the driver says, his accent much thicker than the Devil's.

So it has begun. Before I know it, I will have a Russian accent as prominent as this guy's and will say *do svidaniya* instead of *bye*.

Hey, that might work better with Gia than *cheerio*.

I look up other Russian greetings in case they come in handy. There are many, but the easiest to say is probably *privet*, which is an informal hello.

A text chimes.

It's the Devil.

I store his number as first name Lucifer, last name Satan.

Bella's text comes soon after.

It might be a double standard, but I enter her into my contacts with her real name.

For the rest of the ride, I count the seconds my mind wastes picturing a certain pair of cerulean eyes. At a hundred and thirty-seven, I halt the count, as I don't want even more proof of how mental I am.

When we stop next to NYU Langone, I'm already seven minutes late—and the fact that it's a prime number is little consolation.

Grabbing a hundred-dollar bill and a single, I throw them at the driver and dash out of the car with a shout of "keep the change."

Time to pull off a miracle.

Chapter Eleven

*O*n the way to my destination, I do accomplish a small miracle: I don't knock anyone over during my mad sprint.

Once I get to the meeting room, however, I find it empty.

Bloody hell. Did they leave already?

I sit down to catch my breath.

The door opens and Dr. Piper walks in.

"Sorry to keep you waiting," he says. "The others will arrive shortly."

Hurrah!

Instead of being late, fate has made me look early. Fingers crossed this continues.

We make small talk as we wait for the rest of the administrative staff to arrive. Once they're all in, Dr. Piper gives me a fatherly smile and says, "It's a good thing you reached out. We were talking about your project at the morning scrum."

I smile nervously. "Good things, I hope."

"Absolutely," he says. "We've been talking to the children who are part of the beta test, as well as their parents. The feedback has all been positive. We should discuss the next steps."

Wow. Maybe I won't even need to convince them?

"That sounds great," I say with feeling. "I'd love to talk next steps."

"Glad to hear it," Dr. Piper says. "We've started our due diligence and have involved an external consultant to assist us with the aspects of this technology we're not familiar with." He chuckles. "Which is most of it."

Reasonable. They can't just rely exclusively on my say-so all the time.

"Talking with this consultant, we got an idea for the next step, one that the parents and the children also liked," he continues.

Why do I have a feeling I'm not going to like what he's about to say?

"What idea?" I ask.

"First, I just want to say that a VR pet is a very effective use for this technology, the best even."

My heartbeat speeds up. "Why does it sound like there's a but coming?"

"No buts. Only the truth. You only have the one app, the pet. It's limiting. Kids like video games. The consultant suggested we expand the list of apps."

I gape at him. What he's talking about is a classic in project management. It's called scope creep—

except this isn't even a creep, it's a bloody elephant stampede.

I clear my throat. "Pet therapy is a real therapy. Games aren't."

"The consultant sent us an article about this very topic. VR games have been shown to reduce pain."

Who is this evil consultant? I fight the urge to swear and point out that I already knew about those studies—they were the starting point for my work. In fact, said studies were how I convinced these very people to give my project a chance.

Taking in a calming breath, I speak evenly as I lay out the truth of the matter. "I'm working with limited resources. The pet app is the result of many months of work. Adding more apps is—"

"I'm sorry to interrupt, but we have a solution to this problem already," he says.

"You do?" I fan myself with my shirt, but carefully, so as not to have another nip-slip.

"There's a company that makes games for the tablets the kids currently play with. This company has recently branched out into VR as well. We can introduce you to them, and you can work out a way to put their games onto your platform. Much less work, right?"

Except we needed to be all squared away *today*, and this is the opposite of that.

"It all depends," I say cautiously. "What's the name of the company?"

"1000 Devils," he says. "Ever hear of them?"

I lose my ability to speak and just sit there, holding in a scream.

When I researched the Chortsky name, what little I learned about the two brothers was from the websites of the companies they own.

One of which was a game studio called 1000 Devils.

A game studio owned by none other than Alexander (Alex) Chortsky, the Devil himself.

Chapter Twelve

*H*ow have I gotten so screwed so fast? What were the chances they'd want me to work with that company out of so many others?

Well, 1000 Devils *is* famous for their kid-focused content, and it's local to NYC, so it's not completely out of the blue.

Unless…

No. Can't be.

But what if? Could the Devil be the Evil Consultant? I mean he's the Evil One, so this—

"Are you okay, dear?" Dr. Piper looks at me with a worried expression.

How long have I just been sitting here, mind imploding?

"I'm fine," I lie. "This is something I need to process." For a year.

"Fair enough," Dr. Piper says. "How about we

adjourn the meeting for now? Offline, I'll introduce you to Robert Jellyheim—my contact at 1000 Devils."

Robert Jellyheim. If I had any hope that there's a different game studio called 1000 Devils, that hope is now caput. Robert is my contact at Morpheus Group —a company I can't mention here at all, because porn.

The Devil must be using the staff from his gaming company to help his sister.

I'm so, so screwed.

Everyone leaves the meeting room except Dr. Piper.

"Are you *sure* you're feeling okay?" he asks.

"Fine." I leap to my feet.

"It's just that"—he readjusts his bowtie—"if you *are* sick, I don't think you should visit Jacob and the others."

"I'm not sick, I promise," I say.

Also, he's a genius. Visiting Jacob might help brighten this otherwise rubbish day.

We say our goodbyes, and I navigate to the pediatric long-term care wing.

Bugger. Bobze the clown is here, entertaining Jacob and the others. Even though I don't have proper coulrophobia, and even though Bobze doesn't look like he's escaped from Stephen King's basement, I prefer to stay away. Bobze is the epitome of messiness: every color of the rainbow in his wild wig, disproportionate shoes, and, adding insult to injury, he always carries not one, or two, or three, or five, but exactly *four* balloons.

Realizing I'm famished, I sneak out to the cafeteria and get my hospital usual: seven apples and a pack of twenty-three almonds.

I gobble down the fruit and the nuts, then check on Jacob.

Whew.

No more clown.

Preparing to channel my inner Mary Poppins, I walk up to Jacob. His nose is in a tablet, so I cough to steal his attention.

Looking up, he rewards me with a heartwarming boyish grin. "Hi, Aunt Holly."

Jacob and I are not really blood relations—he's the grandchild of one of my parents' friends. He landed in this hospital after an accident where he broke a number of his bones. With his legs in casts, boredom and pain (in that order) are big issues for him, making him a perfect candidate for my VR pet therapy.

"Hi, kiddo." I muss his hair. "How's Master Chief?"

Master Chief is what he calls his version of Euclid. It also happens to be the name of a character in *Halo*, a video game that Jacob once coerced me to play. Sadly, I could only tolerate the uber-violence for seventeen seconds before I had to bail—and he called me lame, perhaps rightfully so.

Jacob's grin widens. "He grew a few inches and learned a few new words."

No doubt curse words, but I'll leave that for Jacob's parents to worry about.

He tells me about the games he and his VR friend have played, and I gently probe how he'd feel about VR games outside pet therapy. Not surprisingly, he's brimming with enthusiasm for such a scenario, especially if they're to be games of the shooting variety.

Bollocks. I hate to admit it, but adding more games might be a good idea. Too bad it will ruin everything by giving Dr. Piper's team time to learn about the porn connection.

Then again, how much time would it take to port existing games onto a new platform?

"Aunt Holly, are you okay?" Jacob asks.

"Sorry." I smile at him, banishing all errant thoughts from my head—the kid deserves my full attention.

When Jacob and I run out of things to talk about, I combine his clean socks into three pairs, fold the blanket next to his bed into a neat triangle, and chat with a few of the other kids nearby while tidying up their areas as well.

As I exit the hospital, there's a grin on my face. I think I could've been a teacher in another life. Whenever I talk to my pint-sized beta team, I end up feeling supercalifragilisticexpialidocious.

In the cab heading home, I check my phone. No texts or calls from the Devil. Sigh. On some level, I was wondering if he'd set up a meeting to sack me... or text me a dick pic.

I guess the ball is in my court on that—the meeting, I mean, not the nudie pic.

Once home, I follow my routine, but in the background, my mind tries to figure out a way to extract myself from the current kerfuffle.

Just as I'm all set to go to bed, an insane idea congeals out of a horde of equally bad ones.

It's a classic, really. Faust went through it. Brendan Fraser did it in *Bedazzled*. Keanu Reeves also, in *Constantine*, and something like it in *The Devil's Advocate*. Cher, Michelle Pfeiffer, and Susan Sarandon did it in *The Witches of Eastwick*. *Ghost Rider* and *Spawn* did it in the movie and the comics. Katy Perry and Oprah might've done it in real life.

What if I make a deal with the Devil?

Chapter Thirteen

$\mathcal{N}$eedless to say, sleeping on that idea becomes an impossibility. By morning, I'm beyond knackered and require three cups of strongly brewed tea to stay semi-coherent.

On the way to work, I text the Devil what might be famous last words: *Do you have time for a chat?*

The reply is instant: *7:30 p.m.?*

Great, I text. *Where?*

This time, he takes a few seconds to get back to me: *How about my office? You remember—it's the place you decimated.*

See you there, is what I say back, even though my fingers are itching to type out something a lot ruder.

Plan for the meeting: figure out a way not to get fired. Also on the to-do list: no making moony eyes at the Devil, no drooling, and no fantasies of grooming him. Must resist his masculine wiles at all costs.

I'm the first in the office, but I'm brimming with

too much nervous energy to actually do anything useful. One thing leads to another, and I catch myself moving a few desks that look out of alignment, as well as adding/removing pens and other minutia on people's workspaces so that they have nice, prime totals.

The elevator door opens, halting my endeavors.

It's Alison, the manager of the quality assurance team.

"Hiya." I smile at the older woman. "How are you?"

"Hi, Holly," she says. "Did you get my email about a bug my team found with Euclid?"

Skipping the pleasantries—I like that about Alison. "Sorry, no. Haven't had a chance to check my email yet."

"Everything crashes if you feed him four toasts and toss the fetch stick six times right after that. I had a few people replicate this issue on multiple devices."

Four and six. Nasty, non-prime numbers. Of course they crash the bloody app. "I'll look into it, thanks."

She scurries to her desk as I unlock my workstation and jump into Euclid's code.

By the afternoon, I've fixed Alison's discovery and let her know about it.

"I'll have someone retest," she says. Lowering her voice, she adds, "I heard a new rumor, by the way."

I lean in. She's as good at uncovering juicy gossip as she is at detecting software bugs.

"The Chorstkys are moving in," she says. "Maybe even tomorrow."

Yep. That sounds about right—but I don't tell her that. Nor do I mention the very real possibility that I won't be here tomorrow to witness the Devil's invasion. It all hinges on our upcoming conversation.

"Let me know if you hear anything else about the Chortskys," I whisper. "And if you find any other ways to crash poor Euclid."

She promises that she will, and I retrace my steps to my desk—where, unfortunately, Buckley is waiting to speak to me.

I'm not Buckley's biggest fan. He likes to clear his throat a lot—and usually an even number of times.

"Hi, boss," he says and clears his throat twice. "Got a minute?"

This man is an enigma. I got promoted to CTO over him, so I figured he'd hate my guts afterward. Imagine my surprise when he asked me out instead. Of course, I had to refuse, mostly because I don't think office romances are proper, but there was a shallow reason too: I find his asymmetrical body and face aesthetically displeasing.

"I can talk," I say. "What's up?"

He clears his throat twice more. "I was just wondering if you've heard from the new management."

I shrug noncommittally. "Why?"

He scratches his perpetual stubble—a grooming choice that didn't help his chances when he asked me out. "I was wondering if the merger means there will be opportunities for us to move within the bigger organization. Not that I don't like working for you, but—"

"Say no more." I smile at him. "I'll write to my equivalent on the other side and see what they have for you."

"Thanks, Holly," he says and clears his throat just once—a miracle. "I really appreciate this."

As soon as he leaves, I write an email to Robert Jellyheim in which I wax ecstatic about Buckley. If he gets the move he wants, I might just never hear his throat-clearing again.

Since I'm on an email kick, I take a stab at the million messages awaiting my attention. By the time my inbox is empty, it's already past normal working hours.

Just like yesterday, people aren't leaving, no doubt waiting me out again.

Fine. I can use the same leaving trick again. I should eat before the big meeting anyway. And for the record, my going to Miso Hungry has nothing to do with the hope of seeing the Devil there, like the last time.

Nothing at all.

Nope.

I even out a few more desks and move some pens around to get prime totals on my way out too, both because I want to and to get attention. Then I rush to the restaurant.

"To go?" the hostess asks as soon as she spots me.

"Takeout," I say and glance around.

No Devil, no Bella.

Ugh. What's with the wave of disappointment crashing into me? They must not be as much creatures of routine as I am.

Oh, well. Not everybody's perfect.

Food in hand, I return to the empty office and eat my miso soup with forty-seven cubes of tofu and seventeen pieces of scallion. Then I consume the twenty-three avocado roll pieces. Sadly, in my current state, I could just as easily chew on the paper bag the sushi came in as far as tasting any of it goes.

At a quarter past seven, the elevator doors open and the Chortsky siblings step out.

Bella looks even more like she's just come off a runway, and the Devil is somehow even scruffier than usual—so much for those grooming fantasies I was hoping to avoid. *Or keeping my heart rate even and my libido in check.*

"Hi." Bella waves her delicate hand at me in a suspiciously beauty-pageant-like way for someone who's allegedly never participated in one.

I wave back. "Lovely to see you again."

"*Privet,*" the Devil says.

"That means hi," Bella translates.

"Ahoy," I say back to the Devil.

Wait, ahoy? Last I checked, today isn't International Talk Like a Pirate Day. Bloody adrenaline is really messing with my head.

Acting as though ahoy is a normal reply to a Russian hello, the siblings go into their offices.

The next eleven minutes drag on for a year.

Finally, it's time.

Getting up, I head to the Wicked One's office.

Pirates are still on my mind, it seems, because I can't help feeling like I'm about to walk the plank. His door creaks—like the plank—and once I open it, I half expect to see the mess I created yesterday.

Nope. Someone's cleaned it up.

Good. I won't be having my nose rubbed in my sins, like a puppy. Then again, he hasn't replaced the broken keyboard and monitor—and is instead working on a laptop, which must be a lot less comfortable.

Here goes nothing.

I step into the Devil's lair.

Chapter Fourteen

he Prince of Darkness closes his laptop. "Please, sit."

Since the couch is the only place available, I plop there—and do my best not to think about the things a virtual version of him was doing to me last night on this very surface.

The Tempter's cerulean eyes scan me carefully, as though he plans to create a 3D model of me for VR.

Did my eyelashes just bat at him prettily?

Afraid so.

Does that count as moony eyes?

Close enough.

Bugger. Nothing is going as planned.

At least I'm not drooling. Or am I? Would it look weird if I checked?

"Since you might get a reminder about a more important meeting at any second, I'll get to the point," he says. "You're not fired."

"Pardon?"

Wait. What am I doing?

He said I'm not fired.

I heard him just fine—I just didn't expect it.

Also, is it hot in here?

I feel equal parts dizzy and euphoric.

"I said you get to keep your job," he enunciates. "Under certain conditions, of course."

Ah. Here we go. Knowing there's a catch makes me feel better. Otherwise, things would be too good to be true.

"What are the conditions?" I ask.

Is he about to make an indecent proposal?

More importantly, is that something I'm hoping for?

"There are two." He drums his long, masculine fingers on the desk. Is it wrong that I can picture them stroking me? "You're going to help with the integration project," he says, wrenching my mind away from delicious massages. "The issues you mentioned, where the headset and gloves don't work as they should with the suit, will become your top priority."

"Fair enough," I say and mean it. "What's the second thing?"

"Right." He frowns. "This should go without saying, but I will spell it out for you. There will be no more monkey wrenches into my sister's work. If you so much as introduce a bug into the integration code, you're done. If cameras malfunction at any of our offices, that will be it. If a virus infects any of our computers, or critical employees for that matter, you're a goner. If there's—"

"I get the picture," I say. "We have an accord."

"It appears we do." He opens his laptop. "*Do svidaniya*."

Channeling Buckley, I clear my throat. Not getting fired is just the first item on my agenda, but I'm not sure how to proceed.

"We can discuss the details of the integration project tomorrow, after my sister and I officially move in to these offices," he says, clearly misunderstanding my hesitation to leave.

Here goes nothing. "There's something else I wanted to discuss with you."

"Oh?" He pins me with that intense cerulean stare. "Work or personal?"

My skin feels overly warm and tingly. "Work. Strictly professional. Not personal in the slightest."

I force myself to shut up, as methinks I sound like that lady that doth protest too much.

He frowns. "So, work."

Did I catch disappointment flitting across his features? Nah. Must be my overactive ovaries playing mind games.

"1000 Devils has a contract with NYU Langone hospital," I say.

His eyes widen. "I thought you didn't do corporate espionage. How do you know that?"

I remind him that his company website publicly lists him as the owner, and I tell him about my meeting at the hospital and why Dr. Piper informed me about the contract.

"So you want my help getting some games onto the headset?" he asks when I'm done explaining.

"Yes. I figure you'd make even more money from NYU Langone this way. So win-win."

He scratches that cursed stubble on his chin—activating my grooming fantasies once again. "I'm not sure they would pay more. I bet they'd just include VR as a platform in the existing contract—they don't make a distinction between tablets, consoles, or phones at the moment, so this is like that."

My heart feels like a witch doctor has just shrunk it. "So you won't help me?"

A satyr-like smirk illuminates his gorgeous features. "I didn't say that. I think I might help you… for a price."

Here we go.

I can practically envision myself pricking a finger and signing a contract that asks for my firstborn.

My insides start quivering, and not just my ovaries anymore. "What do you want?"

"Two more things," he says, his voice low and deep. "Not work-related this time."

I knew it. The Devil is demanding a deal—one cannot hide one's nature.

"What are they?" I'm impressed with myself. My voice is steady, and the British accent hasn't reappeared.

"Bella is going crazy wanting to know what you

thought of the suit," he says. "I want you to give her a full report. It'll make her happy."

I gape at him. On the one hand, this is not completely unrelated to work, but on the other, it's bonkers.

"I'm not qualified for that," I say, realizing I'm grabbing at straws. "I'm not QA."

"Oh, don't worry," he says. "Bella has a form and everything. Also, she can put you in touch with Fanny —she's got experience in these things."

There's someone named Fanny involved? Poor woman. In England, that means vagina—though here in the US, it means butt, so also not a great association.

Bugger. Now the Devil is making me think about vaginas and butts.

"What else?" I ask noncommittally.

His eyes gleam. "It's my father's birthday tomorrow. I want you to come with me to the celebration."

My breathing quickens. "Like… a date?"

The smirk is back. "Not a real date. A pretend date. My mother has been trying to set me up with random women, and I want it to stop."

That twat. How dare she try to set him up with some harlot? Why I—

Wow. That escalated quickly. For all I know, his mother might be a lovely lady.

"Not a date." I taste the words and find them lacking.

Shouldn't I be relieved he didn't ask for that firstborn—or to father said firstborn? Also, why is it so easy to picture this hypothetical devil spawn? It would no doubt have his cerulean eyes, my oval-shaped face, his—

"So," the Devil says, ripping me out of my hormone-induced delirium. "Have you ever been to a Russian party before?"

I shake my head.

"A Russian restaurant?"

Another shake.

"You're in for a treat, then. There will be amazing food and a show." He looks me up and down. "Just bear in mind, the dress code is pretty formal, so you might want to wear something nice."

Is he saying I'm not wearing something nice *now*? Wanker. Also, he's wearing a hoodie. Pot calling the kettle black much?

"Fine," I grit through my teeth. "I accept your terms."

"Great. I'll text you the details."

Turning angrily on my heel, I head for the door.

With a speed worthy of his supernatural nature, the Devil leaps to his feet and gets the door for me.

Seems that convincing the world he doesn't exist isn't the only trick the Devil tries to pull. He also wants me to think he's a gentleman.

Bugger. Now if I want to leave this place, I'll either have to pass close to him or rudely ask him to move, which I don't want to do.

I take a step forward.

A faint aroma of a yummy tea enters my nostrils, making my mouth water. Oolong, keemun, maybe lapsang souchong, along with something ineffably male.

Another step.

Our gazes fuse.

There's a tumult in my belly—my treacherous ovaries are no doubt trying to choke each other to death.

The closer I get, the more hypnotized I become by his gaze.

Maybe I should back away—or be rude after all?

That would be wise, but I don't do either. Like a doomed star trapped by the gravity of a black hole, I'm drawn to him—which must be why I close the distance.

Leave, Holly.

My feet feel welded to the ground.

Don't do it, Holly.

I rise on tiptoes.

His head dips toward me.

No. No, no, no. Can't do this. Shouldn't do this. If we actually kiss, my ovaries will explode and—

"Oh, sorry," Bella's voice says from just a few feet away. "I'll come back in—"

I don't hear what she says next. Finally tearing my gaze away from the Devil's, I bolt for the elevator.

Thank heavens the doors open instantly—I might've gone for the fire exit staircase otherwise.

As I ride down and sprint for the cab, my mind is

blank, my heart racing madly. It's not until I get home and change my soaked knickers that I finally shake off the shock brought on by that brush with the Devil.

I follow my usual evening routine like a robot, but that leaves room in my brain for errant thoughts. Thoughts like: was he going to kiss me, or did I imagine it? And if he did want to snog, does that mean our fake date isn't so fake?

No. Can't be. I'm sure he doesn't want me like that.

More importantly, even if he did, it can't happen.

After the disaster with my ex, I'm not ready to date. Might never be—though if I were, it wouldn't be the bloody Devil.

There's nothing messier than mixing work and love life, even when a relationship would be deemed appropriate by HR—say, when the two people are in different departments. In this case, though, he's pretty much my boss, so it's definitely against corporate policy. And let's not forget that he's evil—might in fact be the Evil Consultant himself. Worse still, he's untidy.

Speaking of that, why am I even attracted to him?

It's a mystery of Bermuda triangle proportions.

When my routine is complete, I go to bed, but even with the weight of all that recent insomnia pressing against the backs of my eyes, I lie there for an hour before admitting I'm unable to sleep yet again.

Fine. I might as well do something useful instead of tossing and turning for hours.

Getting up, I open my closet to pick out an outfit for the upcoming birthday.

The problem is, my usual philosophy about clothing is going to bite me in the ass. To limit the time wasted on decisions, I wear the same thing every day: one of seven identical white button-up shirts (each with five buttons in the front) and one of seven pairs of identical black pants. Since I was wearing this exact combo when the Devil said to "wear something nice," it implies my usual work outfit won't do. Nor will my home clothes suffice. They're also identical, with the t-shirts and yoga pants optimized for comfort, not "niceness."

Sigh.

I look at the "outlier" section of the closet.

There are three identical dresses left over from when I went out on dates with my ex.

I hope they fit the Devil's "nice" criterium.

I wriggle into one.

Grr. I can't breathe and my boobs look on the verge of bursting out. Seems I've gained some weight.

Bloody hell. I can't have nip-slip number three—especially since I will be in front of the Devil's whole family.

Ugh. This means shopping.

I hate shopping, mostly because if there was such a thing as fashion intelligence, my IQ in it would be something abysmal, like thirty-one.

Oh, well. At least I'm otherwise intelligent enough to know to ask for help.

Getting my phone out, I text *Hi* to my twin. Despite her Criss Angel-inspired, rock-star-meets-vampire appearance, her fashion intelligence is at least three standard deviations higher than my own.

She instantly replies: *You're not asleep? Isn't going to bed at eleven sacred?*

Of course. She doesn't know about my insomnia since I lied to her about the B & E.

Might as well come clean.

Can you do a video call? I ask.

Turns out she can, so I call her and tell her everything, including my lack of appropriate outfit.

When I'm done speaking, she has that mischievous expression on her face that I and the sextuplets learned to dread in our childhood—the one you see before you learn that she hid a dozen alarm clocks in your room, or duct-taped an air horn under your chair, or replaced the cream in your favorite doughnut with mayo.

"Before we talk about shopping," she says, "I have to tell you, I strongly disagree with you."

I audibly sigh. "What do you disagree with?"

"This restaurant outing totally sounds like a date."

I bring the phone closer to my face so she can clearly see my disapproving frown. "No. It's not."

She also brings the phone to her face, so all I see is a giant blue eye. "Is too."

"Is not."

From here, the sophistication of our argumentative techniques regresses all the way down to:

"Yuh-huh."

"Nuh-uh."

The giant eye rolls, then she pulls the phone away from her face. "Agree to disagree?"

I also pull the phone away. "If that's what it takes to get you to help."

"Oh, I was going to shop with you regardless," she says. "I've seen your closet. This is long overdue."

I narrow my eyes at her. "We're only getting what's needed."

Her grin is downright devious now. "Exactly. How about I meet you at your place at nine? We're going to Madison Avenue. You can afford it."

"Tidy," I say without thinking.

"Toodles," she replies hoity-toitily and hangs up.

Bugger. Forgot to warn her there's no way in hell I'm wearing something slutty for the party—which will be her first instinct, no doubt.

As I put my phone on its charger, I realize a slight problem with our plan.

Being the CTO, I've never needed to explain my comings or goings to anyone at the office, but things are different now. Tomorrow is the day when the Devil and Bella are moving into our offices, and they'll surely wonder where I am.

The solution is simple. I type out a text to the Devil:

Will not be in the office tomorrow. Have to prepare for the birthday. If you have a problem with this, I'd be delighted to call the whole thing off.

There. Maybe shopping can now be avoided?

His reply is instant:

See you at the party.

Oh, well. It was too much to hope he'd just call it off. Not that I really want him to do that anyway. Not if my sister is right and there's even a sliver of a chance this thing *is* a date.

Which it isn't.

No way.

And I don't want it to be.

I head to bed, but sleep is again as elusive as an oiled eel.

It doesn't take me long to pinpoint the main culprit. It's the Devil's second demand: sharing my suit experience with Bella. There are so many problems with that, I don't know which is the worst. To start, when I do things, I like to do them properly— and in this case, I lack the QA experience to do the task justice.

I sit up. The problem is pretty solvable. Alison has a training manual for new QA employees.

Firing up my laptop, I look for the manual and hit paydirt quickly.

I start reading.

Fascinating. This is exactly what I needed.

When I'm done, I have a new respect for Alison and her team, but sadly, I'm no closer to sleep—even though some folks would find the reading material I've just finished sleep-inducing.

A part of me is tempted yet again by the suit. An

orgasm might help me sleep, and without sleep, the party ordeal might be that much harder.

No. I'm not going to give in to my base desires, or use the suit as a sleeping aid.

But wait. Why are my legs taking me to the genitalia-decorated backpack?

And why am I taking the damned suit out?

When I lay the suit out on my bed, I readily come up with the reason: I will use it for Bella's report. Yeah, that's it. I didn't finish the demo the last time and thus can't give Bella a complete picture. Speaking of completeness, unlike cunnilingus, coitus *is* something I have done in real life, so I can answer any pesky "did it feel real?" questions.

Yeah, that's it. I'm not doing this because I'm randy, but because the completionist in me demands it.

Jolly good. That's my story, and I'm sticking with it. After all, using the suit with the QA manual in mind will allow me to pay attention to all the little things I might've missed before—like girth, length, and hardness of certain things.

When it comes to the schlong of the VR Devil, it's all in the details.

Once I shimmy into the suit, I go through the same selection criteria as before—with a small difference.

I give the VR Devil a much, much bigger cock.

Chapter Fifteen

*T*he naked Devil simulacra starts dancing, like the last time.

Gulping down drool, I desperately try to look at this as a QA person would.

Nope. I'm now picturing poor Alison having a heart attack, and looking at him this closely makes my distracting arousal worse.

Maybe this wasn't such a great idea.

"Do you want me to give you a taste of what the suit can do?" the demo asks me once more. "Yes or no."

A "yes" teleports the VR Devil next to me, his bigger cock making it hard to stand next to him.

Hard indeed.

How did Bella give the suit such a variety of phalluses without a bunch of hidden dildos?

I'd better not ask her that. She will never shut up

about it if I do. Plus, like with Gia's magic, some things are more fun when they retain their mystery.

Also, is it actually phalluses or phalli, given that phallus is Latin-based and has that -us ending? Must check—along with the plural for penis, another important item on my to-do list.

"Continue?" the demo asks.

When I agree, he cups my breast again.

QA manual? Report for Bella? What is that nonsense? I certainly don't recall anymore.

After a prompt, he squeezes my nipple again.

I'd bet my life this is what it would feel like if the real Devil did it—which he never would.

Another prompt.

He touches my clit—and I nearly come on the spot.

"Do you want to sample the cunnilingus phase? Yes or no."

Gee, I don't know. Yes, sodding please.

The sensation of a wet tongue down under is so real I again dimly wonder how Bella accomplished it.

He licks me once, twice, thrice.

I'm getting close.

He sucks on my clit.

My toes curl.

Almost there.

Please finish. I've been good, I promise.

Nope.

Bugger. It all stops, just like the last bloody time.

Also, I've totally forgotten all about QA.

"Do you want to sample the penetration phase? Yes or no."

I think about this for all of a second. I've never felt this empty before. Never been so ready to receive—

The whole VR world goes red, and a big box appears in the air, "Please charge batteries."

Noooo.

This is what hell must be like—access to a big cock that loses its charge at the worst possible time.

Peeling the suit off me, I locate its charging port.

Whew. Regular USB port.

Feeling a little jealous of the USB hole that gets plugged instead of me, I leave the suit attached to my laptop to charge, then sprawl on my bed and debate if I should wait and resume testing today or finish myself off manually and deal with this another time.

My lids grow heavy, so I close my eyes—I don't need them open to make this decision.

As if it were waiting for this opportunity all this time, sleep pounces and knocks me right out.

Chapter Sixteen

I wake up to the sound of the bloody alarm.

In my dream, the Devil—the real one, not the VR imitation—was just about to finally make me come.

Woe is me. If I didn't know any better, I'd theorize this to be the work of the Wicked One—he's building up my horniness past teenage-boy levels and into the territory where I just might sell my soul for an orgasm.

Wait.

My deal with the Devil. The party.

Gia is going to be downstairs at nine, so I need to get my butt out of bed and start my seven-step morning routine.

———

"So, I have a magic effect I wanted to try out on you," Gia says as we walk into a ritzy department store.

Great universe. Shopping wasn't bad enough; now I have to deal with this too? As children, our siblings and I sat through our share of Gia's beginner magic, with me getting the brunt of it. If I had a dollar for every card I've picked in my life, I'd own this whole store.

"It's a good one," Gia says, no doubt picking up on my hesitation. "And short."

Short? I guess not all is lost. "Go ahead."

"Can I help you?" says a snooty-looking saleswoman before Gia can continue.

"She needs a new outfit," Gia says, nodding my way.

The lady looks me up and down with a look that seems to say, "Boy, do we have our work cut out for us."

"Before we shop, maybe you can participate in a little experiment my sister and I were just about to undertake," Gia says, her stage persona in full force.

The lady looks at her suspiciously, but that doesn't deter my twin in the slightest.

"When I say so," Gia says, "you will think of a two-digit odd number. A number so odd, in fact, that both digits are odd. Okay?"

The lady's nod is more reluctant than my own, but not by much. I also wonder if Gia is blind to the irony of asking us to think of an odd number while acting so odd?

Unless that's part of the trick?

"I have one in mind," I say, since I know how to handle my twin better than the salesperson does.

"I do too," the lady says with all the enthusiasm of someone who's entered *The Twilight Zone*.

With a flash of fire and smoke, a notepad and a pen appear in my sister's hand.

Wow. Gia has gotten much better since the last time she showed me stuff. I have no clue how she just did that.

The saleswoman clutches her chest, no doubt worried the fire alarms are about to blare.

Gia writes something on the pad. "I've just committed myself."

I'm glad to hear that. She's certainly acting like someone who needs to be committed.

She thrusts the pad into the hands of the stunned saleswoman. "On the count of three, you will say your numbers out loud."

She counts to three.

"37," I say at the same time as the helper lady says the exact same thing.

Double wow.

"Check the pad," Gia says.

Yep. On the pad is 37.

Not only did I and a perfect stranger think of the same number, but Gia also knew what it would be ahead of time.

How? She could've guessed I'd say 37—it's a permutable prime because you can make 73 out of it, which is also prime, and I like that sort of thing. Then again, nothing stopped me from choosing 13. It's a twin prime to 11 because they are two apart, and it fits her "both numbers odd" criteria.

The real question is, why did this lady say the same thing? And how did Gia know she would?

"Is it subliminal messaging?" the lady asks.

Rookie mistake. Gia will never admit how she did what she did—not even to someone with identical DNA.

My twin smiles with an air of mystery. "Can you keep a secret?"

The lady nods.

"So can I," Gia says triumphantly.

If I had a dollar for every time I've heard this joke, I'd also own this store.

The lady rubs her temples. "I have a headache. Did you do that?"

"No, but put your hand out." Gia waves her gloved hands over the lady's extended palm and a white pill appears there.

The lady stares at the pill.

"It's Tylenol," my sister says.

"Thanks," the lady says but doesn't put it into her mouth—and I can't blame her in the slightest. "Are you ready to shop now?"

Gia says we are, and before I can argue to the contrary, I find myself shepherded into a fitting room with a strappy black cocktail dress designed for a femme fatale in a James Bond film.

Taking off my clothes and bra, I shimmy into the dress and look in the mirror. "I don't like it."

"Who cares?" Gia asks. "Come out so I can see."

I step out of the fitting room.

The helper lady nods approvingly, and Gia examines me like a butcher about to make a prime cut.

"Too conservative," she concludes, making it sound like a bad thing.

"I'll get something else," the lady says, scurrying away.

I look back into the mirror, then at my twin. "My problem was the opposite. It doesn't look proper."

She rolls her eyes, walks into the fitting room, and gingerly lifts up my perfectly functional beige bra with her gloved hands. "Is this your idea of proper?"

I shrug.

"I assume you have granny panties to match this atrocity?" she asks.

I put my hands on my hips. "Oh, pish posh. Who cares about my underwear? No one is going to see it."

She snorts. "Not with that attitude he won't."

I flush, the thought of the Devil seeing me in *any* underwear making me uncomfortably warm inside.

"How about you grab a dress you like?" my sister says, suddenly sounding conciliatory. "I'll go find some normal underwear for you."

Leaving her to it, I locate something appropriate.

By the time I return, she's waiting for me, hiding something behind her back. "That is something a sadist would ask her bridesmaids to wear," she says, wrinkling her nose at my choice.

Ignoring her, I go into the fitting room and try the dress on.

Outside, I hear her saying something to the salesperson, but I can't make it out.

The dress looks okay, I think. Reminds me of what I wanted to wear to the prom before my siblings talked me out of it.

"I think this is it," I say.

"Show us," my sister says imperiously.

I come out.

The salesperson's eyes widen, and she struggles to keep a professional expression. On her end, my sister just laughs in my face, like a maniac. "This might work as a Halloween outfit," she says when she catches her breath. "You can be Cinderella... before she got the ball makeover."

I huff indignantly. "This isn't a maid outfit."

"Go back and take it off," Gia says. "We'll hand you things to try."

I return to the changing room and strip.

"Start with this." Gia tosses in two lacy atrocities. "You're not going in granny panties."

I hold the items between my thumb and index finger, far away from my body in case they bite. "This is stupid. I'm not here for new underwear."

"Just try it," she says.

To shut her up, I put on her selections.

The so-called panties make me understand why

they call these "butt floss," and the bra pushes my boobs just a few inches shy of my chin.

"What do you think?" Gia asks.

"I look like a French courtesan circa the Middle Ages."

"Which is good, right?" she asks.

I readjust my squished boobs. "It's not proper, but I don't care as much because it will be invisible."

"Great." She tosses in a dress. "Even if no one sees the new undies, you'll feel sexy wearing them."

Does feeling sexy have a lot in common with feeling scratchy? Maybe. Knowing men, they just might find it hot if they saw you readjusting your knickers.

With a sigh, I put on her chosen dress and gape at all the exposed skin. "This will not do."

"Show me," Gia says.

I shake my head. "A streetwalker would hesitate to wear this."

Gia knocks on the door. "Come out."

"No."

"You'll have to, eventually."

No, I won't. I'm just going to change back into—

Wait.

Where are my clothes?

"I hid them all," Gia says before I can ask. "If you want to come out of there dressed, you'll have to do it in that dress."

With a growl, I step out of the dressing booth.

The salesperson and Gia exchange knowing glances.

"You look hot, sis," Gia says, and the lady nods enthusiastically.

I look in a mirror again and frown. "My cervix is showing."

Ignoring me, Gia asks the salesperson for a pair of high heels.

"You're wasting your time," I say when the lady is gone. "I'm not wearing this."

"You are," Gia says.

"Am not."

In déjà vu, we go back and forth until we get to:

"Yuh-huh."

"Nuh-uh."

"You forgot something important," Gia says.

My stomach turns cold at the wicked expression on her face. Surely, she's not going to—

"Yeah, that's right, you owe me one," she says, confirming my fears.

"But—"

"I'm calling in my favor," Gia says ceremonially. "I want you to look hot for your date. That means this dress, professional makeup, this lingerie, high heels of my choosing, and last but not least, a Brazilian wax."

Chapter Seventeen

*I*f her magic career never takes off, Gia can always give law a shot. No matter how hard I try to argue that heels plus lingerie plus dress plus makeup plus wax is five favors, she expertly contends that "looking hot" is just one.

Handing me a shoebox, she makes a summation of her case. "Teaching you lock picking required talking, gesturing, breathing, and much more, but I didn't consider those subparts separate favors. You should be grateful I'm using up my favor for something as selfless as making *you* look good for *your* date."

"Yeah, you're a saint," I say and open the box. "These are fuck-me pumps."

"Show us."

With a sigh, I clickety-clack out of the fitting room and twirl for my tormentors.

"Perfect," Gia says. "Now let's pay and go get you made up."

The makeup artist is so slow with her task she makes a slug seem zippy by comparison.

When it's done, I look like a proper strumpet, with a touch of trollop thrown in—which, of course, means Gia loves it.

After this metaphorical torture is over, we sprint across the street to a salon where a much more literal torture of hot wax awaits.

"The aesthetician will be right with you," says a smiling older woman.

I do a little research on my phone, then look up. "Is she licensed?"

I don't ask for the gender—if it's a man, I'm going to revolt.

"Of course," the lady says, smile faltering.

"When was the last time she got her physical?" I ask.

"Ah, there she is," the now-frowning lady says and gestures at who I presume is the aesthetician.

Tall and broad-shouldered, the woman looks more like a wrestler than a beautician, but hey, at least she should pass any physical with flying colors.

"Good luck," Gia whispers to me. Louder, she says, "She wants a Brazilian."

"No problem," the aesthetician booms in a masculine voice with a thick Russian accent.

Great. The last thing I need is an accent that reminds me of the Devil.

As she leads me to the torture room, I ask her all the standard questions I'd ask my surgeon, like if she drank the night before (no), and if she got enough sleep (yes).

"Do not be twitchy," she booms after my fifth question in that vein. "I take good care of you."

I know she wants to be reassuring, but it actually comes off menacing.

"In here," she says.

I step into a sterile-looking room with a big table in the middle.

"Strip," the aesthetician orders.

Fighting the urge to whimper, "Yes, mistress," I take my clothes off and follow directions until I end up on my back, legs spread, ready for further indignities.

"Nice bush," the mistress says, looking over my pubes approvingly. "Make job easier."

"Thanks?" I mutter. Who knew never trimming myself down there would come in handy?

Muscles flexing, the mistress treats the area with cleaning products and who knows what else while I lie there and remind myself that this is a licensed professional, and that I've survived a gynecologist's office with my sanity mostly intact.

When she applies the first batch of hot wax, I realize my teeth are clenched so tightly I just might need a dentist's visit after this—and wouldn't that put a shit cherry on top of this crap cake.

"Relax," the mistress growls after she attaches the first strip to my skin a few inches below my navel.

Relax? That is what all the doctors say before they do something—

Aargh! The sound emitting from my mouth is as shrill and desperate as that of the proverbial stuck pig would be in this situation—though if anyone waxes pigs before sticking them, PETA should get on it, posthaste.

The door opens and the receptionist lady rushes in, along with Gia and a couple of women I haven't seen.

"Are you okay?" my twin asks.

I redden. Could this be any worse? I guess they could've brought some random men with them. Or my dad. Or the Devil himself.

"She okay," my mistress tells them. "First time always hard."

"No, I'm not okay," I gasp. Giving my twin a narrowed-eye stare, I grit out, "I'll get you for this."

"Oh, you'll thank me once it's all over and you feel like a sex goddess," Gia says and herds all the spectators out of the room.

"Not bloody likely," I yell, but by then the door is closed.

"No worry. I make it better," the mistress says and applies another strip.

How?

She rips. I yelp in pain—but not as loudly.

She bends her head until it's inches away from my crotch and blows gently on the booboo.

Oh, this is what she meant?

Hmm. It does feel better—but at the same time, I really don't feel comfortable with how close her lips are to my clit, or the sensations my clit experiences from that airflow.

"Ready?" she asks.

I nod, resigned.

She rips again, then blows on the smarting flesh.

To stay sane, I count the number of rips and think of England.

After I survive a few more rounds, my tormentor says, "Now more sensitive area. Take a deep breath."

Wait a bloody sec—

Aargh! The pain is so intense I inadvertently squeeze my legs shut, no doubt giving the mistress a flashback to her wrestling career.

"Now look what you do," she says when my legs come apart again. "You glue your vagine shut."

She's right, and the process to undo the damage is probably the most humiliating thing I've ever experienced—including everything that's just preceded it.

"Try again?" the mistress asks when my mistake is finally undone.

I take in a deep breath. "Do it."

She does.

I yelp in pain and swear vengeance on Gia—but my legs stay apart this time.

My yelp is less loud the next round, and even less the one after that. I wonder if I'll reach subspace—a state of mind I read about in the context of BDSM. As the process continues, the subspace never materializes, so I desperately count the rips as I mentally draft a letter to whoever puts together the United Nations Convention against Torture—they clearly missed a technique.

After a century of pain, the aesthetician stops.

Dare I have hope? Is it finally over?

"Get on all fours," she orders.

I furrow my eyebrows. "Pardon me?"

"Doggy style," she says with a deadpan expression. "I finish Brazilian."

Oh, well. In for a penny of indignities, in for a pound of humiliation. I get into the required position, and hot wax is smeared around my bumhole for my troubles.

Can this get any worse?

Yep, sure can.

Though the pain of the rip is less severe, her subsequent blowing on the spot is as close as I've ever come to someone blowing smoke up my butt—sans the smoke.

On rip sixteen, she says she's done.

Sixteen? Not a prime. It's going to drive me mad.

No.

Must let go.

Can't.

Bugger. Am I really going to do this now?

Seems like I am.

Looking over my shoulder as I would at a lover mounting me, I ask, "Can you do one more strip?"

She stares at me like the hair she's just waxed has sprouted from my eyeballs. "Why?"

"Please?" I sound like I'm begging, which no doubt cements her "kinkiest client ever" impression of me for good. "I'll give you an extra tip."

With a slow headshake that clearly means "the shit I do to make money", she applies a little bit more wax to my bumhole, then rips—but without blowing this time.

That's fair. I guess now she thinks things have gotten weird.

Whatever. I got my seventeen rips, so I can leave.

In hindsight, counting wasn't the best idea.

I swiftly dress and pay, then walk out of the place while pointedly ignoring Gia's attempts to chat me up.

"Let me buy you lunch," Gia says after a few minutes of silent treatment. "You seem hangry."

She must feel very guilty indeed if she's willing to part with cash—her magic career doesn't pay all that well.

Let's see if I can call her bluff. "How about Nemo and Chips?" I ask, picking a restaurant near my place that I order from on the days I feel particularly thin and/or nostalgic for the UK. A place I happen to know she hates.

"That fish and chips shop?" Gia asks with an eye roll.

"At least it's clean enough for you," I say. "A-rating all the way."

She scoffs. "Yeah, like no one's ever gotten food

poisoning from fish. But sure, why not? Brits are famous for their delicious cuisine."

Despite the grumbling, she hails a cab and takes us there—a sign of just how guilty she must feel after my banshee shrieks.

When we get a table at the place, I sip my tea and she guzzles her bottled water while giving me unsolicited advice for my upcoming "date"—advice I studiously ignore.

The food arrives. As I bite into my fried Nemo, I frown.

It tastes different than usual.

I hate it when that happens. If a dish has a name, it has to be consistent forever—that's why I always go to the same restaurants.

"What's wrong now?" Gia asks.

I explain.

"Please don't make a big deal out of this," she says. "Pretty please?"

I put my fork down. "Would *you* not make a big deal of it if they spit germs into your food?"

She sighs. "That's exactly what they'll do the next time if you make a scene."

"I'm not going to make a scene." I wave the waiter over.

Gia cringes.

"The fried Nemo was different than usual," I announce. "And I don't mean just the normal variation you can have in pollock."

"Different?" The waiter doesn't seem as concerned as a professional should be.

I explain that I've had the dish countless times, so I'd know better than anyone.

The waiter gets the manager, who offers to make the meal free.

"No," I say. "I want the recipe restored."

The manager gets the chef, who claims the dish is the same.

I challenge him to bring out the ingredients, which he reluctantly does. Then I proceed to taste it all, until I find the culprit: a different brand of beer in the batter.

"That's an impressive palate," the chef says. "I'll be sure to get the old beer going forward."

Whew. Order in the universe is restored.

Since Gia was a trooper through this ordeal, I pay for the meal after all, then magnanimously lie to her face that I had a great time today.

She grins. "Sure, let's pretend you did. Good luck on your not-a-date."

"Thanks," I say, matching her snarky tone.

"Don't mention it." She leans in and lowers her voice to a conspiratorial whisper. "Whatever you do, don't complain about the food like you just did. That's a sure way to turn a date into not-a-date."

"I won't," I say, and it's true.

How could I? I've never eaten at the place where the party is happening, so I don't have a baseline for what the food ought to taste like.

———

When I get home, I check my email. Seems that Buckley has impressed Robert and quickly too; they're having a chat today. Great. The throat-clearing might cease even sooner than I hoped.

There's an email from Alison too, filling me in on the Chortskys' move into the office. Apparently, both gave a speech and everything. She says they promised I'd lead the most important project—suit integration.

Speaking of the latter, an email from Robert gives me a link to the source control with the code I'll need to review. I don't look at said code just yet. I'm not in the state of mind to focus with everything that's happened already, not to mention my anxiety over what is about to happen in a few hours.

Since the Devil is proceeding with his part of our arrangement, I email Dr. Piper and tell him that I'll be able to get 1000 Devils on board. To make sure that actually is the truth, I email the Wicked One and ask him when he wants to meet to talk about the games.

Once my inbox is clean, I can't help but begin to worry.

What will the Devil's family be like? How sure am I that this isn't a date? What if his father doesn't like the gift I picked out—a tiny can of caviar that put me way over my usual birthday gift budget?

Also, what if Bella asks about the suit tonight—a query I now have an obligation to respond to?

Would she bring that up at her father's birthday?

She seems like the kind of person who might.

I level a speculative glance at the suit. It's charged now, so in theory, I could go through that last step of the demo now. It might even be wise. I've got so much pent-up sexual energy in me I might flirt with the Devil tonight… or worse.

If I use that suit now, it would be like that scene from *There's Something About Mary*, where Ben Stiller jerks off as a way to seem less twitchy on the date.

But no. That didn't work out so well for Ben Stiller—the last thing I want is for the Devil to end up with my pussy juices as hair gel. I'm sure I can control myself, and in any case, my post-wax skin is tender down there, so getting rubbed by the suit material isn't what it needs.

So, no sex with the virtual Devil for me… for now. If Bella brings it up, I'll ask her about the testing documents the Devil mentioned. That should delay things until I see her next.

Yeah, that's it. Now the question is: where are those details the Devil promised me? Where is the place and what time is the event?

Dare I hope he doesn't provide them? I obviously can't go if I don't know where to go. But in that case, did I go through all the ordeals with Gia for nothing? Also, why does it seem like I might get upset if—

My phone dings.

Wow. The phrase is "speak of the devil," but thinking of him works just as well.

What's your address?

Since he can look it up in HR records anyway, I text it to him.

I'll pick you up at seven.

I have no words—via text or otherwise. In fact, I'm so flummoxed I visit Euclid in VR, but even that doesn't lower my blood pressure. It takes two episodes of *Downton Abbey* and several chapters of *Emma* to calm me down enough to put on my new clothes and double-check that the makeup still looks tidy.

It does. I'm all set to go.

I just hope I don't die of awkwardness by the time the night is through.

Chapter Eighteen

*A*s I step out of my building, my waxed privates are still on fire, and I feel almost naked in my new dress.

If this is what sex goddesses feel like, it's a marvel they don't commit suicide in droves.

I'm a couple of minutes early for the pickup, so I pace the sidewalk, my new shoes making it sound like I'm tapdancing. My heart rate is through the roof again, and not just because I'm about to see the Devil.

Okay, fine, mainly for that reason.

"Holly?" a deep, sexy, Russian-accented voice says, and I nearly jump out of my skin—an act that would be made easier by how much of it is exposed by the bloody dress.

I turn on my heel and gasp.

It's the Devil, but he looks different.

Better.

Tidy.

Dressed up.

Groomed.

To say he cleans up nice wouldn't do it justice. We're talking drool pooling in my mouth, heat gathering in recently waxed places, and a standing ovation from my ovaries.

His hoodie and jeans have been replaced with a perfectly tailored suit. The stubble is gone. Even the unruly hair is tamed—though not as much as I would've liked. There's some product in there, but all he must've done is run his fingers through those dark locks instead of combing them back, as would've been ideal.

Still, combined, the look robs me of coherent thought.

His cerulean eyes gleam as he gives me an equally thorough once-over. "You look amazing."

"No, you do," I blurt, and an English proverb pops into my head: "When flatterers meet, the devil goes to dinner."

His wicked smirk is back. "Thanks." He gestures to the sidewalk. "This way."

A limo is waiting for us. He gets the door, which makes him somehow look even more dashing.

Must. Stop. Ogling. My. New. Boss.

Doing my best not to flash him any lady bits, I climb into the car, and he follows.

Will he sit next to me?

Please sit next to me.

I mean, don't sit next to me.

He sits across from me.

Good. Why am I disappointed? Also, can he see under my dress from there?

Just in case, I cross my legs.

His eyes suddenly look hungry.

Bugger. Did I accidentally pull a Sharon Stone from *Basic Instinct*?

No. Impossible. I'm wearing knickers.

"Do you want something to drink?" he asks, his voice low and smooth.

I do feel parched, but I'm not sure I can handle alcohol at the moment. Or ever around him. "Is there any tea?"

What am I saying? Of course not. This isn't the UK.

And yet, he grins and opens a cupboard on the side.

Wow. It's tea porn in there. There's every variety I can think of, from black to white to matcha.

I blink. Nope. The tea isn't an illusion. "Why does this limo have so much tea?"

He pulls out a box with Russian writing on it. "Because it's my ride, and I love tea."

"You love tea?" Maybe the fact that he has his own limo should be more of a surprise, but it's not.

His grin widens. "Why can't I love tea?"

"I love tea," I say dumbly.

He winks. Winks! "Now we have this in common."

A shrug is all the reply I can manage.

"What kind do you prefer?" he asks.

"Um, Earl Grey."

He shakes the box he took out earlier. "What about Russian Caravan tea?"

"I've never had the pleasure."

He opens the box and takes a sniff. "Want to try?"

Why was that so seductive—the question *and* the sniff?

"What's in it?" I ask unsteadily.

"It's a blend of oolong, keemun, and lapsang souchong," he says, and now I'm wondering if he's trying to tempt me on purpose.

I mean, a prime number of ingredients listed in that sexy voice of his?

"It's very aromatic," he continues. "Sweet. Malty. Smoky."

Is there such a thing as a nosegasm?

"What do you say?" He shakes the tea box again.

"I want." Great reply. Then again, it's better than "shag me."

He chuckles and reaches into the bar to pull out an ornately decorated metal contraption that reminds me of a funeral urn.

Weird. Does he want to drink a cuppa for his departed grandmother who happens to be inside that thing?

"This is a samovar," he says as he putters with it. "Russians traditionally use these for tea."

Ah. I think I've heard of a samovar. Never thought I'd see it in real life… especially in a limo.

A minute later, he's handing me a teacup on a proper saucer.

As the handover commences, his fingers brush against mine again, sending pleasurable energy through my nerve endings and rendering me capable of nothing more than blowing on the bloody tea.

Then he starts blowing on his, and I watch his puckered lips in fascination. Why do they look so beautiful that way? So kissable? So... lickable?

Eventually, I recover my wits and tire of blowing... the tea.

Taking a dainty sip, I have an honest-to-goodness teagasm.

There might even be a moan.

Those kissable lips curve. "Better than Earl Grey?"

I eagerly bob my head. "I didn't think that was possible. Where can I get this?"

"Online or in Brighton Beach. That's our destination, by the way."

Ah. It's also known as Little Odessa—a part of Brooklyn famous for the high population of Russian-speaking immigrants. Not surprising that his father would want to have his birthday there.

"I think I'll get some and make this tea part of my daily ritual," I say.

"Here." He hands me the box. "Use that for now."

"Thanks." I reverently accept the gift and hide it in my purse.

"Don't mention it. It's just tea."

"Amazing tea," I say.

He smiles widely. "How was your day?"

"Jolly good," I lie. "How was the move into the new offices?"

He runs his hand through his hair, ruining what little orderliness it had. Seriously, would I get arrested if I attacked him with a comb? "All fine," he says. "I finally got a new keyboard and monitor."

Bugger. I almost forgot about the damage I wrought.

"Do you have any biscuits—I mean, tea cookies?" I ask, desperate to change the subject.

"I do, but I don't think you want to ruin your appetite," he says. "My parents have pulled out all the stops with the menu tonight."

"They found a restaurant that lets them change the menu?"

Because that sounds great to me. The problem with restaurants is that you can't get the same thing in all of them.

"Better," he says. "They own the restaurant."

Huh. That didn't come up when I researched the Chortsky name.

"Does it serve Russian cuisine?" I ask.

"Naturally."

"What's it called?"

"The Hut. Heard of it?"

I shake my head.

"It's an abbreviation for The Hut on Hen's Legs

—a reference to a Russian fairy tale in which a child-eating witch by the name of Baba Yaga lives in such a dwelling."

A child-eating witch? I'm not Gia, but that doesn't sound very hygienic… or ethically acceptable.

"There." He points out the window. "That's the place."

As if in confirmation, the limo stops.

Fascinated, I study the restaurant. There's a wooden staircase that leads to the entrance, and around it stand two decorative hen "legs," as per the longer title.

"I hope they serve chicken inside," I say. "Otherwise, Americans might be confused."

He exits and holds the door for me. "Chicken, among many, many other delicious things."

The stairs are rickety, but the door he holds for me is solid.

Inside, the place is downright posh, with lots of marble, fancy tablecloths, and covered chairs—a nice touch since it makes it hard to count the number of legs. Music with a strong beat is blasting loudly enough to vibrate my internal organs, and a pudgy mustachioed man is rapping in Russian on a central stage.

Right. The Devil mentioned food and a show, so a stage makes sense.

The folks inside the restaurant seem to enjoy the song, so I launch the translation app on my phone to get some idea of what the lyrics are.

Boys are the drug poop
At school gave in box
Narcotics suck kvass

Hmm. A lot must've been lost in translation there. What's *kvass*? Not that it would help me understand the lyrics.

Turns out kvass is a fermented drink. If anything, that makes the lyrics less comprehensible. All I can tell is that the song is vaguely anti-drugs, so that's good, I suppose.

Looking up from my phone, I see the Devil grinning as he notices what I'm doing.

"That's a pretty bad translation," he says, peering at my phone screen. "What it should've said is: 'Drugs are the shit I gave at school in a matchbox. Kvass is better than drugs.'"

"That doesn't make sense either. Why would you put feces in a matchbox?"

"It's something we did back in Russia. Stool samples."

Gia would die if she knew. "Why?"

He shrugs. "Maybe to test for parasites?"

Seriously? There goes my appetite.

He leads me to a table in the back just as the music quiets down.

I recognize some people at the table right away: Bella and Dragomir, sitting side by side, clearly as a couple. The rest I don't know, though I can guess. The bespectacled man who looks like the Devil's brooding twin must be the brother, Vlad. The two older people must be the parents. Also guessable is the man who looks like Dragomir's more cheerful copy—must be *his* brother.

The main enigmas are the two women: a pale, cherubic-faced one who's looking adoringly at Vlad, and a striking blonde who's giving me the stink eye for some reason.

"Hope we're not late," the Devil says.

The maybe-parents get to their feet, and everyone else follows their example.

"You're not late, Sashen'ka," codename-mother says with a Russian accent that's molasses thick. "And you really brought a date."

The blond woman's stink eye turns stinkier.

Hold on. The Devil mentioned his mother setting him up. Is this blonde a backup date, in case I didn't show up?

I resist the urge to hiss at her—I've got first impressions to make, after all.

"Everyone, this is Holly," my fake date says. "Holly, this is my brother, Vlad, and that's Fanny." He gestures at his poker-faced doppelgänger and his pretty, round-cheeked date.

The brother nods coolly, but Fanny smiles brightly as she waves.

Wait. So she's the expert tester the Devil mentioned earlier? She looks way too sweet and innocent to have experience with porn-related testing.

"You know Bella and Dragomir," the Prince of

Darkness continues. "And this is his brother, Anatolio."

Smiling, Anatolio comes up to me, bows, then grabs my hand and gives it a kiss faster than I can blink.

A strange sound emanates from beside me.

I blink.

Did the Devil just *growl?*

"It's Tigger," Anatolio says. "That's what my friends call me."

Tigger? Does he like to bounce a lot and have a stuffed bear for a friend?

The Devil pointedly steps between me and Tigger before continuing the introductions. "This is Snezhana." He gestures at the blonde. "She works in a store next door, though I'm not sure what she's doing here." He glances disapprovingly at codename-mother.

The blonde also looks at codename-mother—in her case, with a confused expression.

"I can explain," codename-mother says, not meeting either of their gazes. "I heard that Anatolio —I mean, Tigger—is single, so I invited Snezhana in case they might... get along."

"That's odd," Bella says. "We only told you that Tigger was coming today."

The look the older woman gives her maybe-daughter could melt lead.

Tigger frowns at Snezhana, whose expression makes it clear that this is the first time she's heard of the setup with him.

My earlier guess must've been right. She was originally invited here for the Devil.

Twat.

With a barely perceptible headshake, the Ruler of Darkness says, "Last but not least, this is my mother, Natasha, and the birthday boy himself, Boris."

Boris and Natasha? Huh. They even look like the cartoon characters by the same name.

I catch Fanny grinning—I bet she's thinking the same exact thing.

Before I know what hits me, the mother is hugging me and kissing me on each cheek.

Well, that's a bit too friendly.

As soon as Natasha is done with the smooching, I receive the same treatment from the patriarch—that is, until the Devil clears his throat. Aggressively, I might add.

On my end, I can feel Boris and Natasha's saliva on my cheeks, and I make a mental note to tell Gia that she can never date a Russian. She wouldn't survive such a greeting.

When Boris finally disconnects from me, I dig into my purse, take out the jar with caviar, and thrust it into his hands. "I wish you many happy returns."

He looks at the jar, then at me. Exchanging an impressed glance with Natasha, he booms, "Thanks, Holly. Thank you very much."

He pronounces my name almost like "holy," and

like his wife, he sounds just like the cartoon character who shares his name.

"Sit, everyone," he says. "Drinking must commence."

The Devil catches my gaze and pulls out a chair. "Sit here."

Who knew the Evil One would bring chivalry back from the dead?

I sit.

He takes the chair next to me.

I smell that yummy scent of his—and recognize that it is, in part, that heavenly tea he gave me.

A tea cologne? I may come on the spot.

Snezhana ends up across the table from us, next to Tigger, but neither of them seems interested in each other. Tigger checks out other women in the room like a total rake, while she ogles my fake date.

A very popular UK word that starts with a "c" is on the tip of my tongue.

Natasha looks at Vlad. "I get the first toast. Pour, please."

Vlad grabs a giant bottle of vodka and starts filling the shot glasses in front of everyone's plates.

"Watch how much you pour for the non-Russians," Snezhana says. Her voice turns out to be smoky and melodious, her accent annoyingly sexy. "Can't expect them to keep up."

Tigger's lips quirk. "This non-Russian can drink anyone under the table."

"I meant Americans," Snezhana says, looking right at me.

Boris grins at Tigger. "That sounds like a challenge I'll gladly accept."

"Bring it on, birthday boy," Tigger says good-naturedly.

Boris waves at the passing waiter and says something in Russian.

"Don't," Natasha growls.

"It's my birthday," Boris snaps.

"Fine," she says sharply. "But don't complain to me tomorrow."

The waiter comes back with two glasses the size of flower vases.

"Pour one for me and one for my soon-to-be-drunk friend," Boris says.

With a disapproving look, Vlad pours the two vases to the brim.

"You sure about this?" Dragomir asks his brother.

With a cocky smile, Tigger takes a pickle from a nearby assortment and places it on his plate.

As Vlad continues with the vodka distribution, the Devil leans toward me and whispers, "When he gets to you, tell him to stop before your glass is full."

"Why?" I whisper back.

"It's the custom to drink until you can see the bottom of the shot glass, and since it's my dad's birthday, he'll want everyone to do that. However, no custom says your glass needs to start off full."

Interesting. Now that he's said it, I notice that

Fanny is already aware of these peculiarities—her shot glass is only a quarter full.

When Vlad gets to me, he pours slowly while looking at me, clearly expecting me to stop him early. Unfortunately, Snezhana is also watching, and her superior expression makes the contrarian in me allow Vlad to fill my glass to the brim.

According to a DNA ancestry test, I'm a mix of English, Scottish, Cornish, and Irish. Some of these ethnicities are as famous for their drinking prowess as the Russians—so there.

Eyeing my shot glass disapprovingly, the Devil puts a pickle on my plate.

Is this symbolic of the pickle of a situation I'm in? No, it must be another custom—Snezhana and everyone else get a pickle also.

"I will make my toast now," Natasha says as soon as Vlad is done with his vodka duties. "I dedicate this poem to my beloved husband and soon-to-be proud grandfather." She looks very pointedly at me.

Blimey. Does she know something I don't? Is the Antichrist supposed to come about via immaculate conception?

Done making me uncomfortable, Natasha looks at Fanny next—I guess as another source of a soon-to-be grandchild.

Fanny's cheeks pinken with a mighty blush.

Skipping Snezhana, Natasha levels an even pointier stare at Bella. Then she returns her gaze to her husband—which is why she misses Bella's eye roll.

"My poem is in my mother tongue," Natasha continues. "So, I hope those of you who don't speak it, bear with me."

Snezhana looks triumphant.

Seriously?

I launch the translation app on my phone—I can use modern technology to follow along.

Hopefully.

Natasha begins her poem, and the app tries to keep up.

My support.

Okay, good start.

My master.

Hmm. Hopefully a mistranslation.

My soulmate.

Cute.

My protector.

How many of these "my" bits will this poem have?

My defender.

Okay, we get it, lady. He's a lot of things.

Ever faithful.

Hey, at least the list of "my" is over.

Ever eager.

TMI?

Ever ready to please.

More TMI?

No woman has been as grateful as I to obediently serve at the side of a man.

Is this another mistranslation, or has feminism not

reached Russia yet?

The poem goes on in the same vein, so I quit following the translation and just wait for it to be over —which takes what feels like another hour.

"Now for our American friends," Natasha says when she's finally done. "A shorter toast."

Another one? I'll believe the brevity when I hear it.

"What is the difference between a faithful and an unfaithful husband?" Natasha asks.

Everyone stays politely quiet.

"Huge," Natasha says. "The faithful sometimes feel remorse."

As one, we all politely chuckle.

"So," Natasha says. "Let us drink so that remorse does not torment this faithful husband."

I'm confused. Does she want him to be a sociopath?

Everyone grabs their shot glasses/vases, and I do as well.

Until now, I've only imbibed wine, beer, and cocktails, and rarely at that. I don't like the loss of control that alcohol and drugs bring with them, so I've never really indulged in either.

Well, at least this will be a new experience.

Natasha sniffs her pickle, downs her shot, and eats the condiment with great enthusiasm.

Looking at me challengingly, Snezhana gulps her vodka down without any pickle-sniffing or eating— which must be the more hardcore way.

Tigger and Boris down their gallons of vodka as though it were water.

Okay. How bad can it be?

Sniffing the briny pickle for shits and giggles, I down my vodka.

Holy bollocks of fire!

The magma travels down my esophagus and explodes in a mushroom cloud in my stomach, filling it with unwelcome warmth.

Is this the expected result?

If so, why would anyone do this to themselves?

Desperate to ease the pain, I devour the pickle.

Nope.

Though salty, the pickle isn't an ice slushy, which is what's needed at this juncture.

Is that the look of schadenfreude on Snezhana's face?

Schooling my features, I say as evenly as I can manage, "That was nice."

Boris smacks the Devil on the back approvingly. "That one's a keeper."

Snezhana narrows her eyes and stands up. "The time between the first drink and the second ought to be short."

Natasha frowns at her, but Boris grins excitedly. "Indeed," he says. "Out of the mouths of babes."

"How about we eat something more substantial than a pickle first?" Natasha says.

"After the second one," Boris says. "Traditions must be followed."

Natasha gives Snezhana a glare that seems to say, "That's the last time I invite *you*," and I feel a little schadenfreude myself.

This time, Tigger pours the vodka, and because Snezhana stares challengingly at me again, I let him fill my shot glass to the brim.

Bella stands up. "My toast. To Dad: May you have health above all and happiness."

Are Russians allowed to make a toast that short?

Seems so. Everyone starts downing their shots.

Okay. I guess I have to do this again.

I sniff the pickle and knock back the vodka.

Chapter Nineteen

*S*urprisingly, this shot burns only a fraction as much as the prior one.

Is this why the break between the first and second had to be short?

"You should pace yourself," the Devil whispers in my ear, his warm breath sending goosebumps down my arm. "Say 'stop' sooner the next round."

Excuse me? Is he telling me what to do? He's not the boss of me. At least not in this restaurant.

"Here." He grabs a bowl of something that looks like potato salad and deposits some on my plate. "Eat something."

Since everyone else is digging into the food also, I taste the offering.

Yum. Unlike regular potato salad, a dish I don't care for, this has meat, green peas, and (of course) chopped pickles, which might be why it's so good.

"What's this called?" I ask.

"Oliver salad," Natasha says with a smile. "You like?"

"It's amazing," I say, in part because I mean it and in part because they own this restaurant and have "pulled out all the stops with the menu."

As we eat, the music comes back on. The new song reminds me of the opera the blue alien was singing in *The Fifth Element*, right before things turned too violent for me to watch, except the pudgy singer's testicles seem to be in the way of him hitting the high notes.

Dragomir pours the next round of shots, and I stare defiantly at the Devil as my glass is filled to the brim again.

The third shot goes down even smoother.

They might make an alcoholic out of me yet.

The waiters bring out a hot dish of small dumplings.

"That's *pelmeni*," Natasha explains. "It's a simple food, but my pookie loves it."

The Devil puts some pelmeni on my plate and adds a dash of what he calls *smetana*, which turns out to be sour cream.

The combo is so good I moan in pleasure, which causes the Devil to eye me with a strangely intent expression.

Swallowing the deliciousness, I gush compliments to the chef.

"I have to agree with my husband," Natasha says to the Devil with a grin. "This one *is* a keeper."

"You have to teach me how to make these," I say earnestly. "I'll eat it instead of ravioli."

Natasha is beaming with enthusiasm as she tells me how to make the dish. Then she turns to the rest of the table. "While we're talking restaurant-related things," she says, "your father and I have an announcement to make."

She waits until every one of the Chortsky offspring gives her their full attention.

"We've decided to leave The Hut to the first of you who gives us a grandchild."

With that, Fanny, Bella, and I receive a new round of pointed stares that seem to say, "Are you ovulating yet?"

Snezhana looks on the verge of Hulking out from jealousy. It makes me wonder if it's not my fake date that she wants but this restaurant. She does work next door, after all, and at least according to Hannibal Lecter, we covet what we see every day.

Bella groans. "Mom, please. You know we all have successful businesses of our own, right?"

The Devil and his brother nod, and Vlad says, "When you're ready, we want you to sell this place and enjoy the money yourselves. You've earned it."

"In any case, we're not going to engage in a fuck race for your sake," Bella says, not bothering to lower her voice.

147

Fanny's cheeks turn crimson.

"Sorry you have to witness this," the Devil whispers into my ear.

He thinks this is bad? He should spend some time with *my* family.

"Such language!" Natasha appears on the verge of throttling her daughter. "You're going to upset your father. On his birthday."

Actually, Boris doesn't seem interested in anything but the vodka bottle—he keeps eyeing it like it's a naked woman dancing.

The Devil seems to pick up on this. Grabbing the bottle, he states that he'll pour the next round and fills Tigger and Boris's vases again.

Damn. Didn't I read somewhere that a liter of spirits could kill you?

"To the brim for me," Snezhana says huskily when he gets to her shot glass. "I can handle… all of it."

Is it the vodka that's making me want to scalp the blonde?

No wonder there are so many brawls in bars.

When the Wicked One gets to me, he only pours me a drop—as though I've told him to stop.

Snezhana looks at my measly vodka level with triumph.

Oh, yeah?

"Thanks, sweetheart," I tell my fake date and pat his upper arm—only to feel my breath catch at the hard, sinewy muscle under the layers of cloth.

Damn. The Devil is built.

He gives a slight start at my familiarity but recovers quickly and plays along. "No problem, *kroshka*."

Whatever that word means, the result is a double whammy. Natasha looks clam-happy, while Snezhana gulps down her vodka without waiting for the toast.

I lock eyes with her, take the Devil's fully filled shot glass, and knock it back.

"Holly," he exclaims.

Everyone turns his way.

"It's not the custom to drink before the toast," he says lamely.

Ha. So stealing someone's vodka is okay?

"I'll fix this." Boris grabs the vodka bottle and refills the two shot glasses in front of me, then hands one to his son.

I notice he didn't give Snezhana any, but I don't want to be a snitch.

Putting the vodka down, Boris declares, "I'll make the next toast. Sorry, it will be in Russian."

I ready the app, and while I'm at it, I check the meaning of *kroshka*.

Breadcrumb?

Okay, fine. Then I'm calling him *breadcrust*—or Crusty for short.

Boris starts speaking.

A wife is the most wonderful invention since the discovery of the wheel.

Great. Is this another poem?

A wife is a man's best friend.

Isn't that a dog?

A wife is—

The next part sounds like slurred speech, which might be why the app translates:

—how much is a kilo of kielbasa if you bite off a screwdriver from a locomotive?

I don't follow the rest. I'm suddenly feeling very nice, all warm, relaxed, and eager to party on.

"To my wife," Boris concludes and downs his gallon of vodka.

Tigger looks a bit more apprehensive as he downs his.

I knock back my shot on autopilot—and there's zero burn this time. Has someone switched out vodka for water?

The music starts up again. This time, the singer butchers a familiar song: "Hips Don't Lie" by Shakira.

Doing my best not to think too much about the pudgy dude's hips, I devour the remaining pelmeni as everyone focuses on the countless other delicacies that keep coming to the table.

"Will there be more pelmeni?" I ask the Devil when my plate is sadly empty.

Grinning, he calls over a waiter and tells him something in Russian.

"Why don't you try something else, dear?" Natasha asks me. "There's so much other food."

I hiccup. "When I find something I like, I tend to stick to it."

Natasha glances at her son with a grin. "Admirable attitude when it comes to men, but I'm not sure it's transferable to food."

"It is," I assure her. "We make countless decisions every day. Why add to that stress with unnecessary food choices?"

Before Natasha can argue, Tigger picks up the vodka bottle. "My turn."

Is it me or is his hand a bit unsteady?

"I think the ladies have had enough," the Devil says sternly.

"That's sexist," I say.

His cerulean eyes narrow. "It's biology."

"Well, I want one more," I say stubbornly, and it's true. According to my mental count, I've had four.

I can't end on a four. Five is much better.

Bugger. How many pelmeni did I eat? Also, is that the plural of—

"I want one too." Bella winks at me. "I know we look dainty and frail and all, but we can handle ourselves without a man's supervision."

I've got to hand it to Dragomir. He nods approvingly at her words.

"I wasn't being sexist," the Wicked One mutters. "Not on purpose, anyway."

"I'll have a little more too," Fanny chimes in. "Also, I volunteer for the toast."

Natasha nods approvingly, and Snezhana says something incomprehensible… maybe in Russian.

"Your wish is my commando," Tigger says. "I mean, commander. I mean, command."

Dragomir shakes his head at his obviously buzzed brother but says nothing.

Once everyone has their shots, Fanny stands up, her cheeks red. "I wanted to salute our hosts, Natasha and Boris. Thank you for creating such wonderful children." She looks adoringly at Vlad. "And thank you for being so welcoming. Amen."

Wait, that sounded more like she said Grace.

"I'll drink to that," Boris slurs and swallows another vase worth of vodka.

Ignoring the Devil's disapproving stare, I finish my fifth shot.

Ah, smooth. Prime vodka is the best.

"Ladies and gentlemen," says the pudgy singer from the stage. "It's showtime."

Right. There was mention of a show.

The lights dim, and semi-naked burlesque dancers take the stage.

What happens next reminds me of Cirque du Soleil, only rated R. The dancers perform impressive acrobatics, but the miracle is that their tiny outfits stay on. No doubt glue is involved.

To his credit, the Devil looks completely uninterested in all the flesh on display. Same is true of Dragomir and Vlad.

Boris, on the other hand, is drooling, while his

drinking buddy/nemesis Tigger is clapping with equal enthusiasm.

When the show is over, the singer returns to the stage.

"We start our dancing program with a White Dance," he announces.

Bella winks at me. "That means the ladies invite the gentlemen."

A vaguely familiar melody blasts out of the speakers.

Bella executes a dramatic bow before Dragomir, and Fanny shyly asks Vlad if she could have this dance.

The men accept, and the two couples head to the dance floor.

Do *I* want to dance? I've been known to say that dancing is an excuse for public cuddling and dry humping, but it looks really appealing right now.

Natasha is inviting Boris. Some random girl from another table is inviting Tigger. Snezhana's eyes are like the laser sights of the Terminator's gun as they zero in on my fake date.

Yeah, no. That's not happening.

I leap to my feet.

Wow. Is the room a little wobbly?

No matter. Curtsying in front of the Devil, I shout, "Wanna dance?"

"It would be an honor." The Ruler of Darkness rises gracefully to his feet.

Snezhana halts in her tracks.

Yeah, she better.

On the stage, the pudgy singer belts out in broken English, *Holy water cannot help you now.*

It probably can't. After all, isn't what I'm about to do a colloquialism for ill-advised behavior?

I'm going to dance with the Devil.

Chapter Twenty

*T*he Evil One takes my hand.

Golly.

The heat of vodka has nothing on this. My palm feels like it's been branded.

He leads me to the middle of the dance floor and assumes a ballroom stance.

I join him.

He pulls me against his powerful body.

Until now, I hadn't realized just how tall and broad-shouldered he is.

It's intoxicating.

We start to sway to the music.

The aroma of tea mixed with something deliciously masculine makes my head spin as cerulean eyes pin me like a butterfly. And speaking of those little flying bastards, they're having an orgy in my stomach and need to stop it.

To break the hypnotic pull of his gaze, I burrow closer and hide my head in the crook of his neck.

Oh my.

There's a hardness in his pants, and it's the size of the proverbial flashlight.

A massive flashlight.

The Devil is happy to see me, that's for damn sure.

Did I underestimate his manhood in VR?

Maybe. What's worse is my lady boner is just as ready.

Before I realize what I'm doing, I lick his neck.

Lick. His. Neck.

Not good.

Not proper.

I totally should've masturbated before coming here. The urge to lick him again—or worse—is strong.

His entire body stiffens, and the skin on his neck breaks out in goosepimples.

I pull away, only to get caught in his gaze again, the blue depths now dark and heated.

I no longer have any doubt what the Devil's favorite sin is.

I audibly gulp.

The heat flaring between us is as scorching as the fires of hell.

On the stage, the pudgy singer belts out, "Seven devils all around me…"

Seriously, universe? I recognize these lyrics. It's

from my playlist of songs that have prime numbers in their titles—"Seven Devils" by Florence + the Machine. Sure enough, if I count Bella's and Vlad's significant others as part of the Chortsky clan, there are indeed seven of them. All around me.

I meet my devil's eyes again.

If the Tempter means to seduce me, consider me succumbed to his charms.

I dampen my lips.

Pupils dilating, he bends his head.

I rise on tiptoes.

Our lips are a millimeter apart.

"Borichka!" Natasha screams in panic.

What the bloody—

Boris crashes between us.

The Devil and I spring apart, and Boris grabs onto me as he falls to his knees, his face burrowing into my crotch.

"Dad, what the hell?" my maybe-not-so-fake date exclaims, grabbing for his father.

Boris doesn't respond. He's channeling Winnie, the bear dog—the smell of my crotch must've driven him into a stupor.

"Does this mean I win?" Tigger asks, his speech slightly slurred.

His brother gives him the stink eye before helping the Devil drag Boris off me.

"Why don't we girls go powder our noses?" Natasha says, her voice overly bright. "Let the men help the birthday boy to the table."

Yeah. Great idea. I have a feeling Boris might put on a show any second—maybe even a recreation of that scene from *The Exorcist*. And if that happens, there might be a chain reaction across the restaurant —a horrid visual.

Fanny and Bella must be on the same wavelength because they join us in the stampede for the loo.

The place turns out to be fancy, with a bathroom attendant and everything. She's broad-shouldered and vaguely reminds me of the mistress from the salon, but I don't fret because I have no pubes left.

Getting into the stall to drain my lady lizard, I'm shocked by how pleasant the endeavor turns out to be.

I must've needed to go badly. That, or this is an effect of vodka no one ever talks about.

Exiting the stall, I wash my hands and accept a towel from the mistress clone.

Okay. Time to face the Devil again.

I turn toward the door and find Snezhana blocking my way.

Damn. She's a blond ninja, this one.

"You and Alex will never work." Every word coming out of her mouth is slurred. "He needs to be with someone of his own kind. Like me."

I scoff. "I didn't realize Alex was a bitch."

Where did that come from? I'd expect it from Gia or my other sisters, but not me. Alcohol clearly agrees with me.

Slight problem: Snezhana doesn't like my retort.

Nostrils flaring to the point where her nose hairs show, she takes a step toward me.

"I think it would be best if you left," Bella says coldly from my right.

"Yeah," Fanny says in a softer tone from my left. "And just so you know, Holly and Alex make the cutest couple."

Snezhana doesn't seem to care about their words, or the fact that she's outnumbered.

She takes another menacing step my way.

Oh, well.

I've never been in a fight in my life, abhorring violence as I do, but I guess today is the day for a lot of firsts.

Balling my hands into fists, I jut out my chin. "Bring it on."

Chapter Twenty-One

The buff bathroom mistress steps in Snezhana's path. "No one is bringing on anything in my bathroom."

"Stay out of this," Snezhana growls.

"Bella already told you to leave," the toilet mistress booms. "Scram."

Snezhana lunges at her. Before I can blink, the mistress has her upside down in a wrestling grip.

Snezhana is literally kicking and screaming as the bigger woman carries her out.

"Wow," Fanny says, her blue eyes huge. "That got intense."

"Some people are bad drunks," Bella says philosophically. "I'm sure she'll be petrified at her behavior once she sleeps it off."

I grin at them both. "Thanks for having my back."

"Of course," Bella says. "What are friends for?"

She called me a friend. Bugger. I'm not too drunk to forget about my transgressions against Bella's dream. Once she learns about them, she won't think of me as a friend. In fact, she'll ask the toilet mistress to toss me out as well.

There's a sound of a flush. The farthest bathroom stall opens and Natasha steps out, frowning. "I heard a commotion."

Bella talks to her in rapid-fire Russian, and as she goes on, Natasha's frown deepens.

"I'll have words with Snezhana's mother," Natasha says decisively when Bella is finished.

"You do that," Bella says. "Better yet, you shouldn't have invited her in the first place."

Natasha starts washing her hands, her movements jerky and clearly impaired. "I can't believe the girl had a chance to be with Tigger and blew it so badly. I love my son to death, don't get me wrong, but that boy—"

"Mother, I think you might've had enough to drink," Bella says. "You're married, remember?"

Natasha sniffs. "Married doesn't mean dead."

"I disagree," I find myself saying. "Not with the married means dead part, but the other thing. Your son is superior to Tigger in every way."

Why did I just say that?

Bella grins at me. "I'd say you may have also had enough vodka for today."

I bob my head. "Probably. I don't think I can handle two more shots in any case, and six would surely kill me."

"Six?" Fanny asks, looking confused.

"If I had one more, that would be six," I say. "Needs to be seven. Or eleven."

"Right, the 7-Eleven." Fanny nods solemnly, but there's a hint of a smile dancing in her eyes. "In solidarity, I'll stop drinking too."

"Same here," Bella says.

"No more vodka for me either," Natasha declares. "I'm going to be too busy dancing with Tigger now that his date is gone."

With that pact in place, we return to the table, where we find Boris with his head next to his plate, loudly snoring. Tigger—who clearly won the drinking contest—is surrounded by two women from another table. The trio of the Devil, Vlad, and Dragomir are speaking animatedly in Russian.

Blimey.

If a plain chap looks good with vodka goggles on, the Devil is downright beautiful, as befits the brightest and most powerful of all the angels.

Would he mind if I sat on his lap instead of my chair?

"Back to your husbands," Natasha barks at Tigger's entourage, and they scram. Natasha then bats her eyelashes at the younger man and says huskily, "How about a dance?"

Tigger rises, albeit a bit unsteadily, and leads her to the dance floor.

"How about we go keep an eye on them?" Bella asks Dragomir. "I don't want your brother as my stepfather."

Dragomir grins, and they head over to the dance floor, with Fanny and Vlad on their tails.

Should I dance with the Devil again?

"Here," he says, pulling out a chair for me again.

Spoilsport. No dancing and now I have to sit on my own bloody chair? Next thing I know, he'll ask me to join a nunnery.

Sighing, I plop into the chair a little too quickly, and the restaurant spins around me.

"I got you more pelmeni," he says. "Eat. Food slows down alcohol absorption."

"That takes the cake." I grab a fork—the thing is heavy for some reason. "The Devil is worried I might be sloshed."

Wait, did I say that out loud?

Yep.

He quirks an eyebrow. "The Devil?"

I hiccup. "That's what I call you. Well, also Crusty—but that one's so recent I haven't used it yet."

He shakes his head. "As much as I don't like the sound of 'Crusty,' I just might prefer it to 'the Devil.'"

"Seriously?" I attempt to spear a dumpling, but the bugger slithers away—must be all that butter and sour cream.

He grabs my fork, expertly nails the morsel for me, and hands the utensil back, our fingers brushing orgasmically in the process. "Back in Russia, kids would tease us with variations on that theme because of our last name," he says. "So it's something of a sore spot. At least 'Crusty' is original."

I blink at him owlishly. "But you named your dog Beelzebub."

He shrugs. "That name isn't known in Russia, and it's okay to call your dog something you wouldn't want to be called yourself. Besides, I don't want the assholes from my past to have any power over me—that's why I named my company 1000 Devils."

"Ah. The Devil is your Holy Hymen." I bring the fork to my mouth and close my eyes, enjoying the flavor explosion that is the pelmeni.

When I open my eyes, he's eyeing me with confusion. "Holy hymen? Didn't you say you've had 'coitus'?"

Flushing, I swallow the pelmeni. Why did I open my big mouth?

"Not that it's any of your business, but no, I'm not a virgin," I say in a low voice. "Holy Hymen is what the kids called me back in the day. On account of me being Holly and having the last name of Hyman."

"Ah. So you do understand." His face hardens, his cerulean eyes tightening dangerously. "Give me the names of the assholes who insulted you."

I have to blink at him again. Is he serious? "Um, I

don't remember them now. In any case, I'm sorry—I didn't mean to press on your sore spot. You're Crusty going forward. Or however you say 'crusty' in Russian."

The dangerous look in his eyes fades, replaced by a bemused expression. "How did you arrive at 'crusty?'"

"You called me breadcrumb, so I decided you should be breadcrust—or Crusty."

A wicked grin curves his lips. "You know, in Russian, crusty is synonymous with hard."

Hard? My breath hitches as heat streaks down my spine. "Why did you call me breadcrumb?"

"*Kroshka* also means *little one*," he says. "I'm sorry if it sounds like I was infantilizing you. That wasn't the idea."

"I… see." I look him up and down. "How do you say 'huge one' in Russian?"

His grin widens. "How about you just call me Alex?"

"Alex." I taste the word.

"Or Sasha. That's another diminutive of Alexander, which is my full name."

"No." I trace a finger along his strong chin. It's a little scruffy already. "I like Alex."

His gaze darkens as he catches my hand in his strong grip. "Is that so?"

I dampen my lips. "I like Alex a lot."

He looks hungry—and not for the pelmeni.

Before I can think better of it, I wrap my other hand around the back of his head and pull it toward me.

His whole body stiffens, and his head doesn't budge.

Insulted, I release him and draw back—and then I see why he's so still.

Dragomir and Bella are coming back from the dance floor, along with Tigger, Natasha, Vlad, and Fanny.

I guess the Devil—I mean, Alex—isn't into PDA.

"No dessert?" Natasha asks no one in particular as she sinks into her chair.

Alex's cerulean eyes are trained on my face, the expression in them hotly intent. "Not yet."

Natasha waves over a waiter and gives an order.

A cornucopia of desserts is soon brought out, along with tea—the same wonderful kind I tried in the limo.

As I put the last lump of sugar in my cup, they bring a plate of pelmeni and set it between all the cakes, candy, and fruit.

"Is that for me?" I ask Natasha.

She nods. "I had the chef make it. This type is called *vareniki*. Try it."

I get one and taste it.

Yum. It's not filled with meat, like regular pelmeni. Instead, the stuffing is sweet cherry, and I can totally see it as dessert.

"Does anyone know any new Vovochka jokes?" Fanny asks shyly.

"That's a boy who's the butt of many Russian jokes," Alex whispers in my ear, making my neck tingle. "As a bonus, it also happens to be the diminutive form of my brother's name."

"I know one," Natasha says. "Vovochka comes home with an F in math. 'Why?' his father demands. 'She asked me what's 2 times 3, so I said 6.' 'That's right,' the father says. 'Then she asked me what's 3 times 2?' 'What the fuck is the difference?' the father asks. Vovochka sighs. 'That's exactly what I said.'"

Chuckles all around.

"I have one too," Bella says and darts a glance at her sleeping father. "The mother is trying on a fur coat. Vovochka says, 'Mom, don't you understand, that coat is the result of the suffering of a poor, unfortunate animal.' She looks at her son sternly. 'How dare you speak of your father like that?'"

More chuckles.

Vlad goes next. "'Why is the flounder flat?' the zoology teacher asks. 'She had relations with the whale,' Vovochka says. 'Out,' the teacher says. 'Now let's continue. Who knows why the crawfish has such big eyes?' From the door, Vovochka says, 'Because he saw the whole thing.'"

When the jokes run out, everyone enjoys dessert for a while. I wonder if alcohol gives you munchies, the way cannabis does. I'm enjoying my vareniki a little too much. Like 137 sit-ups too much.

As I reach for more tea, I feel someone loom over me and look up.

It's Tigger.

With a courtly bow, he hiccups and says, "May I have this dance, milady?"

Alex's teacup smashes into the table with a bang. "No, you can't." The words come out in a growl.

"Hey," I say indignantly. "Why are you speaking for me? What if I want to dance with him?"

I don't, but still. Who does he think he is?

"Dude, relax," Tigger says to Alex. "It's just a dance."

Alex launches to his feet and steps between Tigger and me. "She's here with me."

I leap to my feet as well. "I'm still here. Why are you talking as though I'm not?"

"I know she's with you," Tigger says. "I just—"

Dragomir barks something angrily at his brother, but I don't catch the words.

Still ignored, I debate stomping my foot in frustration but decide against it.

Tigger raises his hands. "Chill, people." He looks at Alex. "Sorry, man. Didn't mean any disrespect. Plenty of dance partners at other tables." He hiccups and winks at me. "Alas, milady, a dance is not in the cards. If you had an equally attractive sister, maybe I'd dance with her."

I push Alex out of my way. "As a matter of fact, I do. How about I give you her number, so you can—"

"Hey." Bella gently pulls on my elbow. "Mind going to the bathroom with me?"

I let her lead me away, and when we're out of everyone's earshot, I say, "I was just going to give Tigger my twin's number, so that——"

"I suggest you sober up first," Bella says. "Then, if you still think that's a good idea, you can ask your twin if she wants to be set up."

That's a good point. The men aren't the only ones who've let vodka mess up their thinking. It might be impacting me a little bit too. Gia would be pissed if I pimped her out without her permission, the way Natasha seems to do with her kids.

I shudder. When Gia gets pissed, her pranks get mean—like the time she rubbed half the objects in our middle school with hot pepper powder.

"Now," Bella says with a grin. "Tell me about the suit."

Ah. Of course. It's been seconds since I've been made to feel off-kilter. Speaking of, is my walking off-kilter? I seem to be bumping into people a lot.

Bella is still looking at me expectantly, so I say, "Not much new to tell. The batteries died before I could experience the last phase. I read some QA manuals, so I can document it better if——"

"I was hoping you'd say that." She pulls out a stack of papers from her purse. "Fill this out when you're ready."

I glance at the first page.

There are questions like, "Was orgasm achieved?"

and "How many times?" But nothing about, "Do you have the lady equivalent of blue balls?"—which is where I am.

What would you call that condition? Blue ovaries? Blue clit?

"Fanny's helped me with that document," Bella says as she opens the door to the loo. "And I'd really appreciate your help as well."

I read more of the questions as I use the facilities and then wait for Bella by the door.

"Can you give us a moment?" Bella says to the bathroom attendant.

With a huff, the bathroom mistress leaves.

"So," Bella says with a mischievous grin. "I have a gift for you." She digs into her purse and pulls out a giant dildo.

I nearly drop the testing document.

Does vodka cause hallucinations?

Nope. My new boss is really standing there with a dildo.

A gift. For me.

As if to add to the surrealness, Bella clicks a button on the side of the silicon shlong, and it hums to life and begins to vibrate with all the enthusiasm of a jackhammer.

"Enjoy." Turning the vibration off, Bella thrusts the dildo into my hands.

I gape at it. Besides being enormous, it's blue with chrome swirls and a red mushroom top—which combine to remind me of Optimus Prime from *Transfomers*.

Bella frowns. "You don't like it?"

"I'm just a little stunned," I say, my tongue feeling strangely heavy in my mouth.

"I made it myself," Bella says. "Not sure if Alex mentioned it, but I own a sex toy company called Belka."

Huh. That would've been a fun conversation between Alex and me:

"Did you know my sister makes fake cocks?"

"Why, no, I didn't. Tell me more. Spare no detail."

Hey, at least this explains Bella's interest in the VR suit—it's the logical next step for a sex toy company owner.

"Thank you." I stash Optimus deep in my purse. "It's very thoughtful."

It must've been the right thing to say because Bella beams with pride as she prances back to the table, which has been cleared of everything but tea and coffee.

Spotting me, Alex leaps to his feet and pulls out my chair.

I know I'm supposed to be upset with him, but it's difficult when he's being so gentlemanly.

Vlad stands up. "We're going to head out."

Smiling at me, Fanny follows his example. "It was great to meet you."

I fight the urge to ask her if she also got a dildo from Bella, or if I'm special. "Nice to meet you both."

Bella glances at her still-snoring father. "I think Dragomir and I should head out as well."

Dragomir nods and rises to his feet. "Great to see you again, Holly. Sorry about my brother." He glares at the dance floor, where Tigger is sandwiched between Natasha and some random middle-aged woman from another table.

"It's okay. All he did is ask me to dance." I look at Alex pointedly. "I took it as a compliment."

Is that a growl from Alex?

"I'll see you at work." Bella kisses me on the cheek. "Bye."

"*Do svidaniya*," I say without a second of hesitation.

"See?" Alex says with a devilish smirk. "You're already saying goodbye in Russian. How long before you acquire our accent?"

I can't help but grin.

His expression turns serious. "Are you ready to leave, or do you want to finish your tea?"

My heartbeat speeds up. I hadn't given much thought to how this night might end, but now all sorts of X-rated scenarios are performing the Kama Sutra in my brain.

"I'm ready," I say breathlessly.

"Great." He extends his hand to me. "Let's go."

Pulse quickening further, I clasp his palm.

It's big, warm, and callused, and I never want to give it back.

"Bye, Dad," Alex says to the sleeping Boris. "Bye, Mom!" he yells toward the dance floor.

Natasha waves, and we head out, hand in hand.

The walk to the limo happens as if in a dream.

He holds the door for me again, and I slide inside. He joins me and, unlike before, sits next to me.

Blimey.

Is this about to turn into a real—and really hot —date?

Chapter Twenty-Two

*N*ow that he's inches away, I drink him in with my eyes.

The man is the visual equivalent of crystal meth for the ovaries.

"Have I told you how amazing you look tonight?" he murmurs, his eyes greedily scanning me back.

Heat rushes over my skin as I slide closer, emboldened both by the alcohol and by the obvious hunger in that cerulean gaze. "The subject might've come up."

His voice turns husky. "You also smell delicious."

"Not as delicious as you." I lean in and shamelessly breathe in the yummy tea aroma that's been driving me insane all night.

He cups my chin and stares into my eyes.

Losing the fight with my self-control, I reach out to tame his unruly hair—which turns out to be deliciously smooth and silky, cool at the tips and warm closer to his scalp.

His breath hitches at my touch, his eyes darkening, and he retaliates by tucking an errant tuft of my hair behind my left ear.

The heat inside me intensifies, and the limo begins spinning.

Like two magnets, we're pulled to each other by a force greater than ourselves.

Our lips fuse.

Time seems to stop.

The kiss is good. Scary good. I'm drunk on all the sensations it wrenches out of me. He tastes like that delicious tea, his lips soft and warm, gentle yet merciless in demanding a response—a response that makes me feel completely out of control.

The limo is spinning like a NASA training module now, and an inferno is raging in my core. A touch of a feather applied at the right place would probably make me come.

This has to be some kind of vodka side effect. No mere kiss can feel like this.

Panting, I slide my hands down his back.

His muscular, broad, impossibly strong back.

He pulls away.

What the hell?

My ovaries are so far on the blue spectrum they just might turn violet and then green.

The limo stops.

Ah. We've arrived.

I glance out the window.

Indeed. My place.

Heart pounding, I turn back to face him. "Come up with me."

He tucks another strand of hair behind my ear, his touch sending another bolt of heat down to my core. "I can't." His voice is hoarse, his tone deeply regretful.

"You can't?" I look uncomprehendingly at the bulge in his pants.

He sighs. "I want you to issue this invitation when you don't have pure vodka in your veins."

"I'm not drunk." Bugger. The words have come out slurred.

His gaze turns sympathetic. "How about I help you get inside?"

Aha. Loophole. All isn't lost.

He exits the car without any sign of inebriation.

I climb out after him, my treacherous body feeling weirdly heavy and clumsy.

He steadies me by the elbow as I step out.

Hmm. My knees feel wobbly. Must be all the bloody hormones stirred up by the bloody kiss.

He gently tugs on my elbow. "Let's go."

I enjoy the feel of his strong hand supporting me as he leads me to my door. Unlocking it, I smile as seductively as I can. "Let me make you some tea?"

There. Who can refuse the lure of a good cup of tea?

The look on his face is that of a parched man who's crossed the desert. "I'm not thirsty."

I grind my teeth. "Fine. Don't need you anyway."

He quirks an eyebrow.

"I have the suit, remember? There's always virtual Alex."

His lips flatten. "Virtual Alex?"

"Yeah, that's right. That bloke is a lot more accommodating than the real thing."

His eyes narrow. "You should just go to bed."

I lift my chin. "What? Jealous of a little competition?"

"That suit is my company's property," he says flatly. "I'd like it back. Now. Right away."

With a growl, I stumble inside and almost trip over my pentagram-shaped coffee table before he catches me.

So *now* he comes in? Wanker.

I pull out of his grasp and dash to the bedroom. Hands shaking from anger, I pack the suit into the penis-decorated backpack and throw it at him.

He adroitly catches the projectile and gives me an annoying smirk. "Thank you." He puts the backpack on his back. "Rest now."

Grr. Why is that commanding tone turning me on?

Time to get serious. I plop onto the bed in a hopefully seductive pose. Of course, I may also look like a drunk lump. "Last chance to join me," I slur—again, hopefully seductively.

His nostrils flare. "I need to borrow your door key."

"My key?" Sexy pose forgotten, I jerk upright. "Why?"

"So I can lock the door on my way out," he says, enunciating each word as though I've suddenly lost forty-seven IQ points.

"I can lock my own door, thank you very much."

He shakes his head. "You might trip on that witchy table again."

"Not witchy. I just like five-pointed furniture."

"I'll leave the key in your mailbox," he says. "Does it lock?"

I nod jerkily.

He extends his hand. "Be a good girl now."

Ugh. I scramble off the bed, dig through my purse, and slap the key onto his palm.

"Good. Now sleep tight." With one last heated once-over, he turns on his heel and leaves without shutting the bedroom door.

Fine. I don't need him and his real sodding cock. Or the suit.

I have his sister's dildo.

Actually, I should think of it as my dildo now. Or as Optimus Prime.

I almost yell the bit about the dildo after him but contain myself at the last moment.

What if he goes all caveman jelly and steals the dildo?

Can't have that. Blue ovaries must be appeased.

I'm going to lie here and wait until I hear him lock the front door before pouncing on the dildo.

I wait.

Is he gone?

Better wait a few extra minutes. I can't have him catch me with my pants down again.

I yawn.

Maybe it won't hurt to close my eyes for just a second?

The moment my upper and lower lashes meet, sleep hits me like a bomb and I pass out.

Chapter Twenty-Three

*I*s that Big bloody Ben?

The sound has to be at least 127 decibels—loud enough to cause permanent damage to my ears.

Oh. It's my alarm clock.

I slap the snooze button before my eardrums explode.

What the hell? I'm nauseated, and my headache is sporting a migraine.

Bugger. I know what this is.

Hangover.

But that implies inebriation.

Oh, no. It's all coming back to me—especially the part where I came on to Alex at the end of the night.

What was I thinking? Talk about making a mess.

With great effort, I sit up, realizing dimly that I'm fully dressed.

The room spins around me. A fly passes by, sounding like a buzzsaw.

How drunk was I that I feel this awful? Are those things directly proportional?

By the time I get to my feet, the headache worsens.

Hey, at least I seem to be walking straight.

I go through the motions of my morning routine until I find myself in the kitchen.

Hmm. There's a Gatorade in my fridge.

I didn't buy that.

Did Alex get it for me?

Unsure if I should be upset that he let himself in or pleased that he was concerned about my electrolytes, I chug the drink until my stomach is about to burst.

There. Now if I take a barrel of Tylenol, I might be able to go to work.

———

I take a cab because public transportation would probably make my brain explode today.

A few blocks from home, my phone begins to vibrate.

"Hello?"

"Hey, sis," Gia shrieks. "How was the date?"

"Ugh." I move the phone a few inches away from my ringing ear. "Lower your voice."

"What are you talking about?" she shouts even louder. "I'm practically whispering."

I tell her about what happened, and with each word that leaves my mouth, greater mortification and horror set in.

I kissed Alex… then threw myself at him, like a hussy.

I pretty much sexually harassed my boss.

"So," Gia says when I'm done with the whole awful story. "What are you going to do now?"

"No clue. Somehow salvage my career?"

"I meant about him. Are the two of you dating now?"

"Not bloody likely. We still work together."

And that's just the tip of the messy iceberg. In any case, who says he'd want to date me? After all, he refused my advances after that kiss. If it had been as hot for him as it was for me, he wouldn't have.

"Fine. I won't push this," Gia says with a dramatic sigh.

Has hell relocated to Antarctica?

"Great, thanks."

"I just hope you're not too hungover for the lunch you owe me."

I bring the phone back to my ear, certain I misheard her. "What lunch?"

"With our parental units," she says, and I can almost hear the eye roll. "Crystal and Harry Hyman. Chicken sexer and penetration tester. Remember them? The reasons we're so messed up?"

If we *are* messed up, it would be thanks to our siblings as much as our parents, but I don't say that, opting for a horrified, "Is that today?"

"You know it is," Gia says. "And no, you don't get out of it by playing the hangover card."

"Fine," I grumble. "I wish the headache was a pain in my ass instead—it would help me pretend to be you."

"That makes no sense. Unless you're talking about anal. No, not even in that case."

"Good. Making no sense should also help me pass for you."

"If you want them to believe you're me, don't attempt to make jokes, especially like that," she says. "And avoid the Britishisms. Also, a friend of mine is going to bring you a bag with supplies."

"Supplies?" I feel an absurd pang of jealousy at the mention of a friend. Despite our identical genes and upbringings, and even with all her studious germ avoidance, Gia has a much better social life than I do... in that, she has one.

She snorts, happily oblivious to my thoughts. "Were you going to show up in the same outfit you wear to work?"

I glance down. Yep. I have my usual on—as it should be. "I didn't even think about that. I guess I'm more like you today than I realized."

"Har har. The bag will have some clothes, a wig, and makeup."

I feel my headache intensifying. "Great. I'm

looking forward to looking like Morticia Addams… if she'd joined a motorcycle club."

"I'd watch that," Gia says. "Also, show them magic. Do that thirty-seven thing I showed you the other day."

"Sounds good." I know she wants me to ask how she can be sure our parents will think of thirty-seven when I do the trick, so I resist the temptation. "What about Tigger?"

"That's Bella's boyfriend's brother?" she asks.

"Right. Do you want to be set up with him?"

"Of course not," she says. "He sounds like a manwhore, and that's the last thing I need."

The urge to argue is strong, but I decide to be a nice sister and resist it. After all, she's mainly skipping lunch with our parents so she won't be pressured into dating.

"Fair enough," I say. "Let me know if you change your mind."

"I won't," she says firmly. "Anyway, I'd better go."

"Do svidaniya."

"Well, that's new," she says, and with a bye, she hangs up.

Chapter Twenty-Four

I step out of the elevator on my office floor and cringe at the racket my coworkers are creating. Holding my ears, I sprint for my desk before anyone asks me something stupid, like, "How are you?"

As I run, I notice something weird. There are extra chairs next to the desks of the developers.

What's that about?

Launching my email, I grimace at the sight of my inbox. You skip one day, and the stupid thing overflows.

I start by checking if I have anything from Alex. If I'm fired, I will at least be spared the rest of the inbox, not to mention the abominable cacophony of my coworkers.

The first email is about the games for the hospital. Alex suggests we meet with Dr. Piper and his people, so he can make sure everyone is on the same page. I'd be happy about this if it weren't for the fact that this email arrived yesterday—hours before my improper behavior.

As if to add to my job-related anxiety, the next item from Alex is a lot more sinister.

A meeting request.

Location: his office.

Agenda: blank.

Time: an hour from now.

Bugger.

Should I even bother with the rest of the inbox?

I think I will. I need something to do if I don't want to go crazy for the next hour.

First things first, though. If I keep my job, I want the meeting with Dr. Piper to happen ASAP, so I email him about it—the window before he associates my work with porn is closing fast. Then I check if I have anything from Bella; after all, she's also my boss, and according to Alex, this is more her company than his.

There's just one email from her, also from yesterday. Apparently, Bella and Alex have decided to implement something called pair programming—a technique that's proven highly effective at 1000 Devils. She says if I have good arguments against it, I should talk to her right away, and that if some developers prefer to work alone, exceptions can be made.

This must be what the extra chairs are for.

Though I have some idea of what pair programming is, I read up on it some more.

Also known as pairing, it is as the name suggests: two programmers sit side by side and work together. The driver types the code, while the other person, the navigator, reviews the code as they go. Naturally, the roles are frequently switched.

Why have I never tried this? According to research, code quality goes up when you do this, and it leads to everyone on the team sharing knowledge better.

Jolly good. If I'm not fired, I'll be curious to see how this pairing thing works out.

Someone clears his throat. Twice. "Hi, Holly."

Rubbing my throbbing temples, I look up.

I should've guessed by the throat clearing.

It's Buckley.

"Hi," I say. "What's up?"

He clears his throat twice more. "I just wanted to say goodbye."

"Oh?"

A single clearing of the throat. Thank God. "I got the move I wanted already. The new management are fast."

"Ah." I do my best not to look *too* pleased. "Congratulations."

He clears his throat twice more. "Today is my last day."

He's at seven throat clearings now. How do I get him to leave things at that?

"Great," I say. "I wish you the best."

I wave goodbye.

Nope. He clears his throat twice, as though he's intentionally trying to drive me mad. "We should stay in touch."

"Sure," I say. "Will do."

Not bloody likely.

Giving me an unprofessionally lingering look that I definitely won't miss, he clears his throat yet again and leaves.

I pretend that it doesn't bother me that his throat clearing total is ten.

Not bothered at all.

Nope.

I'm as Zen as eleven Hindu cows. As cool as seven cucumbers.

Okay, fine. I need something more absorbing and stimulating than checking email, and I know just the thing—the code Robert emailed me the other day. If I keep my job, I'll be working on suit integration, so I might as well have a look.

I didn't think my headache could worsen, but here we are. The code itself is good, elegant even, but it's not tidy.

I frantically make sure all the lines are indented by four spaces, and then I fix spelling errors in the comments until I get a reminder about the upcoming meeting with Alex.

Bugger. Almost forgot. Forget fun, time *really* flies when you're cleaning up.

Before I get up from my desk, I type out the command to submit the cleaned-up code into the shared repository; otherwise, if my computer dies, my work will get lost. I do this carefully because I once gave the whole team a heart attack when I messed up this step and made it look like a year of hard work had disappeared. Fortunately, I had all the code they thought we'd lost stored locally on my computer, so I redid the code submission and everyone stopped freaking out.

Is it my imminent meeting with Alex, or is the term "code submission" vaguely BDSMy? Also, is BDSMy a word?

Grr. Why am I pondering linguistics? Alex and my fate await.

As I rise to my feet, the pain in my head sharpens to a throbbing.

Well, there's no helping it.

I speed-walk to the office I broke into and knock.

"Come in," Alex says, his sexy accent in full force.

I take a deep breath and step inside.

Chapter Twenty-Five

At a glance, I see that he indeed got himself a new monitor, a keyboard, and even an extra chair. What really commands my attention, though, is the man himself.

Though I doubt he shaved this morning, he's not as scruffy as usual thanks to the grooming from the prior day, and even his hair is less of a mess—all enhancing the scrumptiousness I should ignore.

Would getting fired by someone this hot hurt a little extra?

Hard to say.

Speaking of hard, he totally was last night. Throbbing hard, like my headache.

Ugh. Shoot me now.

"Hello," I say when I realize I've been standing there mutely for far too long.

His expression is unreadable, which makes him

look like his brother, Vlad. My palms grow sweaty, my stomach tightening into a knot.

"*Privet,*" he says.

An informal hello? Maybe that's a good sign?

"I—I think I know why I'm here," I stammer.

He lifts his right eyebrow the smallest fraction of a millimeter. "You do?"

I bob my head. "I'm sorry about last night."

A crease shows up on his forehead. "You are?"

"I behaved unprofessionally." I cast a yearning glance at his guest chair. I'm not sure if it's the hangover or this encounter so far, but my legs feel like jellified rubber.

"Sit." He makes it sounds like an order.

I gladly obey. "As I started saying, I'm sorry about my unbecoming behavior. It won't happen again."

His expression grows even harder to decipher. "It won't?"

"I promise. Please let me keep my job. I—"

"You think I asked you here to fire you?"

Now his face is easy to read. The angry expression states that if he didn't think I should be fired before, he's considering it now.

I swallow hard. "You didn't fill in the agenda on the meeting request."

His cerulean gaze darkens. "So you assumed you're getting fired? Is your opinion of me that low, or are you trying to be as pessimistic as a stereotypical Russian?"

Whew. I guess he's not firing me. My sigh of relief is audible. "What did you want to talk about then?"

"Suit integration." He turns his screen my way, and I see the code I just tidied.

"Oh."

A hint of that wicked smirk appears on his face. "Specifically, I wanted to talk about how we're going to work on the code."

"We?"

He's not about to say what I think he is, is he? That would be unthinkable. Like letting a bear into a honey storage facility. Like—

The smirk is clearly there now. "I want the two of us to pair."

Chapter Twenty-Six

*H*e means pairing as in the programming technique, but images of us copulating invade my brain and refuse to leave. Or more accurately, they never really left, but now they're at the forefront.

He turns the screen back toward himself. "Pull your chair closer."

Wait. Now?

We're pairing now?

He looks at me expectantly.

I guess that's that. We're pairing.

Binary gods help me.

I drag my chair over until I'm close enough to detect his yummy scent.

"You just submitted some code," he says, turning his focus to the screen. "Let me sync so we're looking at the latest."

Is it normal to notice how sexy his fingers are as they type out those commands? I picture them dancing around my body instead of on the lucky keyboard keys, and my breathing quickens. The way he just pressed that C key—

"You've made some files look nicer," he mutters, his attention still fixed on the screen. "It's easier to understand what's going on. Thank you."

Damn it. Why does that praise flash me back to last night's kiss?

"No problem," I manage.

"Do you want to drive or navigate?"

"I want to drive," I say quickly. Thankfully, I don't add "you crazy in bed."

Bugger, my thoughts are an inch away from becoming an article in *Cosmo*.

He scoots his chair away, and I slide in behind the keyboard.

"How about we work on that issue you mentioned to my sister?" he says.

"Sure. Can you help me navigate to the relevant file?"

He tells me where to go, and we review things together. Unfortunately, his proximity and the hangover make it extremely difficult to concentrate.

If this pairing is to go on, I'll need to aggressively hydrate… and masturbate.

Once we open the file, I scan for any low-hanging fruit when it comes to smoothing out the issues I saw. I find something and he agrees the change would help, so we work on it as I battle the urge to kiss him again.

Who knew coding could be so sexually frustrating?

"We'll need to test this," he says when I declare that I'm done with the change.

I nearly fall off my chair.

Test. As in use that suit?

I spotted the initial problem while canoodling with the replica of him in VR, so that's how I imagine the testing he's talking about. Except this time, I'd have to strip in front of him and—

My phone rings.

Ignoring it, I close the file.

The stupid thing rings again.

"You should take that," he says. "I have another meeting soon anyway. We'll pick this up in the afternoon."

So the X-rated testing is going to happen in the afternoon.

Jolly good. I'm so calm now.

The phone rings again. Stammering something incomprehensible, I finally accept the damn call.

It's security from downstairs. Someone's left a package, and I need to pick it up.

"See you later," Alex says when I explain that I have to go.

"Do svidaniya," I say on my way out.

"Do *skorovo* svidaniya," he says with a grin.

In the elevator, I pull out my phone and learn that *skorovo* means *imminent*.

Yep.

More pairing and testing is imminent—assuming I survive this lunch with my parents.

Chapter Twenty-Seven

*P*ackage in tow, I return to my floor.

I have to kill some time before lunch, so I decide to fill out as much of Bella's questionnaire as I can.

Damn.

Some of those questions are X-rated, to say the least. I hope no one stops by my desk—or questions why I'm blushing so profusely.

Questionnaire complete, I decide it's time to prep for lunch, so I sneak into the loo to try on whatever is in Gia's package.

No, not loo. Bathroom.

Must watch my Britishisms at that lunch.

In the box is my vampire makeover: a black wig, a bottle of foundation a shade too pale, a pair of biker boots, a dark lipstick, and an outfit consisting of black jeans, a black long-sleeved top, and a leather vest with metal studs on it. There are also fancy black gloves that will serve double duty, making it seem like I'm worried about germs while also covering the lack of black nail polish on my hands.

By the time I'm done putting it all on, I look enough like my twin that my own mother would not be able to tell us apart—which is the goal.

Hiding my own stuff in the now-empty box, I prepare to head out, only Bella walks in and does a double take.

"Wow. I've heard of Casual Fridays, but never of Goth Thursdays."

I grimace. "It's a long story."

She grins. "Let me guess. Your hangover is as bad as mine, so you've decided to look the way you feel."

"That's not a bad guess," I say, smiling back.

Her grin turns wicked. "So did you and Alex pair?"

Blushing through the foundation, I nod. Then, since I'm flustered anyway, I pull out her naughty form and thrust it into her hands. "That's as much as I'll ever be able to fill out. Alex took away the suit."

She chuckles. "Not surprised. Even as a kid, Alex never liked sharing his toys."

Am I the toy here, or is it the suit? Or maybe she's talking about virtual Alex?

"I've got a thing." I glance at the door.

"Me too." She heads for one of the stalls. "Bye."

I sneak a look at my phone and sprint back to my desk, ignoring my coworkers' startled glances. Dropping the box with my normal stuff by my chair, I hurry to the elevator.

Wait a sec.

Did I just see Alex in the corner of my vision? Hopefully not—I don't want to explain my look to him most of all.

To my relief, the elevator arrives quickly, and from there, the trip to Miso Hungry is uneventful.

My parents are waiting at a corner table when I step inside.

They don't see me yet, which is good.

I walk over to the hostess.

She doesn't seem to recognize me.

Sweet.

"Hi," I say. "I know I look different today, but I'm the customer who asks for forty-seven cubes of tofu in her miso soup."

"Ah," she says a bit too loudly. "That is a nice look for you."

"Thanks. I'll be sitting there." I point at my folks. "When I order miso soup and rolls later, can you make them the way I usually get them?"

She nods.

Great. Maybe I'll pull this off.

I approach the table. "Hi, Mom. Hi, Dad."

When he was young, Dad looked like Bob Dylan —or so Mom says. Nowadays, he looks more like a hobo, with a wild beard and a creepy silver ponytail that sticks out of a beanie that hides his bald spot. A well-fed hobo—his belly looks like Mom's right before the sextuplets aliened their way out of her. In contrast to Dad, and despite growing eight human beings inside her, Mom's stomach is flat, her hair is shiny, and her skin is smooth. She looks like she could be my older sister, which makes me optimistic about aging gracefully.

Note to self: must not give Dad grief about his eating habits, as that is something Gia wouldn't do.

Or would she?

Mom leaps to her feet and folds her hands together, yoga style. "Namaste, sunshine."

Sunshine? Is that sarcasm? I look like a creature of the night that sunshine kills.

"Thing 2." Dad's smile is goofy as he pats my shoulder.

Score. He called me Thing 2. The deception is working thus far. I'm actually Thing 1 on account of being the oldest, though that simply means I beat Gia by a few seconds in our race out of Mom's vagina. The sextuplets are Things 3 through 8, so I'm very lucky. I'm not Thing 4, or Thing 6, or—shudder—a very nonprime Thing 8.

"I'm sensing tension," Dad says. "Are you uncentered? Care for a shoulder rub?"

"We eat first," Mom says in the motherly tone she perfected while dealing with eight growing monsters —I mean, girls.

With a slight pout and a sigh, Dad plops back into his chair. He's a huge people pleaser, so denying him the chance to give a shoulder rub is like taking s'mores away from a starving hippie with the worst case of the munchies in cannabis history.

Mom sits, so I take the remaining chair, which happens to face the door.

"How are things going?" I ask, eager to keep the conversation as far away from my person as possible. "Did you do anything interesting while in town?"

"Things couldn't be better." Mom opens her menu. "Last night, we saw a burlesque performance. Afterward, your father turned into a beast."

And so it begins. I bet if I were to take a drink each time Mom says something that makes me want to poke my ears out, my current hangover would seem like a tickle.

"How are things in Thing 2's land?" Dad asks. "Still following your dream?"

"Yeah," I say. "Magic is great."

If they buy this, the rest of the lunch will be a breeze. Though I always try to be supportive of Gia, I can't help but see her magic more as a hobby than something a grownup does to pay bills on time.

Dad nods approvingly. "I so much admire what you're doing."

I carefully lift an eyebrow—the heavy layer of foundation on my forehead feels like it might peel off at any second.

"Manifesting your dreams," he clarifies. "I still haven't quit my day job."

"Your day job lets us travel like this," Mom says reassuringly. "Plus, as a penetration—"

"Mom." I glance worriedly at the hostess. "Please don't make penetration-related jokes, I implore you."

Dad tugs on his beard. "It just sucks working for *the man*."

The waitress comes over, and we order. As soon as she departs, I offer to show my parents a magic trick, since Gia would've done so by now.

To my deep annoyance, they think of the number thirty-seven when prompted—Gia manages to do magic without being at the scene.

"That was great." Dad pours the three of us little platters of soy sauce. "Reminds me of that video I sent you the other day."

Interesting. He sends Gia videos of magic tricks? The last thing he sent me was a theoretical computer science treatise on NP-hardness (where N and P stand for Non-deterministic Polynomial-time and not, say, Naked Penis.)

"Yeah, great video," I say. "Thanks."

To prevent more magic talk, I stuff a piece of avocado roll into my mouth and pretend that it's bigger than it is.

Mom picks up a piece of sushi with her chopsticks. "I'm sorry to move the conversation away from magic, but there was something I wanted to talk to you about."

I tense but try to hide it. The last thing I want is a shoulder rub from Dad. "What's up?"

"We're worried about your sister," Mom says.

Rolling eyes is Gia's bread and butter, so I give in to the urge. "Which one?"

"Your twinsie," Mom says. "Obviously."

Bugger. They're worried about *me*? I mean, the real me? Also, what's with that "obviously?" If you pick a sextuplet at random, she's bound to be more of a concern than I am. Unless Mom means "obviously, Holly's troubles are a conversation to have with *Gia*."

Yeah. I'm sticking with that.

I fake Gia's mischievous grin. "What has my Posh Spice clone done now?"

Did that sound like Gia?

Both parents frown.

Great. Now they're upset with me for mocking my own self.

"She seems off," Mom says.

"Not living," Dad says. "Merely existing."

I narrow my eyes at him. "What did you smoke today?"

He waves a dismissive hand. "Ever since Beau came out, she—"

I miss what he says next because I'm caught off-guard by my ex's name and the accompanying tightening in my chest.

I do my best not to show anything on my face. I have to act as Gia would. Actually, she'd scowl, so I do that. She hates Beau on my behalf. To cheer me up, she admitted that she'd broken into his house after our breakup and added laxatives to everything in his fridge.

"I think she's fine." I dip a piece of avocado roll into the soy sauce. "Apart from needing a better wardrobe, of course."

There. It's like I was born for this role.

"She hasn't dated anyone since Beau," Mom says. "You know how important orgasms are, and I don't think she's getting them."

I grit my teeth. Does she think Beau was giving me orgasms? "My own sex life isn't exactly flourishing. How can I help her?"

Crap. Both are looking at me funny. Not good.

"I mean, I obviously play with myself," I add, figuring Gia can talk like this in front of Dad without feeling suicidal. "I'm pretty sure Holly does too. Just a prime number of times per day."

Boom. Where is my Oscar?

Mom sits up straighter. "You really think so?"

You'd think I'd told her that her daughter discovered a cure for cancer instead of a dildo.

"Totes," I say. "I'm more worried she'll get carpal tunnel from all that masturbation."

"That's a relief," Mom says. "Of course, the real goal is getting a human being to deliver those orgasms."

I'm Gia. Gia should be embarrassed, not me.

"Because love is lovely," Dad adds.

"Right. Holly and I will get right on that," I say with Gia's signature sarcasm. "Real human. Got it."

"Let me know if I can help in any way," Mom says with an earnest expression that makes me doubt my sarcasm skills. "I have decades of experience with the most toe-curling, mind-boggling, tantric sex in the universe. If you need any advice, I'm always here for you."

"*We* are," Dad corrects her.

Why didn't I order Fugu—the Japanese dish made out of the deadly puffer fish? The sweet release from tetrodotoxin might be preferable to this conversation.

"Thanks, guys," I force myself to say.

Dad scratches his beard. "If you put out loving energy into the world, the karmic balance will always be in your favor."

Did the waitress sneak him a fortune cookie?

If I weren't pretending to be Gia, I'd remind them that this isn't just about orgasms for them. I suspect they want a son-in-law, and a grandson if they're really lucky. Their desire for a male child is widely known. It's why they underwent that fertility treatment all those years ago—the one that yielded them six more daughters instead.

That's what made Dad believe in karma. He's convinced he must've been a serial killer in a prior life.

"So, we have some news," Mom says.

Please don't say you're starting a sex commune. Or a nudist colony. Or opening your marriage.

"We're staying in town for an extra few weeks," she says.

Whew. "That's great, Mom. You should see *Mary Poppins* on Broadway."

Mom and Dad exchange glances.

Bugger. Gia would've recommended a magic show. Or a mentalism show—like there's a difference.

Well, the nanny is out of the bag now. If I backpedal, it will look even more suspicious, so I just stick a piece of food into my mouth and chew.

The restaurant door jingles.

I glance at the newcomer, and my heart leaps into my throat.

It's none other than Alex Chortsky, my maybe-fake date and definitely-not-fake boss.

Chapter Twenty-Eight

I swiftly look away.

Maybe he didn't see me? Or saw me but didn't recognize me in my Gia guise?

The chance is there but low if he saw me like this in the office.

My phone dings.

I check it instinctively.

It's a text from Lucifer Satan: *Is that you?*

I'm an idiot. I just looked at my phone, confirming his suspicions.

I throw a panicked glance toward him.

Yep. He's coming this way.

There are so many problems with this, but Gia's deception is the biggest—and that, unlike my dignity, is something I can still protect.

Grinning like a loon, I wave at him. "Alex! It's me, Gia. Over here."

With a frown, he picks up his pace.

Parents turn. Dad scratches his beard while Mom begins to drool.

"Gia?" Alex says, clearly confused.

"I know." The loonie grin is approaching Joker levels. "I'm usually much paler, but you know how it is. I was in the sun for a whole five minutes today."

Everyone chuckles nervously.

"Mom, Dad," I say. "This is Alex."

They look at me expectantly.

Right. At this point, one usually explains the relationship between one's self and the person they're introducing.

What do I say?

Then it hits me. I can do Gia a huge favor—and get back at Alex for parading me in front of his parents the other day.

"Alex is my boyfriend," I say nonchalantly. "I asked him to join us. Surprise!"

Alex blinks but seems to go along with it. At least he doesn't refute my claim as he drags a chair from another table to ours.

My parents gape at him with shell-shocked expressions.

Wow. Do they consider Gia completely undatable?

"Alex, this is Crystal and Harry Hyman, my parents."

Alex shakes Dad's hand, then kisses Mom on the cheek in the Russian style.

She looks like she might lay an egg. Breathlessly, she stammers out, "How did the two of you meet?"

"Alex works with my twin," I say. "Obviously, *she* couldn't date him; his name doesn't have a prime number of letters."

In reality, I *can* live with the letter count in "Alex" because I really like the way it sounds. Also, I can appease myself with the knowledge that his parents call him Sasha, which *is* five letters long.

Alex sits down. "Yeah. Dating Holly would not be appropriate, would it?"

Mom doesn't seem to be listening. Judging by the looks she directs toward "my boyfriend," it will be her turn to be a beast tonight.

"You seem tense," Dad says to Alex.

Alex shrugs. "It's not every day I meet the parents of a woman I'm dating. Plus, there's an important project I'm working on with Holly, so…"

"Say no more." Dad leaps to his feet. "This will recharge your energy for the week."

Before I can shout something like SOS, Dad's hairy fingers are digging into Alex's shoulders.

I'm Gia. Gia should be mortified, not me.

Dad's massage is so vigorous his ponytail comes within an inch of hitting Alex in the face. Also, Dad is making odd grunting sounds. What is that? Is he so out of shape that even squeezing his fingers is difficult for him? Or is he trying to create a vibration effect for Alex, like a fancy massage chair or a cat?

Mom looks on jealously, but probably not because Dad is getting handsy with someone who's not her. I think she wants to be touching Alex herself... and maybe not just his shoulders.

To his credit, Alex's face doesn't show what he must be really thinking. There's only a hint of a smile dancing in his cerulean eyes.

"Sir," the waitress says to Dad with exaggerated politeness. "Could you not do that in here?"

Is she being homophobic? Unclear, but she does get results. Dad slaps Alex on the back, then plops back into his chair, muttering something about the dumb bondage of societal norms.

"What would you like?" the waitress asks Alex in a tone that makes me think she shooed my dad away to get rid of competition.

"For Holly's father to never, ever touch me again" is what I expect Alex to say, but he simply asks for a sushi lunch special.

"Your accent," Mom says huskily. "Where are you from?"

With a delectable smile, Alex explains that he was born in Murmansk, a city in the northwestern part of Russia.

Mom and Dad pepper him with questions about his hometown, and I learn that it was the last city founded by the Russian Empire. And that it's cold even for Russia, with bitter winters and short, cool summers.

"When would you recommend someone to visit it?" Mom asks, her eyes still annoyingly moony.

"I wouldn't recommend visiting at all," Alex says.

"But if you really want to, I'd say always visit Russia in the summer. And check out Moscow before you bother with Murmansk."

"Is your whole family here?" Mom asks.

He nods, then tells them about his parents and siblings. "My grandparents stayed behind," he says in conclusion. "That was before video conferencing, so I missed them a lot." He looks wistful. "They're gone now."

I feel the urge to kiss the sadness off his face. Bugger. What's wrong with me? He's not *really* my boyfriend. Seeing him vulnerable isn't supposed to give me the feels.

"I'm sure they feel your love wherever they are," Dad says to Alex reassuringly. "Love transcends time and space."

To his credit, Alex doesn't roll his eyes. Instead, he asks, "What about your parents?"

"Florida," Mom and Dad say at the same time.

Alex smiles. "That's pretty much the opposite of Russia."

Before anyone can say anything else, the waitress comes back with Alex's food, and he attacks it with gusto—Dad's massage must've stimulated his appetite.

"What do you think of Gia's magic?" Mom asks when Alex slows down his sushi devouring to match everyone's pace.

He gives me a questioning glance. "She's... amazing."

"He's being kind," I say. "In reality, whenever I

perform for him, he begs me to tell him how I did it. Not knowing drives him crazy."

Mom and Dad exchange another look.

Bugger. Did that not sound like Gia?

"What's it like to work with Holly?" Mom asks, her blue eyes shifting between me and Alex.

"She's brilliant," Alex answers with a sexy grin. "My sister and I are lucky to have her working with us."

Aww. I'm sure he's just playing along, but it's still nice to hear.

Dad beams with pride. "I like to think she went into the computer science field because of what I do for a living."

Alex picks up a piece of tuna. "Which is?"

Ugh. Dad was clearly angling for Alex to ask that question.

"I'm a penetration tester," Dad says with the usual relish. "But it's not as dirty as—"

"Oh, I know what penetration testing is," Alex says, not batting an eye. "And this makes sense. Holly did show me some tools of your trade recently."

Thanks, Dad. Let's remind my boss about my attempted sabotage.

"Right," Dad says eagerly. "She borrowed some of my stuff. Glad it was useful."

"Is it strange to date one twin while working with the other?" Mom asks.

Hmm. I don't like this line of questioning one bit.

Alex shrugs. "They're so different it doesn't matter."

Mom looks at me unblinkingly. "And Holly's idiot synchronies don't bother you?"

"It's idiosyncrasies," I say sternly. "And Holly doesn't have any."

"She doesn't?" Mom's eyes narrow. "What about the prime mania?"

"You made that up," I say.

"Prime mania?" Alex asks, intrigued.

"My sister just likes prime numbers, that's all," I say. "Anyone mathematically inclined will have favorite numbers."

Alex nods. "I'm partial to the Fibonacci sequence. There are actually primes in that sequence, like 2, 3, 5, 13, 89, 233."

Can I ask him to marry me right here and now?

"Fine," Mom says. "If you claim her number obsession is normal, surely wearing and eating the same thing isn't."

Am I ready for matricide?

I take in a calming breath. "She just wants to organize her life so as to limit the number of mundane decisions each day. That way, she can focus on what's bloody important."

Mom's eyes narrow further.

Bugger. Have I just betrayed myself?

"I think Holly is smart to do what she does," Alex says, and I want to kiss him—more than usual, that is.

"Didn't Albert Einstein always wear the same thing for the same reason?"

Moving like a cobra, Mom grips my wig and yanks it off with a triumphant expression.

Bloody hell.

"Hello, *Holly*," Mom says with a stern emphasis on my name. "Care to explain?"

Chapter Twenty-Nine

*B*ugger.

Gia is going to kill me.

Dad looks betrayed. "Thing 1?"

I pick up my untouched water glass and gulp down half of it under everyone's penetrating gazes. "I'm sorry. I owed Gia a favor."

Mom shakes the wig over her sushi. "That doesn't explain this at all."

My skin burns with heat—and not the nice, Alex-related kind. "Gia thought you'd drill her about her nonexistent love life, but apparently, today is Worry About Holly Day. Which sounds like a holiday. The worst holiday ever. If I—"

Alex puts a reassuring hand on my elbow, unleashing a hive of horny bees in my stomach.

Dad tugs on his ponytail. "Sorry about that, kiddo. It comes from a loving place."

Mom looks at Alex's hand on my elbow. "So, which of our daughters are you dating?"

Before I can say none, he says, "Holly."

My hand is trembling as I pull out of his hold, grab my glass, and greedily gulp down the rest of the water, crunching on the ice as I go.

I know Alex is lying, but the bees in my stomach are lactating honey nevertheless.

Or is it pooping honey?

Peeing?

No, I vaguely recall David Attenborough saying something about regurgitation of nectar, so I guess it's more like puking.

I put the glass back down.

Isn't it weird that we all eat honey and never question its insect origins? Spider webs might taste like cotton candy, but I'd never know because that seems like a gross thing to eat. Yet bee vomit is great with tea.

Actually, spiders aren't insects. They're Araneae, though that doesn't make their—

I realize everyone is looking at me expectantly.

"Can you repeat the question?" I ask sheepishly.

Mom's frown finally softens. "I didn't ask anything. I was just saying you two make a very cute couple."

Blimey. The bees are getting buzzy again.

"Thank you," Alex says. "My parents said the same thing."

And now the bees are puking enough honey to survive a long, cold, Russian winter.

Mom's smile is mischievous—this is who Gia inherited hers from. "You've met his parents? Things must be serious indeed."

Golly. We have met each other's parents—and I always thought that if a guy ever met mine, that would be the end of the relationship.

Wait. What am I even saying? Alex and I don't have a relationship. He needs me for a work project, which must be the only reason he's not running away screaming. Still, he's being a good sport about this whole thing, I have to give him that.

"We should head back." I glance at Alex. "Coding awaits." And we'd better escape quickly because it's just a matter of time—seconds, probably—before Mom inquires about our sex life and begins dishing out shagging advice.

"Before you go..." Mom bats her eyelashes at Alex. "You wouldn't happen to have a brother, would you?"

Alex grins. "As a matter of fact, I do."

I suppress a groan. "You're married, Mom, remember?"

Mom chuckles while Dad looks zero jealous, making me wonder if they've opened up their marriage after all.

"It's not for me, dear," Mom says with mirth in her voice. "I wanted to circle back to Gia."

Ah. Pimping out my twin. What else is new?

Alex pulls out his wallet. "In that case, I'm sorry. My brother is already taken."

Yep. Given the way Vlad was looking at Fanny—her face, not her fanny, though I'm sure he looks at it too—he's all settled.

I rummage in my purse for my own wallet and realize I never took out Bella's dildo.

I mean, *my* dildo.

"Gia is too picky," I say as I carefully bring out the wallet without sending the dildo flying into Mom's face. "I offered to set her up with Alex's sister's boyfriend's brother, but she refused."

"Why?" Mom asks.

I toss forty-one dollars on the table. "Said he was a manwhore."

"Oh, please." Mom directs a worshipful look at Dad. "Your father was a player in his day, but I—"

"We really don't want to hear that," I say, tugging on Alex's sleeve.

I'd bet a thousand quid the rest of Mom's sentence was going to be "tamed him with my pussy."

"It was a pleasure to meet you, Crystal," Alex says and gives her another peck on the cheek. "And you, Harry." He shakes Dad's hand.

Though she's never worn pearls in her life, Mom clutches the place where they would be as she gasps, "The pleasure was all mine."

Dad clears his throat.

"I mean ours," Mom amends hastily.

Right. Like we could forget the pleasure Dad took in touching my pretend date.

"Bye," both parents say in unison.

"Do svidaniya," Alex and I say, also in unison, before rushing out of the restaurant.

———

"Thanks," I mumble weakly as we get into the elevator in our building.

"What for?" he asks, his lips curving in that devilish way of his.

"For pretending to be my boyfriend."

His smirk grows more wicked. "Pretending?"

The doors open, and he gestures for me to come out.

I do so on unsteady legs, so shell-shocked I can't think straight.

Of course he was bloody pretending. He can't be my boyfriend without my being aware of it.

Right?

Chapter Thirty

"*R*eady for our testing?" he asks, following me out of the elevator.

With effort, I pull together my scattered wits. "I need to call my sister first. It's best she hears about the lunch disaster from me."

He nods. "Come to my office when you're ready."

In a daze, I watch him stride away. Then I step into the first empty conference room and dial Gia.

"Hey," she says. "How was your lunch as me? Did you feel much, much hotter?"

"I'm sorry," I say, and explain what happened.

Gia sighs. "I should've known." To my relief, she doesn't sound overly pissed. "You're a shitty liar."

"Sorry again."

"You know what this means, right?"

"What?" I can already tell I won't like it.

"You still owe me. And this time, I think I'll use you in one of my upcoming illusions—unless even just standing on a stage without talking is too much deception for you to handle?"

"I'll help you with your bloody illusion. I said I was sorry."

"Fine. I'm going to call our parents and grovel."

"Good luck," I tell her and hang up.

"What's with the outfit?" Alison asks when I exit the conference room.

Bugger. Forgot about my Gia guise.

"Long story," I answer and rush to my desk to grab the box with the change of clothing.

De-vampirefied, I head over to Alex's office, my heart pounding and my legs wobbly once again.

When I step inside, a suit my size is sprawled on the couch. Next to it is a bigger suit that must be for him.

What the hell? We're testing at the same time?

I picture him creating a replica of me in VR, and every inch of me catches fire.

Alex looks away from his screen. "Ready?"

I gulp.

I suppose there's no help for it.

My face feeling like fresh lava, I reach for the buttons of my shirt with trembling fingers.

He frowns. "What are you doing?"

I blink at him. "Last time I used the suit, the instructions said to do so nude."

His eyes darken and rake over my body, as if he's picturing me exactly that way. When his gaze returns to my face, spots of color burn on the edges of his high cheekbones. "We're not going to be testing the features that require that." His voice is tinged with hoarseness. "I'm keeping my clothes on, and I suggest you do the same."

Oh. Okay then. I don't know whether to be mortified or relieved. There may be some disappointment mixed in too.

He walks up to the bigger suit.

"Hold on," I blurt. "You're doing it at the same time?"

"Why not?" he asks, his eyes gleaming.

The man is a bloody enigma.

Not asking any more questions, I get inside the suit.

Like before, there's a single app in there, labeled Demo.

Bollocks. Even with clothes on, seeing naked Alex —assuming that's who I want to assemble—will be awkward with him here. Not to mention, I'm already jealous of whatever VR woman he'll create for himself.

No helping it.

I launch the Demo.

I find myself in a white room again, and at first, it seems like the demo has skipped right to the cock selection.

Except these shimmering, multicolor phallic objects aren't penises, or peni, or penes—I still haven't looked up the proper plural. They aren't dildoes either, though I guess anything can be a dildo if you're brave enough.

They're swords.

Laser swords that remind me of lightsabers from *Star Wars*, and metal swords of various kinds, everything from broadswords to katanas. The variety is not quite as exhaustive as with the cocks, but close.

Is this a demo of some weird fetish?

I choose a blue laser sword because it seems like the least sharp one. Even though I doubt I can be penetrated with it while my clothes are on—or that penetration is even part of what's about to happen—it's still better to be safe than sorry.

The sword feels good in my hand, and when I slice from side to side, the shimmering blade hums.

Neat.

Suddenly, Alex appears in front of me.

Not the real one, but a close approximation—and, sadly, dressed in a tunic and a black cloak.

"Good choice," he says and salutes me with a red laser sword.

"Are you real?" I ask.

"Yep."

"How?" I look down and see I'm wearing an outfit identical to his.

"This is a multiplayer demo. I had my team at 1000 Devils prepare it. This is a small portion of a game we put out on another VR platform, but Robert's people have adapted it to the full suit."

"Wow." I wave the sword in a wide arc. "This will make the testing so much less awkward."

"That's the point," he says. "Want to spar a little?"

Without answering, I stab him.

Or try to.

He parries my attack and slashes at my leg—which the suit turns into a slightly unpleasant pressure on my thigh.

He throws down his sword. "Now tell me, did our code change help with the issue you saw?"

"Let's see." I let go of my sword as well. "Come over and try to grab my shoulder while I catch your wrist. That should approximate the wonky part of your sister's demo."

I'm glad my VR face doesn't show my real-world emotions. The previous demo's Alex tried to grab something a lot more private than my shoulder.

He saunters over and reaches for me.

I grab his wrist and hold, enjoying the solid feel.

How in the world am I turned on by this?

Why is my real-world heart racing from touching his avatar?

"Better?" he asks.

"Very nice," I murmur.

"So the fix helped?"

Oh. Right. Work stuff.

I let go of his wrist and step back. "Yeah. A little better. Lots of work still to do." I reach out and touch his chest, doing my best not to hyperventilate at the warm sensation. "Slight timing issues abound."

He nods. "How about we fix more of them?"

"Sure." I reluctantly drop my hand. "Though I think there are so many, we might want to write them up and delegate a bunch to my team."

"Of course." He reaches for his head and disappears.

I reluctantly take off my headset as well, then wriggle out of the suit.

"Ready to pair again?" he asks.

I pull up a chair to his desk. "Can I drive?"

He lets me, and I spend some time describing the issues that need fixing and assigning a bunch of tasks to the appropriate developers.

The exciting—and terrifying—thing is that Alex insists "we" keep a bunch to work on "ourselves."

"Don't you have some responsibilities at 1000 Devils?" I ask.

He shrugs. "Bella needs me. We have to get the suits ready for production."

I turn from the monitor to meet his very distracting cerulean eyes. "So who will be porting the games for the hospital project?"

"My people at 1000 Devils. There's actually a dedicated team for that."

A peculiarly warm sensation unfurls in my chest.

Must be hope about the VR pet therapy. It can't be joy at the prospect of working side by side with

Alex for the foreseeable future. Because that wouldn't do. Not at all.

"That reminds me," he says. "I wanted to see your VR pet therapy for myself."

Would it look unprofessional if I jumped up and down with glee?

I love showing off my work to anyone even remotely curious, but the idea of Alex seeing it tickles me on a different level. I wonder if this is what a single mom might feel when a guy she's been dating finally meets her child for the first time. Except, of course, Euclid isn't a real child, and Alex and I aren't dating.

"I'll be right back," I say and hurry out of his office to get a headset and gloves from my desk, the ones with my Euclid setup.

"Mind if I stream what you'll be doing to your monitor?" I ask Alex when I'm back.

He doesn't mind, so I set it up.

"Ready?" I ask.

Alex puts on the gear, and I walk him through which app to launch.

"Wow," he says when the purple otter-meets-Tele-tubby creature shows up in front of him. "Aren't you a cute one."

"Hi, Holly," Euclid sing-songs. "I mished you."

I smile. Just seeing my little VR pet on Alex's monitor gives me a jolt of joy.

"He thinks I'm you," Alex says with a grin.

With the headset on, he can't see me staring at his lips, so I allow myself to enjoy that sexy smile.

On the screen, Euclid's fur turns a mix of colors that indicates confusion. "What are you talking about? You can be so shilly."

I walk over and rise on tiptoe to whisper into Alex's ear. "Of course he thinks you're me. It's not like there's a camera inside the headset."

How did I resist the urge to lick that ear?

"You're right," Alex says.

"I'm always right." Euclid turns a proud brown shade. "That means you really are shilly."

Wow. Very good response. The cool thing about AI is that it can sometimes surprise you.

Grin widening, Alex bends down and fluffs Euclid's fur until it's a happy purple again. "You're right, little one. I can be very silly indeed."

Hey now. Was that a dig? After all, Euclid thinks he's talking to me.

"I'm ravenoush," Euclid says and does his hungry dance.

"What do I do?" Alex mouths.

I again enjoy whispering the instructions into his ear. Also breathing in his scent.

I'm not being creepy. Not at all.

Looking almost giddy, Alex extends his hand to get the digital snacks to appear on his palm. Then he feeds Euclid each and every one with an enthusiasm that rivals mine.

Bugger. My ovaries are aching as I watch Alex do

all this, and they go into overdrive when the two start to play fetch and I see the joy on his face.

If this little test is anything to go by, Alex would make a great daddy to some lucky little human.

Perhaps a little human that I make for him?

Wait. What? I've never had these kinds of thoughts about a man before. It's way creepier than sniffing him, if we're being honest.

"I'd better go," Alex tells Euclid reluctantly. "I have a friend waiting for me."

Euclid's fur turns several shades of gray before settling on a light teal. "Shee you later. I wove you."

Alex hugs him. "Love you too, bud."

Okay. I'm officially a puddle of swoon.

Alex looks reluctant as he removes the headset.

I hide improper feelings as quickly as I can.

"Amazing job," he says when he can see me again. "He's the next best thing to mainlining oxytocin."

I feel all floaty all of a sudden, like I've just mainlined oxytocin myself. "Little known fact," I say without thinking. "Oxytocin can produce more frequent and more powerful orgasms in women. Most people think it's just for fostering feelings of bonding, but it does so much more."

Blimey. Why did I just rattle out all of that? I need to get myself off, and soon. Orgasms are too much on my mind, so much so I'm talking about them with my boss like the creep I'm turning into.

Or my mom.

Alex chuckles. "Don't tell Bella. Knowing her,

she'll start wondering how to incorporate Euclid into the pleasure functions of the suit."

All the blood leaves my face. With everything going on, I've almost forgotten about the porn-shaped sword of Damocles hanging over my VR pet project.

He frowns. "I'm kidding. She wouldn't actually do that."

"It's not that," I say. "I'm just worried NYU Langone will not work out." There. It's actually the truth... just not the whole truth.

He walks over and tucks a stray strand of hair behind my ear. "We're going to kill at that meeting tomorrow. I promise."

I fight the tsunami of oxytocin to raise a questioning eyebrow. "Tomorrow?"

"Well, yeah. Weren't you copied on the invite from Dr. Piper?"

"No." I grab the headset and gloves. "I'll be right back."

I sprint to my desk, stash the gear, and check my inbox.

Sure enough, there's an invite for a meeting at NYU Langone tomorrow morning.

The jittery excitement I feel as I dash back clears away whatever remained of my hangover.

"Want me to walk you through my strategy for the meeting?" Alex asks as I come in.

"Yes. Please."

He puts up a presentation on his screen and

explains that someone on Robert's team prepared it for him.

Note to self: learn to delegate better. I totally would've done the presentation myself by staying late, and then I would've felt like rubbish the next day.

Alex walks me through the presentation, which includes the games they plan to pitch for phase one— all kid-appropriate and the furthest thing from porn.

"When can all this be ported to the suit?" I ask. It's the closest I can come to, "Do you think this can be finished before they somehow find out about the porn connection?"

Alex closes the presentation. "Robert is comfortable with a pretty aggressive timeline."

If I didn't already want to kiss him (again), I'd want to kiss him now.

But no.

Professional and proper is my new motto.

"So," Alex says. "What are your plans for the rest of today?"

"I'm game for us to pair," I say.

Bugger. That didn't sound either professional or proper.

"Great." He takes his seat. "Can I drive?"

We begin to program together, and I lose track of time. Whenever he explains the logic behind his code changes, I feel myself getting deeper into trouble. If my inappropriate attraction to him was mostly physical at the start, I'm now just as drawn in by the way his mind works—and that's not good. That way dwell feelings that I'm not ready to have for anyone, let alone my boss.

When we switch and I get to drive, things aren't that much better. Alex has a dangerous habit of telling me how clever he thinks I am. There's only so much praise I can take before I strip off my clothes and beg him to ravage me on the couch.

Or on the desk.

Maybe right in this chair?

"I'm starving," Alex says, pulling me out of my licentious thoughts.

I glance at the clock in the corner of his screen.

It's eight. Way past my usual dinner time.

As if to confirm that, my treacherous stomach rumbles like a bloody motorcycle.

"That's it." He jumps to his feet. "The least I can do is buy you dinner."

Dinner?

All I can do is flap my eyelashes at him in shock.

"Let's go." He holds the door for me.

Mind spinning, I step out of the office onto the now-empty floor.

Bella pops her head out of her office. "Hey, guys."

"*Privet*," I say. "We're going to dinner. Want to join us?"

Boom. Inviting a guy's sister makes the dinner not a date.

"Thanks, but I already ate." She winks at me. "You two go on ahead."

Bollocks. She's playing Emma again.

I guess this is happening.

As he herds me to the elevator, Alex asks what food I'm in the mood for.

"Sushi," I say without thinking.

Ugh. Could I be any more boring and predictable? To make this worse, my parents flat out told him I eat the same thing all the time.

"I'm so glad you suggested it," he says, sounding earnest. "I want their chicken teriyaki."

Whew. It's going to be stressful enough resisting the temptation to turn this clearly professional dinner into a date.

We walk into Miso Hungry.

The usual hostess isn't here, which is reasonable. It is late.

"Welcome back," says the waitress from earlier, her gaze glued to Alex's face. "Your usual table?"

He nods, but when we sit down, he whispers, "I don't think I've been here often enough to get a usual table."

Well, this *is* the table where he sat with Bella when I saw them, and I guess anything related to Alex is burned into this waitress's memory.

Twat.

She comes back, and when I ask for my usual, she makes a confused face.

I'd bet anything she knows it. She just wants me to say it out loud in front of my not-a-date.

"Three avocado rolls with one piece held back," I

grit out. "A miso soup with forty-seven cubes of tofu and seventeen pieces of scallion."

I expect Alex to smirk, but his face is completely unaffected—like he hears people order prime numbers of food items all the time.

"How many pieces is the teriyaki cut into?" he asks with apparent seriousness when it's his turn.

"Eight?" The waitress's smile is a little too chummy for my liking.

"Please tell the chef to make that seven," he says, again completely deadpan.

She raises an eyebrow. "Your order comes with a soup. Do you also want—"

"Yes," he says. "Same number of tofu cubes and scallion for me, please."

This is it. I'm going to propose to him and get fired.

No. Get it together, Holly.

I excuse myself to go to the bathroom, and when I get there, I stare into the mirror, chanting a single mantra:

Do not fall for him.
Do. Not. Fall. For. Him.

Chapter Thirty-One

*W*hen I return from the bathroom, Alex pulls out a chair for me—a gentlemanly gesture that wreaks havoc on my determination to keep things professional between us.

The waitress comes back with a little pot of green tea.

He pours a cup for me first, then one for himself.

Seriously, he needs to do something rude and soon. Else I'm not holding myself accountable for any creepazoid behavior.

Like dry-humping him right on this table.

"What gave you the idea for VR pet therapy?" he asks.

I blow on my tea—and pretend I don't see him staring hungrily at my puckered lips. "As hard as it is to believe, I grew up on a farm, surrounded by animals—and I don't mean just my sisters."

He chuckles.

"It was insane," I continue. "Untidy, chaotic… Yet after I left, I realized that a part of me missed the animal companionship—and hanging out with my twin sister didn't help that go away."

He laughs.

"What I like about VR in general is how everything in it can go away when you take off the headset, leaving no messes behind. When I thought of a VR pet, I hoped it would tap into that need for companionship, but would let me keep my living space ordered. And it's worked out exactly as I hoped."

He nods. "What about the hospital? Why did you decide to partner with them?"

I take a sip of the tea. "I had my appendix taken out when I was ten. It was the worst time of my life, and the only thing that made it semi-bearable was my dad's Game Boy. VR is a bit like that Game Boy, but much, much more effective as a distraction—and studies prove it."

Alex looks intrigued. "What games did you play?"

"At that time?" I strain my memory. "One with Mario and one with Kirby."

He looks disappointed. "Any falling block puzzle games?"

"Not then, but I've played *Dr. Mario* since. Why?"

"I was hoping you'd say *Tetris*," he says. "I might be slightly obsessed with that game."

The waitress comes back with our soups and lingers next to Alex a few seconds too long.

"Your *Tetris* obsession is somewhat logical," I say

when she finally leaves. "You own a video game company, so you're clearly into games—and *Tetris* was created in Russia, your country of birth."

He picks up his spoon. "You know a lot about it considering you've never played."

I blow on the soup, mostly to see if he stares at my lips again—and he does. "I have played it, just on the PC."

"Ah, good. Did you know *Tetris* can improve spatial reasoning and help with anxiety?"

Huh. He sounds like my mom when she touts the benefits of orgasms.

"Surely *Dr. Mario* has the same advantages?" I ask.

"Doubt it." He grins. "What's your favorite tetrimino?"

I wrinkle my nose. "I don't like the very idea of tetriminos. Sorry."

There's a hopefully joking look of outrage on his face. "Why?"

"They're all four squares," I say apologetically. "If I'd designed that game, I would've made them pentominos."

He rubs the stubble on his chin. "You don't think five square shapes would've made the game too difficult?"

I shrug. "Difficult could mean more fun."

He seems to seriously consider this, then shakes his head. "I just can't picture that version of the game becoming as popular as the original."

I swallow a spoonful of soup after making sure

there's a prime number of tofu and scallion pieces in it. "What's *your* favorite tetrimino?"

"The T-block, hands down." He makes a T in the air with his index fingers, conjuring up inappropriate images of one of those fingers going into me instead. "The T can bridge gaps, square up edges, and set up places you can put Z- or S-blocks."

"Interesting." What's really interesting is that I somehow find his explanation erotic.

"Yeah," he says animatedly. "You can also stick a T into otherwise impossible holes with a T-Spin maneuver."

Okay, now I feel less like a weirdo for getting turned on. I mean, sticking things into holes?

I clear my suddenly parched throat. "I thought the I-block is what everyone prefers. It's long and straight and helps you clear four lines at once."

Is this flirting? I did just talk about something long and straight. Add in hard, and I might as well be talking about his cock.

"I'll agree that the I-block is better than J and L," he says. "But it has nothing on the T."

"I'll take your word for it."

He smiles. "If you had to choose a tetrimino, which would you go for?"

"A square. It's symmetrical, nice and tidy."

He nods approvingly. "Dependable choice, especially early in the game."

The waitress brings out the main course, and he pours soy sauce for me when she leaves.

"How did you get into *Tetris?*" I ask before sticking the first avocado roll piece into my mouth.

"When I was a kid back in Russia, we didn't have a computer at home, but there was a business nearby that rented computer time by the hour. I think my love of games and coding goes back to that time and those games—of which my favorite was *Tetris.*" He smiles. "I guess now it's nostalgic. Reminds me of Russia and all that."

Since he's brought it up, I pepper him with questions about growing up in Russia, which was still the Soviet Union when he was a child. The stories he tells me about Perestroika and the wild corruption of the nineties are equally chilling and fascinating, and the more he talks, the more I feel like I understand him—which is terrible for my goal of not falling for him.

"What about you?" he asks. "What was it like growing up with so many sisters?"

Of course. Many people ask this out of the same kind of curiosity that makes them slow down at a scene of a car accident.

"For someone who likes order as much as I do, it was unadulterated hell," I say honestly. "Going to college abroad felt like getting out of jail."

"The college being Cambridge, right? You didn't do a year or two in an American school first?"

"Nope. It was the UK from the start. As you can tell by my occasional verbal slips, I loved it there."

"And yet you came back here." He looks at me

with so much interest I feel equal parts giddy and unsettled.

"Not surprisingly, I wanted to work in VR," I say, averting my gaze to hide from the naked intensity in his. "The best job I found happened to be in New York, so I took it. My whole family is in this country as well, so that was a variable too."

He covers my hand with his. "I know it's selfish, but I'm glad you took the job."

Wow. His skin is touching my skin, and the warmth of it destroys what passes for my resolve in a heartbeat.

If we weren't in a public place, I'd jump him.

"I'm glad too." I stop avoiding his gaze and get lost in the cerulean depths.

"Will you be having dessert?" the waitress asks, wrenching me out of my trance-like state.

"No." I reluctantly pull my hand free.

"Just the check please," Alex says.

She glares at me and stomps away.

Oblivious to her anger and the cause of it, Alex asks, "Have you been back to the UK since you finished college?"

"Unfortunately, no. But I have watched every non-violent movie and TV show set there, from all the entries in Masterpiece Theater to *The Office*."

He cocks his head. "What's your favorite?"

"*Downton Abbey*, of course."

"I haven't seen it." He rubs his stubble again. Is that why he doesn't shave, to have something to touch? I'm going to have stubble in a place he can touch soon—

"—is it any good?"

The question acts like a cold shower. "Is *Downton* bloody *Abbey* any good?"

Was my voice a tad too shrill there?

He raises his hands palms out. "Hey, I didn't mean any offense. I just thought it was about a bunch of rich people having tea in a fancy castle."

"That's like saying *The Lord of the Ring*s is just a bunch of social rejects on a hike."

He chuckles. "I guess I'll have to see it now."

And afterward marry me.

No. I seriously need to stop this.

"Here you go." The waitress slaps the bill on the table.

As I dive into my purse for my wallet, I see Alex reach into his pocket with a frown.

"What?" The question carries a good dose of challenge in it.

"I thought it was clear the dinner would be on me," he says, plunking down his credit card.

I match his frown with one of my own. "I can pay for myself, thank you very much."

"I don't doubt it. But when you work late and your company feeds you, that's on their dime." He pushes the credit card toward me, and I see that it's his business one, not personal.

"Fine." I'm about to put my purse back, but it slips out of my hands.

Bloody hell.

The open bag hits the floor—and, of course, the dildo rolls right out of it.

I suppress a horrified yelp.

Please don't let him see.

Please, for the love of virtual reality, don't let him see.

I lean down to get the purse, my eyes following the path of the escaping dildo.

Wait. What's this shadow over it?

Bugger.

It's the waitress.

She's heading back to our table.

"Wait!" I shout at her, but it's too late.

She steps on the dildo, trips, and flails her arms in desperation.

I leap to my feet to catch her, and in the corner of my eye, I see Alex do the same.

Only we're too late.

She faceplants.

We rush over to check if she's okay.

By some miracle, she is—which is good, but it doesn't answer the next question that becomes rather urgent for me.

Where the bloody hell is my dildo?

Chapter Thirty-Two

*A*lex gets the sushi chef to take care of the poor waitress, then signs the bill and drags me out.

I leave reluctantly. The dildo was a gift from Bella, but more importantly, I'd like to be able to come back to Miso Hungry one day, and I won't be able to if they find that dildo.

A limo is waiting for us.

I'm so flummoxed I let Alex shepherd me into it without so much as a, "Where are we going?"

Just as I recover enough wits to ask the question, Alex pulls something from his pocket and hands it to me. "I believe this is yours."

Of course.

It's Optimus Prime, the dildo.

It didn't disappear. Alex found it and hid it—as though that would minimize my shame.

For a second, I'm surprised I don't sink through the floor of the limo and get run over by the cars behind us.

It would be a relief if it happened.

"Thanks," I stammer and violently thrust the dildo into my purse.

"Bella's gift, right?"

Face on fire, I nod.

He grins. "She gifts stuff like that to everyone. For what it's worth, it means she likes you."

She likes me because he didn't tell her what I tried to do—else she would've shoved that dildo up my bum.

"Do you mind if I ask you for a favor?" he asks, his expression suddenly serious.

Is the favor sexual?

Cheeks flushing even hotter, I realize we're sitting next to each other exactly the way we did when we kissed.

My breathing quickens in anticipation, and I instinctively dampen my lips. "What did you have in mind?"

"At the meeting with the hospital tomorrow, don't let Dr. Piper and the others know that I'm part of Morpheus Group."

His words are like an ice compress to the face. My flaming blush recedes. "They don't know?"

He shakes his head. "Bella is both the official and the de facto head of the venture. I was originally there to help her secure funding, and now I'm just supporting her."

"So you *are* worried they'll associate 1000 Devils with porn. Didn't you say it *wasn't* porn?"

And if he's worried, I was justified to be worried as well.

He rubs the back of his neck. "It's not that. I don't think Dr. Piper would care about 'porn,' as you call it. But he is a very thrifty administrator, and would make an argument for incorporating your VR pet project into our existing contract. To him, I'm 1000 Devils, so if I'm also Morpheus Group, he'll see an opportunity to save money."

"So this is about money?"

"Exactly."

I massage my temples. "Isn't that playing loosey-goosey with your contract?"

"Not really. Even if he pays extra for your project for the remainder of our current contract, he can pounce when it gets renegotiated."

"So you don't think he'd care about what the suit will be used for?"

Alex shrugs. "I can't be sure, of course, but it's a moot point anyway because I don't see how he'd find out. The suit isn't out yet, and won't be until your VR pet trial is well underway. If the trial is a success, we can talk to Bella about spinning off your project as a separate venture, so there should never be an issue."

I feel floaty, like I've taken off a thirty-pound weight vest I've been wearing all day.

If what he's saying is true, my worries were groundless. I didn't need to break into his office and attempt that sabotage. I didn't need to owe my evil twin. I didn't need to jeopardize my relationship with Alex and Bella—not that I knew there was a relationship to be had at the time I broke in.

Alex must read some of my thoughts on my face. "I'm sorry. I should've reassured you when we spoke after your break-in. I was upset then, and there wasn't a good time later."

"You're apologizing to me?" I grab his hand. "I'm the one who is sorry. I should've talked to you guys instead of acting so rashly."

He squeezes my palm, his fingers warm and strong around mine. "Water under the bridge."

Uh-oh.

My eyes lock on his lips, and a familiar magnetic pull draws me toward him.

He leans toward me as well, his lips about to fuse with mine.

The limo stops a little too jerkily, yanking me out of the sexual trance.

Blinking, I draw back.

"Your place." He nods toward the window, answering the question I never got the chance to ask.

"Jolly good," I mumble.

His eyes glint. "Do you want to stay with me a little longer?"

I swallow hard. "I do. But I shouldn't."

His face turns solemn. "I understand."

Why is he being so bloody professional and accommodating? If he pushed even a little bit, I'd kiss him and not look back. More than kiss him, in fact.

I reluctantly grab my purse. "I guess I'll go?"

"If that's what you want." He comes out of the limo and holds the door for me.

I get out clumsily and stand there, unsure how to say goodbye under the circumstances.

Would a kiss on the cheek be inappropriate?

"See you tomorrow at the hospital," he says with a wave.

Unsure of what I'm doing, I snatch his hand from the air and give it an awkward shake.

Great job. Maybe I should curtsy or kiss his ring while I'm at it?

The corners of his eyes crinkle—he's obviously trying not to laugh at my expense.

Mumbling "do svidaniya," I beeline for my building. A part of me is grateful he didn't push. This is how things should be between us. Professional.

I just wish being a saint didn't feel so crummy.

———

Once home, I run through my usual routine on autopilot, my mind already on tomorrow's meeting—except I'm more worried about seeing Alex again than the fate of my project.

Ugh. What is wrong with me?

Getting into bed, I decide to finally do something about my raging hormones. If I don't sleep tonight, I will jeopardize tomorrow, and that can't happen.

So, the big question is: dildo or au naturel?

Before I decide, I check my lady parts to make sure the irritation from the waxing is gone.

Yep. I'm smooth.

In fact, I really like this look. It's like a clean-shaven guy versus a scruffy one. I think I'll keep everything neat and tidy like this going forward. I can't believe I didn't think of it before—I might need to thank Gia, after all.

In any case, the best part is that the lady wank is *on*. And I might as well use Optimus Prime, for novelty and all that. Also, since Alex touched the dildo today, by dodgy transitive property, it'll be as if *he'll* be touching my bits.

And just like that, I'm as ready as can be.

I wash and sterilize the dildo—because restaurant cooties—and turn it on.

Wow. The vibration is strong. Twice the power of my toothbrush, and that thing packs major hertz.

Deciding to touch it to my clit before attempting any penetration, I bring it into position.

Blimey.

I come in a fraction of a millisecond.

Things must've been pent up in there.

Should I go on?

No. Feeling sleepy now, must take advantage.

Turning off the dildo, I hug it to my chest, the way I do with the plush toy of Optimus Prime.

Sleep comes instantly, but I dream of cerulean eyes and inappropriate behavior all night long.

Chapter Thirty-Three

$\mathcal{I}$'m all nerves as I step into the meeting room at the hospital the next day.

Wow.

Alex is clean-shaven again and is wearing a suit—just like the day we kissed.

Focus. VR pet project. Not here to lust.

I manage to sit my horny ass down and reply to the preliminary niceties.

When the talk of weather and such is done, Alex starts his presentation—and I want to kick myself for not masturbating a lot more the day prior. I'm as randy as I've ever been, and that's not a state I want to be in during such an important meeting.

"This is great," Dr. Piper says when Alex is done. "I'm glad we went down this path. Now VR therapy will be even more comprehensive."

I want to jump up and down. My dream took a little detour, but it seems to be back on track.

The rest of the meeting is spent on Q&A. When we adjourn, Dr. Piper asks Alex to stay back to discuss 1000 Devils' business.

As I exit the room, Alex sneaks a wink at me—which is like an injection of aphrodisiac right into my clit.

This is ridiculous. And the worst part is that I have no idea if I should wait for him. We didn't come together, which implies I shouldn't. We're also pretending not to work at the same company—another reason I shouldn't.

But it's a friendly thing to do, isn't it? Or is that my hormones talking?

Whatever. Since I'm here, I might as well visit Jacob.

I buy a candy bar for Jacob and a tea for myself, then make my way to the pediatric long-term care wing.

To my relief, no clowns lurk in my path. However, when I get to Jacob's room, he has a VR headset on—must be using VR pet therapy as we speak.

I should leave him to it.

Just as I start to turn, he takes his headset off, spots me, and shines that boyish grin at me. "Hi, Aunt Holly."

"Hi, kiddo." I hand him the candy. "Were you just playing with Master Chief?"

"Did you say Master Chief?" says a familiar Russian-accented voice from behind me.

I turn.

Yep.

It's Alex.

"How did you——"

"Dr. Piper told me where to find you," Alex says. "And who is this?"

"Jacob, this is Alex," I say to the boy.

"Hi, Jacob," Alex says in the friendly tone he used with Euclid the other day. "It looks like you're as big a fan of *Halo* as I am."

Jacob's eyes light up. "*Halo* rules."

With matching grins, the two start an animated discussion about some gibberish. I recognize only a few words, like *grunts*, *jackals*, and *plasma beams*.

As they talk, I tidy up around Jacob's bed, bundling his clean socks into three pairs yet again and folding the blanket next to his bed for what feels like the one hundred and thirty-seventh time——as cute as kids are, they wreak havoc everywhere they go.

When everything is to my satisfaction, I settle into a chair to watch the two of them, and as I do, the feeling I got when Alex interacted with Euclid comes back with a vengeance.

He *would* make a good dad. An awesome dad.

Blimey. My ovaries are going to turn into a tuna melt.

"Do you want to see clips of me playing?" Jacob raises the tablet.

Alex eagerly agrees, and a minute later, a vicious shootout is on the screen. I sip my tea and force myself to follow along despite the violence.

Jacob is good—or at least, he stays alive for an entire five minutes of an apocalyptic firefight. Then some guy in a blue spacesuit kills him with a plasma sword.

As Jacob's character lies there vanquished, the asshole who killed him starts squatting up and down over his head.

Alex frowns. "Is he—"

"Yeah," Jacob says. "He's teabagging me."

I choke on my tea. "He's what?"

"It's also called corpse-humping," Alex says. "It's a kind of victory dance meant to insult and aggravate the person you just killed."

I roll my eyes. "Boys."

"You know who that is?" Alex asks Jacob, frowning at the screen.

"Yeah. We go to school together."

Alex's frown turns threatening. "How about you and me team up one of these days? I promise I'll make that guy regret his unsporting behavior."

Huh. I can suddenly picture Alex as an enforcer for the Russian mob.

"For teabagging my friend, you die," he'd say with a thicker accent and swing a bat at the poor guy's knee.

Jacob is thrilled at this opportunity to team up, and they exchange the prerequisite info.

"Do you play anything else?" Alex asks once they run out of *Halo* stuff to talk about.

Jacob eagerly rattles out a list of games he likes,

but Alex looks a bit put out by the end—maybe because *Tetris* is not on the list?

"What about *Tetris*?" Alex asks, confirming my suspicions.

Jacob shakes his head. "Old."

"What about *War of Sword*? That's new."

"Yeah," Jacob says. "I've been meaning to try that one. Is it any good?"

Alex nods. "*Tetris* is my boredom-killing game, but if I'm stressed, I like to turn off my phone and just quest in *War of Sword* for hours."

"Okay then." Jacob searches the name of the game on the tablet. "Maybe I'll try it."

Maybe I will as well. I'm curious.

A nurse shows up with a tray of food.

"Ah, lunch," Jacob says eagerly.

We watch him eat and talk about everything under the sun—but especially his VR pet, which turns out to have grown a little more.

He might be feeding his friend a bit too much, but in VR, pet obesity has no harmful side effects.

"We'd better go," I say when Jacob finishes his lunch and appears eager to get back to his games.

"It was nice to meet you." Alex extends his hand to the boy.

Jacob shakes it solemnly. "You too."

"Bye," we all say in unison.

When we step outside, Alex looks at me with an unreadable expression.

"What?" I ask.

He nods at the limo that's just pulled up to the curb. "Would you join me for lunch?"

Are those bees in my stomach or am I simply peckish? "Sure!"

Oops, may have sounded too eager there.

He opens the door for me. "I know a place that specializes in pelmeni."

"Sounds great," I say and climb inside.

To my disappointment, Alex sits across from me this time.

No, wait, he's right to do that. It's the proper way, even if the seating arrangements are the only proper things on this ride—my thoughts are anything but.

"Tea?" Alex asks.

Since it's my favorite kind, I say "yes, please" and get treated to samovar-brewed heaven in a cup once again.

"So how did you and Jacob meet?" Alex asks, sipping his tea.

A smile splits my face. "His grandparents know my parents, and they brought him to my parents' farm while I was visiting. When I came across him, he was petting Spock, my favorite Kirk's dik-dik."

It's Alex's turn to choke on his beverage. "What was he petting?"

"Kirk's dik-dik," I say, grinning. "Dik-diks are these tiny antelopes. My parents rescued Spock and his family from a bankrupt zoo."

I take out my phone and locate Spock.

"See?" I show him my screen with a cute creature

that's about a foot tall despite being fully grown. Like other dik-diks, Spock has pretty eyes and sharp little horns on his head.

Alex leans within kissing distance of me and peers at the screen. "Adorable. Is this a male or a female?"

"That's Spock. He's a male. Unlike some of the other critters on the farm, dik-diks are pretty docile." I meet his cerulean gaze. "They're famous for mating for life."

That last bit charges the air between us until it feels like every tiny hair on my body stands on end.

Is he about to kiss me?

Please kiss me.

Wait, no. What am I thinking? Propriety must be maintained.

"You realize what we're looking at there," I blurt. "Right?"

"What?" he murmurs, his gaze on my lips.

"A dik-dik pic," I say and thank Gia for coming up with that particular pearl a few years back.

That startles him into a laugh. Eyes crinkling, he says, "Oh, yeah. And this one looks horny."

I groan. That's another one of Gia's.

The limo stops.

Whew. Kiss avoided.

I should be happy, but I'm not. I'm disappointed.

But I shouldn't be.

We exit in front of a building with a drawing of a giant pelmeni outside. It's called Pelmennaya, which Alex translates as "the place you get pelmeni."

How creative.

Once we're seated, Alex orders for both of us—twenty-three pieces for me and thirty-one for him.

"Do you want to stop by 1000 Devils after this?" he asks. "You've been talking to Robert over email, but it might be nice for the two of you to meet face to face."

"Sure," I say.

Does he want to show me his life's work? Because I want to see it, and for all the wrong reasons.

Bugger.

I can't believe I need to remind myself of this again.

Whatever this lunch feels like, it is *not* a date.

Chapter Thirty-Four

The problem is, just reminding myself that it's not a date doesn't make the feeling go away, and Alex doesn't help matters. Whenever I try to steer the conversation toward work, he pulls out random bits of Russian wisdom, such as, "Talking business is not good for one's digestion."

So, we talk about each other instead, and each new tidbit I learn about him is like an extra knot added to a rope wrapping around my heart.

"I hope this place delivers," I say when I'm done gobbling down my portion of the pelmeni.

"They do," he says and gives me a piece from his plate. "That's just one, so still prime, right?"

I eat the piece. "Yes. Thank you."

He scratches his clean-shaven chin—an evil move that's clearly meant to direct my attention there. "I've been wondering... Do you like prime rib?"

"Not every day, but yeah. Dad used to make a great one on the farm."

"What about prime-time TV?"

I see where he's going with this, so I smile and nod.

He grins. "Do you use Amazon Prime?"

"Yep, I subscribed to it as soon as the program was introduced."

He takes out his wallet. "How deep does this love of primes go?"

I shrug. "I prefer the UK government to the US one because I think *Prime Minister* sounds much better than *President*. Does that answer your question?"

"It does—and makes me wonder: do you use a prime broker?"

I shake my head with a grin.

"Ever see the movie *Prime Cut* or play Nintendo's *Metroid Prime*?"

"Neither."

"Do you own a Prius Prime?"

"I don't have a car."

"Ever take out a subprime mortgage?"

"No."

He scratches that sexy chin. "Are you interested in primeval history?"

I chuckle. "Now you're pushing it."

His grin broadens. "How about the primaries?"

"Nope."

"Privates? As in soldiers, of course."

"Nope. I'm not especially keen on soldiers, though some private parts might strike my fancy."

Ugh, stop flirting, Holly.

He laughs. "What about primates?"

I lick my lips. "I like some apes, sure, but not because of primes."

Seriously, stop flirting—or whatever that was.

He pins me with an almost predatory stare. "I'm sure primates like you too."

Is he saying that—

The waitress comes with the check, and he insists on covering it again.

"Ready?" he asks when we get into the limo.

"For what?

He smirks. "For the 1000 Devils offices, of course."

———

A traffic-filled ride later, we step out of the elevator in front of a plaque that proudly states, "1000 Devils."

The contrast with my company's offices and these is stark. There are bright colors all over, and I hear laughter in the distance—like in a petting zoo.

"We have some fun traditions here," Alex says and leads me into a walk-in closet to the side. "Let's gear up."

I blink, looking around.

Instead of clothes, there are nerf guns.

Lots of nerf guns.

Hey, given my recent experiences, these could've been cocks or dildos.

"Take this one." Alex hands me a sturdy-looking gun. "It's good for a beginner."

I accept the gun and watch him pick out a rifle.

"What do I do?" I ask when we step out of the armory.

A dark smile dances on his lips. "Shoot anything that moves."

With that, he shouts something like *hoorah* and rushes forward.

I sprint after him. I guess when in Rome, you have to act like Jacob's peer.

The first bullet—or dart—whooshes by my ear two seconds later.

Wow.

Do these hurt?

I sidestep the next projectile and shoot back at the attacker, a forty-something, red-headed bloke with a belly reminiscent of Dad's.

Bam.

The guy is grunting and rubbing his left eye.

Oops.

A new attacker leaps out of the corner.

Alex lunges in front of me and takes the projectile in the chest. Had that been a bullet, chivalry would've been the cause of my boss's untimely demise.

Since nobody's shooting at me for the moment, I get a millisecond to take in the office space—and hate it with all my tidiness-loving passion. The desks stand

in a haphazard manner. Nerf gun ammo is everywhere. And what's worse, there are four chairs next to
many of the desks.

The net effect is overwhelming, and that's before
armed people leap at me from every direction. My
guess is, someone took the whole 1000 Devils
branding a tad too far and gave this place the feel of a
satanic ritual.

The next attacker joins the fray, a lady about
Alison's age.

I shoot her with dart two and three.

Double oops. One of my darts hits her groin,
another her right boob.

More attackers join in.

A cloud of darts is flying my way.

I duck behind the nearest desk.

A throat clears above me once, twice.

Wait. I know that sound.

I look up.

Yep. I'm face to crotch with Buckley.

In the heat of battle, I didn't even notice him
there.

"Hi." As I leap to my feet, I catch a glimpse of the
code on his monitor. It looks misaligned, and I have to
fight the urge to push him out of his chair and tidy it
up, and then do the same with the anarchy that is his
desk.

Buckley clears his throat twice more. "Hi, boss."
With a goofy grin, he smacks himself on the forehead and clears his throat two more times. "Sorry.

Force of habit. I guess you're not my boss anymore."

"Right. Sorry. No time to talk," I rattle out and rush into the gunfire.

That proves it. I'd rather be shot at than listen to Buckley's throat clearing.

Another enemy dart whooshes by my ear.

I respond with dart number four and shoot the next person with the fifth.

On the next shot, my gun makes a weird clicking sound.

Must be out of ammo.

Hey, at least it was on the fifth shot and not fourth or sixth.

I drop the gun and raise my hands, hoping that will make the assault stop.

Nope.

A shower of darts flies at me.

I cringe.

There's a blur of movement, and Alex is suddenly in front of me, taking the projectiles in the back.

Wow.

My heart is hammering as if I were in a real firefight—and Alex's proximity isn't helping matters.

He's so close I can smell his tea scent and feel the warmth coming off his big body.

He looks down.

I look up.

Slowly, he bends his head and—

"That's enough shooting," someone says nearby, and Alex jerks away.

I turn to face the messiest man I've ever seen in my life.

His Hawaiian shirt is wrinkled, his hair is disheveled, and his glasses are warped—as though he microwaved them by mistake.

"Robert," Alex says with a grin. "This is Holly. I believe you've spoken over email."

As Robert walks by Buckley's desk, he accidentally knocks over a pen holder.

"Sorry," Robert says and bends to pick up the pens.

"It's okay." Buckley clears his throat a few times. "I got this, boss."

As Robert shakes my hand, I make sure Buckley actually picks up the mess—not that it would help this place become magically ordered.

Alex must sense some of my discombobulation. He insists we talk to Robert in a meeting room and chooses one that's blissfully tidy—no doubt a place where they hold meetings with clients and the like.

As we settle around the table, Alex gives Robert an overview of the conversation at the hospital and a list of games in the scope of the project.

"What about *War of Sword?*" Robert asks. "It would be a good fit for the target hardware."

Alex sighs. "Too violent for the target demographic. Maybe in a later phase."

"Wait," I say. "*War of Sword*—the game you like so much—is one of yours?"

Robert nods so vigorously his warped glasses nearly fall off his nose. "It's Alex's baby."

"More of a passion project," Alex says. "The idea was to make a game for myself and see what happens."

"Yeah," Robert says with a measure of pride in his voice. "Financial success is what happened."

"Tidy," I say. "Now I really want to see it."

Robert and Alex exchange excited looks.

"We have a room for that," Alex says. "Want to see it?"

"Of course," I say, though now I'm not so sure.

The room better not be as much of a mess as the rest of the floor.

Leaving Robert, Alex and I head over there, and when we enter the room, I blow out a relieved breath. It's empty, the only furniture being a dresser-like thing in the corner.

Alex walks up to the dresser and pulls out a pair of VR headsets. "Are you okay using gear made by your competition?"

I nod. "I have that brand of headset at home. It's one of the few besides ours that fit my head."

He hands me the equipment, and I put it on.

"Are all these games made by you guys?" I ask as I take in the cluttered dashboard.

"Yep," Alex says. "The icon with the sword is what you want."

I start the game and let Alex walk me through character creation.

Minutes later, I'm an elf female with facial features not so different from my own, just cartoony. As my weapons, I choose a bow with arrows, plus a thin, one-handed sword.

When I start the game, I show up in a medieval village, and Alex tells me to go into the inn and grab a chair.

"This is a multiplayer game," he says as I comply. "I'm about to join you."

Excited, I look at the inn entrance. A minute later, he walks in.

His avatar is a minotaur, horns, hoofed feet, and all. More importantly, it's a shirtless, muscular minotaur—with a face that looks eerily like Alex's.

Bugger. Now I'm turned on by a half-human, half-cow. Next thing you know, I'll have a fetish for lactating men.

"Hi," the minotaur says, and his voice comes at me twice—from the headset speakers and from real Alex.

"You look horny," I say and wince. He made the same joke about the dik-dik just hours ago.

He's kind enough to chuckle before handing me a ball of yarn.

"With that in your inventory, you'll be able to find me no matter where I am in this world."

As I put the yarn into my travel bag, I realize a horrific fact I hadn't noticed until now.

It's my elfin hands.

They only have four fingers each.

Why? Bloody hell, why?

It's not like elves are known for their non-prime number of fingers. Quite the opposite—they're supposed to be long lived, which a four-fingered elf would not be on account of being suicidal.

"I'm going to join a friend in battle," Alex says. "Shake that yarn to follow me."

"Sure," I say uncertainly.

Usually, I'd be anti-battle, but maybe this will work out in my favor—someone just might chop off a finger on each of my hands in the upcoming fight.

A girl can hope.

Alex disappears. I take the yarn out and give it a shake.

Whoosh.

The inn around me is gone… and is replaced with a scene from hell.

Chapter Thirty-Five

*T*he forest meadow is littered with body parts, the gore made that much worse by the fact that all the hands and feet have four fingers and toes.

I shudder. It's not just the elves that are thusly cursed, it turns out.

With a cacophony of sounds, a menagerie of creatures is tearing each other apart. Despite the cartoony looks, the violence feels vicious and brutal, too much so for me.

Something leaps out from behind a tree. I yank my sword from its scabbard and behead what turns out to be a fellow elf.

So, this is an elf-eat-elf world.

Far in the distance, Alex is ripping into someone with his minotaur horns.

Bugger. My gag reflex cannot take a second more of this.

I remove the headset and try to even out my ragged breathing.

Alex pulls off his headset as well and looks at me worriedly. "You okay?"

"Yeah," I lie. "Just a little bit of VR sickness. It will pass."

He hurries over to the dresser and brings back a bottle of water and a pill. "Take this."

"What is it?" I ask.

"Dramamine."

"No, thank you. I'll just drink the water." I take the bottle and chug it greedily until the images of four-fingered limbs are but a distant memory.

"Feeling better?" he asks.

I nod.

"Want to take the rest of the day off?"

I shake my head.

"How about we head back to work?" he suggests.

"Great idea," I say, and that is what we do.

―――――

"Do you want to pair?" he asks when we step out of the elevator back at our offices.

I glance at my desk. "Let me check my email first, then I'll pop in."

"Deal." He heads over to his office.

When I finish with my inbox, I don't feel ready to face Alex just yet, so I move some of the misaligned desks and remove objects from them to make sure there's a prime total.

"Want to organize my office?" Bella asks as she catches me putting Alison's stapler into a drawer.

I try to hide my eagerness. "Can I? Right now?"

"Maybe another time." She grins. "I'm pretty sure my brother is waiting for you."

Gulp. She's right.

"See you later," I say bravely and head over to Alex's office.

If he's annoyed at having waited, he doesn't show it.

"Will you drive?" is all he asks, and when I say yes, he lets me. A few hours later, he takes the reins.

Just like the prior day, pair coding with Alex is a type of sensual torture. I lose track of time, and he again drags me to Miso Hungry at eight p.m.

In déjà vu meets wet dream, this dinner not-date feels just like a real date would—and I have to constantly remind myself not to do or say anything inappropriate to my boss.

The temptation is huge.

Heroically, I resist it, and he gives me a limo lift once more, where it's a miracle we don't kiss again.

At home, I take out all my sexual frustration on Optimus Prime—until its batteries die.

Then and only then, I fall asleep.

———

The next few days follow the same formula: I get to work, check my messages, and pair code with Alex until lunch. He then insists on taking me to Pelmennaya. Afterward, we work together some more and have dinner at Miso Hungry.

Each day I get a lift home and each day we almost kiss—but don't. And each day Optimus Prime has to pick up the pieces.

"The suit integration is progressing so well," Bella says to me one morning as I'm checking emails at my desk. "You guys are amazing." She proceeds to tell me how she's tested the suit in every blush-inducing detail.

"Anyway," she says when her TMI avalanche is over. "Alex is no doubt pining for your company."

Before I can respond, she sashays away, so I rejoin Alex and the whole coding-lunch-coding-dinner-limo-wanking cycle happens once again.

And then again. And again.

Chapter Thirty-Six

As the weeks pass, I get to know Bella better, and I learn just how brilliant she is. On her end, she's treating me more and more like a friend, which propels my girl crush on her into ready-to-stalk territory.

I dread the day she learns of my original intent to harm her dream product.

In fact, I pray she never will.

The worst part, however, is that each passing day chips away at my resolve to stay strictly professional with Alex, especially since on each limo ride, he seems on the verge of kissing me but doesn't.

It's getting to the point where I'm not sure if I'm grateful for his restraint or pissed off.

"I need a favor," Alex says as I'm about to exit the limo the following Friday evening.

Wow. Is this it? Are we about to throw the bloody propriety out the window?

I'm ready. Or am I?

Bugger. Must answer.

"What's up?" I ask, failing to sound casual.

"You know what, never mind," he says. "It's not appropriate."

Yes. Yes. Yes. Seems he finally has the decency to make an indecent proposal.

I lean forward. "Please. What did you want to ask me?"

He sighs and rubs his forehead. "Okay, so this Sunday morning, my parents' restaurant will be closed for repainting, and Bella wants to stage an intervention for my father about his drinking."

Bloody hell. That's not what I thought he'd say at all. In a heartbeat, I go from wanting to hump him to feeling terrible for him. "Has it gotten that bad?"

He frowns. "He never used to pass out the way he did at his birthday, but Mom says it's happened twice since."

I want to reach out and give him a reassuring hug but manage to resist—I've gotten pretty good at controlling my urges lately.

"Do you want me there with you?" As horrible as the idea of this event sounds, if he needs me, I'll be there.

"No. Dad's going to be upset as is. If someone who isn't family turns up, he'll just storm out."

"I see," I say and instantly feel guilty for the relief washing over me. "Then what's my role in it?"

"My usual pet sitter will be away for the weekend," he says.

I blink at him, not sure what that has to do with anything.

He pinches the bridge of his nose. "It's too short of a notice to look for someone else, but I want someone there with Beelzebub."

My eyes widen. "You want me to babysit your dog?"

Images of nip-slips or worse flit through my mind —his puppy deserves that demonic moniker.

"You know what, never mind," he says. "Now that I hear it out loud, I realize how weird it is for me to ask you this."

Not weird if he sees me as a friend or more—but I don't say that. Instead, with a will of its own, my mouth replies, "I'll be glad to help. You just caught me by surprise, that's all."

He looks at me so intently my stomach flutters. "You sure?"

"Quite sure." I wish I were as confident as I sound.

"Great." He flashes me a grin that makes me feel like my upcoming torture is worth it. "You'll have to let me do something for you as thanks."

The X-rated images from my evenings with Optimus Prime are suddenly at the forefront of my mind. "Like what?"

He hesitates for a second. "How about I make you dinner?"

He will cook dinner for *me*? The proverb states that the way to a man's heart is through his stomach, but I might not be immune to the reversal of that—which makes this a bad idea. "You don't need to do that."

"I insist. Besides, it might be good if you came the day before, so I could show you where all his stuff is. This way, we can sleep in on Sunday morning—I know I'll need the extra zzzs."

So a dinner Saturday night? A dinner he'll prepare himself? Why does that feel so much more date-y than all the non-dates we've had?

"What time?" is all I trust myself to ask.

"When do you usually eat dinner?"

"7:09," I blurt.

He smiles. "Of course. That's a prime time to eat. 7:09 it is—though maybe come a bit earlier so we can start at that exact moment."

"Spiffy," I say, a little lightheaded. "How about I come over at 6:31?"

"Perfect. I'll have the limo waiting for you at 6:13."

I hope I don't feel as I do now tomorrow, or else I won't be able to eat.

"I'll see you tomorrow," I say and scramble out of

the limo before I do something I'll regret—like asking if he wants to come up or giving him a pentagram-shaped love bite on his neck.

Or both at the same time.

Chapter Thirty-Seven

I barely sleep that night, so I spend most of Saturday re-watching *Downton Abbey*, rereading *Pride and Prejudice*, and interacting with Euclid.

None of it calms me down.

No matter how many times I remind myself that tonight's dinner isn't a date, my blood pressure refuses to normalize. I feel off-kilter, unable to focus on my usual routine. I even skip lunch, which might turn out to be a good thing if Alex's cooking is subpar— hunger being the best spice and all that.

Maybe I'll calm down if I research what's customary when visiting a Russian home?

Nope.

Knowing that you should take your shoes off and not shake hands over a doorway isn't that helpful.

Then again, I do see a useful tip about bringing a

gift—something I almost forgot about. Apparently, a box of candy is traditional.

Hmm. I don't have a box, but I do have a stash of individually wrapped Fry's Turkish Delight that I ordered from the UK. Hopefully, the key is the candy part, not the box part. I put nineteen of them into my purse.

When it's closer to prime time, I groom my lady bits, taking care of all the fine hair that's reappeared since the wax—not because I'm planning on Alex seeing my bits but because that puppy might rip my knickers off instead of my bra this time. If that happens—and if Alex happens to look—I want to make sure things look tidy down there.

Another question occurs to me: what does one wear to a dinner her boss is cooking?

After a long deliberation, I decide I can't go wrong with the outfit Gia forced me to get for the birthday party. Also makeup wouldn't hurt. And nice shoes. And for consistency's sake, I make my hair look nice as well.

When my phone alarm rings at 5:57, I examine myself in the mirror and nod approvingly.

I'm as ready for this not-a-date as I can be.

———

The burly limo driver opens the door for me when I approach.

"Thanks," I say.

"No problem," he replies with a heavy Russian accent.

A tea is waiting for me inside the car—a nice touch.

I catch the guy texting something to someone—probably letting Alex know he's picked me up. Then he closes the partition between us, and I'm left hoping he doesn't text more as he drives.

By the time we stop next to Alex's building, I feel so jittery it would take a week of *Downton Abbey* to calm me down.

The chauffeur opens the limo door for me.

The skyscraper in front of us is sleek and shiny. The guy leads me into the lobby and waves at the security guard before escorting me into an elevator. Without a single word, he presses the button for the 107th floor before turning to leave.

"Do svidanyia," I say.

Finally, a smile from the taciturn man. "Do svidaniya."

The doors close.

I hold my breath all the way until the doors open right into an apartment where Alex is already waiting. At that point, the breath escapes in a loud gasp—and not because the place is a posh penthouse that must've cost millions.

Like me, Alex got dressed up and is wearing a suit similar to the one he wore at the restaurant, only even more stylish. Bespoke, perhaps?

There's even a tie. A tie!

I force my mouth to close before any drool leaks out.

He's also clean-shaven again, like he was at his father's birthday. Yet even *that* isn't the reason I have to fight the urge to rip off that suit and shag his brains out right here and now.

The problem is his hairdo.

The black locks are neatly slicked back—exactly the way I've always fantasized about.

He's the very epitome of tidy.

Knickers-dropping, nipples-hardening, mouth-watering kind of tidy.

Bloody estrogen hell.

How am I supposed to act all proper now?

Chapter Thirty-Eight

"You look amazing," we both say in unison.

He grins. "Ivan told me you dressed up. You really didn't have to." I can almost hear the unsaid, "But I'm glad you did."

So that's what that text was about? I guess I have the driver to thank for prompting Alex to clean up as nicely as he has.

Suddenly, a loud bark echoes in the large hallway, followed by the clickety-clack of puppy claws on hardwood floors and then the sound of something crashing.

The koala-bear-meets-dog creature rushes at me, his tail wagging so quickly you can barely see it move.

With a Russian curse, Alex leaps for his pet, but Beelzebub dodges him and jumps on me, rising on his haunches so we come face to maw.

Instinctively, my right hand covers my crotch and my left covers the top of my dress.

No more wardrobe malfunctions at his paws, thank you very much.

Since the puppy can't make me expose my nipples or clit, he settles for doing to me what I've been dying to do to his master—licking my face like I'm covered in peanut butter.

If Bella were here, she'd probably give the eager puppy a voiceover that would say something like, "You're yum. So yum. Want to play? Want to chase flies? I'm Beelzebub—that's the Lord of the Flies, you know. Do flies like bacon? Do you want some bacon? I live for bacon. Is your name Kevin?"

"Bad boy," Alex says sternly, pulling Beelzebub away. "We don't lick guests."

We? Alex can lick me, no problem. Hell, I'll take a dog licking again if that's a prerequisite.

"Sorry about that. You can wash your face in there." Alex gestures at a door down the hall.

I start to take off my shoes as per the Russian etiquette, but Alex says that I don't have to. When I insist, he hands me a pair of slippers. "These are Bella's, but she won't mind if you use them."

I'm glad I insisted. Taking shoes off is clearly important enough that Bella keeps slippers here.

Properly slippered, I hurry over to the loo, wash up, and reapply my makeup.

When I come back out, Alex is alone.

"I put a treat inside a special toy," he explains. "He'll be trying to dig it out for a while, so we can enjoy the peace for now."

I look around.

The hallway is littered with dog toys of every kind.

The urge to tidy is strong, but I fight it and look at the walls for help.

Surprise surprise. Everything is covered with posters featuring *Tetris Payout, Super Tetris, Tetris Plus, Tetris 4D, Tetris League*—the list goes on and on.

"I didn't realize there were so many versions of the game," I say as I look from one to the next.

Alex beams with pride. "Come, let me show you something."

He leads me into a large room that can only be called a man cave—though there's a serious presence of said man's best friend as well, in the form of half-chewed bones and toys.

Must not tidy. It would be as crazy as kissing his neck.

"See that?" Alex points at the wall next to a giant TV.

Wow. Every single video game console I've ever heard of is attached to that TV, and inside most of them is a *Tetris* game, some from the posters I just saw and some not.

I guess this collection makes sense—video games *are* his passion.

His phone beeps.

"It's 7:01," he says. "Let's head to the kitchen so we can start dinner on time."

As I follow him from room to room, I realize just

how huge this penthouse really is—especially for New York City.

Game developers clearly make bank.

The kitchen turns out to be the only tidy room in the house. There are flowers and candles on the table —all very date-y if you ask me.

He pulls out a chair for me, and as I take a seat, I look at the two plates in front of me.

One contains twenty-three pieces of avocado roll, while the other holds the same number of pelmeni.

Tearing my eyes away from the feast, I look up at him in wonder. "You made this?"

"Well, yeah." He sits across from me next to a similar spread. "I wasn't sure which food you prefer on weekends, so I went with both."

"Good call," I say, salivating like one of Pavlov's dogs. "I think I'll go wild and have both."

He grins. "I think I'll do the same. Crazy town."

I attack the pelmeni first.

Yum. Usually, I don't like variation in recipes, but this batch is different in a good way.

I tell that to Alex.

"I added a secret ingredient to the recipe from my parents' restaurant," he says.

"A secret ingredient?" I taste the avocado roll— and it also tastes better than usual, but more subtly so. "Is there one in the roll as well?"

"Yep. And I guess now I have to tell you what it is," he says with mock reluctance.

I match his tone. "It's only the polite thing to do."

"Fine. I figured since we're having Japanese and Russian, why not fuse the two—so I put a touch of ginger into the pelmeni and a little bit of sour cream into the rice in the rolls."

"Ah." I taste another piece of each. "That *is* what you did. You clearly have a backup career as a chef. I'm not usually a fan of dishes tasting different. I hate it actually. But I love these."

He covers my hand with his and smiles. "I guess I have the magic touch."

Oh, yeah. The magic of his touch shoots zings of awareness throughout my whole body and makes my breath catch in my throat.

"Sorry." He pulls his hand away.

"It's okay," I choke out, and it takes all my willpower not to add something like, "I really, really, *really* enjoyed that."

"I'm glad you like it," he says.

The touch? No, he means dinner. Bollocks, that neat hair is making it difficult to think.

"I do like the food," I say when I've unscrambled my brain. "But now there's a problem: I won't be able to eat the regular versions of these dishes going forward."

Just like if any other man touched me the way Alex just did, it would also feel inadequate.

Bugger.

I'm ruined for other chefs *and* men.

He pulls out his phone and types out a message. "I just sent you the exact recipe for the pelmeni, and

I can talk to the folks at Miso Hungry about the rolls."

"Thank you," I say and stuff my mouth before I can say something improper, like, "Can I repay your kindness with my body?"

"You're welcome." His gaze is warm on my face. "I have to admit, I enjoyed making this for you."

My heartbeat quickens. "Have you cooked for other women before?"

Good going. As subtle as a bull in a china shop.

His eyes gleam a rich, dark blue. "Only the ones I've dated."

"Oh." So I'm the first one he's doing this for without dating? To be honest, I don't like the idea that he's dated anyone, but obviously he must have. Figuring I might as well keep going with the inappropriately personal questions, I ask as casually as I can, "And how many was that?"

He bites his lip in concentration.

Crikes. Is the number astronomical? It could be. A guy like this must have women falling at his feet.

Those twats.

He's still thinking?

Why, oh why did I even ask this? Why ask something you might hate the answer to?

"Six," he finally says.

Oh.

Well, six is not bad. I mean, it's a terrible number in and of itself, but as far as former exes go, it's nice and low, which is good. Also, this means that if I

somehow became his girlfriend—a pleasant fantasy—
I'd be his seventh.

As in, a prime girlfriend.

I like the sound of that.

Or is a prime girlfriend another term for wife? If
it's not, it should be.

"There were some dates and such outside those
six," he continues. "But only those relationships got to
the cooking stage—and all but one didn't go much
further than that. That last one lasted a couple of
years but then petered out."

"Why?" I ask. What I mean is: *Why would any sane,
warm-blooded woman let you escape her clutches?*

He shrugs. "She didn't like me being into video
games."

I gape at him.

No. Not a joke.

"But that's your passion," I say, a bit too vehe-
mently for propriety. In a calmer tone, I add, "You're
brilliant at it."

"Thank you." He leans forward, his gaze intent on
my face. "I guess she just wasn't the one."

My pulse is pounding in my ears. "I guess not."

It might not be a kind thought, but I'm super glad
she wasn't the one—whoever she was. I don't care if
it's selfish, but if I can't have my boss, nobody should.

"What about you?" he asks.

Bugger. I guess I started this. "I haven't cooked for
anyone."

I stuff my face again in the hopes he'll leave it alone.

Nope.

He tsk-tsks. "You know what I meant."

The food tastes bland now. Taking a deep breath, I tell him about the clusterfuck that was my relationship with Beau.

As I speak, something about the sympathy and understanding in his eyes makes me share more than I ever have with anyone.

"I was a late bloomer, so I didn't date much in high school or college. I just didn't click with a lot of guys, you know? So when I met Beau a couple of years after graduation, I was so relieved I ignored a lot of the red flags. All of them, really. We dated for months before we so much as French-kissed, but all I cared about was that he was a mathematician who also liked routine." I grimace, still mad at myself. "I didn't know he was gay, obviously, so I just didn't feel wanted. First, he treated my hymen as if it were actually holy. Then, once we'd finally done the deed, he didn't want to do it again for ages—nor do things like go down on me or even kiss me much. We eventually broke up, and when he came out the following year, it was a relief, because it explained so much. Still, I haven't been in a dating mood since."

Alex's jaw flexes. "That fucker. I can't believe I'm mad at a guy for *not* wanting to do things to you, yet here we are. Not to steal lines from Rhett Butler, but 'you should be kissed and often, and by someone who knows how.'"

I grab my glass with water and chug it. This is beginning to feel even more like a date than the time he kissed me.

Well, since I was the one who bollixed professionalism with my tale of woe, I should be the one to fix it.

But how? Ask for more food? I'm kind of stuffed, and he looks to be done. Maybe I should talk about something gross—like snot, or squares of even numbers?

Since nothing comes to mind, I ask for something that's interesting but not in a sexual way. "Can you show me your *Tetris* skills?"

He grins. "I'd love to, but how about I show you all the dog stuff first?"

Duh. That's way less sexy than *Tetris*. Why didn't I think of that?

We finish up what's on our plates, and I take a raincheck on his offer of tea—a testament to how truly stuffed I am. He seems to be just as full, as he accepts my gift of candy without eating any.

I then help him tidy up the kitchen—an activity that turns out to be way too erotic for my comfort. Seeing him dry the plates I washed is a definite turn-on.

When we're done, he shows me where the dog food and bowls are, then leads me out of the kitchen while explaining more doggy stuff, including when to walk the furry beast.

"Speaking of Beelzebub," he whispers as we enter what looks to be his home office.

The sleeping pup is curled on the carpet around some ball—must be the toy with the treat inside.

Aww. Beelzebub is clearly dreaming about chasing something—his paws are moving in the air and he makes little barking sounds.

Okay, so puppies may be unpredictable and messy, but they sure are adorable… especially when they're asleep.

"Come," Alex whispers. "I owe you a *Tetris* demonstration."

We tiptoe into the man cave and close the door so as not to wake up the puppy.

Alex fires up his Xbox.

His version of the game is called *Tetris Effect: Connected*, and it's a work of audiovisual art that's more of a full-fledged psychedelic experience than a block puzzle game.

Aesthetics of the game aside, watching Alex play is a trip in itself.

This is what Mozart must've looked like at the piano in his prime.

I was so, so wrong when I thought this would be a safe, nonsexual experience. It's the opposite. This is even hotter than watching Alex code.

Every time he clears four lines at once—which is

called a tetris—the game shows a celebratory anima-
tion of fireworks. It makes me picture him entering me
the same way the I-block enters the hole that is its
destination, and the fireworks that will result from that.

Bugger.

Between the tidy look, the dinner, and this, I
should get a medal for not attacking him. A pink star
for suppressing libido under extreme temptation.

Maybe I can sneak to the bathroom and rub out a
quick one?

"Check that out," Alex says, bursting my wank-
bubble. "Jacob says he's playing that guy who deserves
a comeuppance. Should I switch to *Halo*?"

"Sure," I say.

A moment later, there are armed people in
colorful spacesuits on the screen.

"There," Jacob's voice says from the speaker, and
his character shoots at a guy in the distance holding a
big rifle.

Alex's character rushes for his prey, somehow
dodging all the bullets, then pistol-whips him in the
face.

"Wow," Jacob says excitedly. "That was
awesome."

And it was. I'm even hornier now. This must be
tapping into whatever cavewomen used to feel when
their men would protect the tribe—or fight other
cavemen for them.

All I know is I want to jump his bones, but I can't.

Not while Jacob can hear—not to mention all the usual reasons.

To stay sane, I grab a box with dog toys and pick up a chewed-up duck from the floor to drop in it.

Alex looks up from the game. "Are you cleaning up?"

"Is it okay if I do?"

He grins. "Be my guest."

Jolly good. I channel my sexual frustration into the cleanup.

When all the dog toys are in the box, I sort Alex's haphazard video game collection by console, genre, and year of publication.

Oh yeah, this is nice. Too nice, in fact.

Cleaning up always puts me in a good mood, which in this context is having an aphrodisiac effect.

Bugger.

I should head home or else.

"Wow, thanks," Alex says, and I realize he's turned off the game and is staring at my handiwork in awe. "I've been meaning to do that forever—but I doubt I would've used such a clever system."

I'm a volcano of lust that's about to explode.

He means what he said, I can see it—which makes him the rarest of unicorns: a person who welcomes my tidying efforts instead of finding them annoying.

Well, that does it.

While I coded with him all these weeks, I stood strong.

When he dressed up and slicked back his hair, I managed to keep my knickers on.

As I watched him play *Tetris*, I was already on the verge of giving in—and he didn't help matters by vanquishing that bully in *Halo*—but I withstood the temptation.

His liking my tidying is what pushes me over the edge.

If I don't kiss him now, I'll forever regret it.

Closing the distance between us, I grab his tie and pull his mouth to mine.

Chapter Thirty-Nine

*O*ur lips clash.

Holy primes.

Who knew snogging could be this blinding? I wondered if maybe the last kiss seemed so amazeballs because of the alcohol I had coursing through my system, but no. If anything, this time is better—and the bar was already sky high.

Our tongues dance.

The room seems to spin, this time without the help of vodka.

He lightly bites my lower lip.

My nipples are so hard they hurt, and the heat in my core is reaching 1373 degrees.

He pulls me closer, and I feel his erection against my belly—which makes me want to rip off his pants so I can see it, taste it, and shove it deep inside me.

After what feels like an hour of make-out bliss, he

pulls away and cradles my face in his big hands. "You sure about this?"

"Your bedroom," I gasp. "Now."

He replies with an affirmative growl, then sweeps me up in a bridal carry and strides out of the room.

"I'm on the pill and clean," I whisper. There, if the word *bedroom* didn't clue him in as to my intentions, that bit should make things crystal clear, shouldn't it?

"Me too," he says raggedly. "I mean clean, not on the pill."

My blood turns lava hot, my knickers drenched. This is real. It's happening. His reply means, "Why yes, Holly, I will shag your brains out, thank you very much."

Approaching a closed door, he kicks it open and strides inside, then gently deposits me onto the bed.

As I frantically peel my clothes off, I take in my surroundings with relief. The bedroom is even tidier than the kitchen—and that pushes my already-insane arousal into frightening territory.

Do I need to worry? I've heard of people laughing to death, so can you get so randy as to hurt yourself?

That question is put to the test in the next few moments. Alex rakes his cerulean gaze over my body and growls, "You're gorgeous."

I can't speak as I watch him strip off his suit and shirt.

Bliiiiimey. This is like staring at the sun. The delicious muscles I chose for VR Alex pale in comparison to the real thing. I guess my imagination—and digital technology—were not ready for this level of male perfection.

He steps out of his pants.

Here, too, the powerful muscles exposed to my gaze leave the VR version in the dust.

And then he takes off his boxers.

There's an ache in my jaw that makes me realize my mouth is open to the width of a python about to swallow her prey.

Speaking of pythons, Alex's cock is bigger than any available as choices in that VR selection. I think it would feel more at home in the other app—the one with all those swords.

Why am I not scared?

His erection dwarfs Optimus Prime—which means that honorable title should be transferred over.

Yep. Henceforth, *that* is Optimus Prime.

Or just Prime for short—the only short thing about it.

Alex approaches the bed. "I'm going to taste you." The hunger in his gaze underscores the roughly spoken words.

I swallow hard. "Taste me?"

Muscles flexing, he climbs over me and slides his callused palm down my thigh. "I want to make you burn as you never have before."

No words. Speechless.

He drags his tongue up my calf.

I barely hold back a moan.

His tongue continues the trip over my knee and up my thigh until he finds the apex between my legs.

The moan escapes my throat now.

This isn't fair. He can't just start this sexcapade with my deepest, wildest fantasy.

His tongue goes flat against my clit.

Balling the sheets in my hands, I come with a choked cry.

He looks up with a wicked smile, then goes back down and licks me once, twice, thrice—and another orgasm energizes my every nerve ending.

Whew. I'm glad I came on lick number three and not four.

He doesn't stop, though, and I can feel that sensual smile of his against my sex.

Another lick. Two. Three. Four.

His is a bloody clever tongue.

Before giving me lick number five, he teasingly abandons the clit in favor of my folds—which I don't include in my count.

Gritting my teeth, I buck against him, desperate for a release. He gets the hint and returns to the clit for a lick number five—but I'm not there yet.

Lick six.

Closer but still no cigar, which is fine. I don't want to come on a non-prime.

Okay. Now a lot is riding on this next lick. If I don't come then, I'll have to survive the next four licks until we get to the eleventh.

He must know what I need because he makes lick seven slow and languid.

Yes! Finally. My toes curl and my moan sounds closer to a scream.

Before he can resume his ministrations, I wriggle out from underneath him.

He looks up, a question in his eyes.

"My turn for a taste," I pant. "Lie back."

He does.

I kiss and lick his face the way I've always dreamed of doing, then press small, teasing kisses to his neck before gliding my tongue over the hills of his pecs and down the washboard ridges of his abs until I'm at the base of Prime.

Looking up to meet his ravenous gaze, I ice-cream lick up the whole hard, massive length.

Like a tomcat enjoying a stroking, he closes his eyes in pleasure.

Is that a bead of pre-cum at the tip?

Curious, I lick it off. It's yummy—and a prelude to what it would be like if he came in my mouth, which is another fantasy of mine.

In response to my attention, Prime grows impossibly harder.

I wrap my lips around the head and let it slide deeper into my mouth.

It's like silk over steel.

"Fuck," Alex groans.

Encouraged, I swirl my tongue around the head—

three times clockwise, then three times counter-clockwise.

He grabs my shoulders, his strong fingers digging into my flesh.

I do seven clockwise swirls as he squeezes my shoulders almost to the point of pain, and then I do seven swirls in the other direction.

Breathing hard, he pulls me away. "I want to be inside you," he rasps, his accent the thickest it's ever been.

"Me too," I gasp. "I mean, you inside me, not me inside you."

With a hint of that devilish smirk, he recaptures my mouth in a kiss, and without our lips unlocking, he arranges me on my back.

My heart hammers in my ribcage, my senses utterly consumed by him, by his scent, his feel, his warmth. It's like I'm surfing through an ocean storm on the wave of our kiss, his body over mine the only harbor from the sensual upheaval, his lips the only anchor keeping me safe.

He enters me, and I feel like bursting into fire-works, the way the game did earlier, when he'd make a tetris with a long, hard I-block.

His first thrust is too gentle, so I grab his steel-hard glutes and pull him into me.

His pupils dilate, and the second thrust is faster and deeper.

My body curves and bends, molding against his.

"That's it," he growls, and the third thrust is

better still. The fourth is pretty good also, considering the number.

On the fifth thrust, I moan in pleasure. An orgasm is coiling in my core, but it's far away, which is frightening because what if it falls on the wrong count?

I moan on thirteen, and nineteen, and by thrust twenty-three, he's pistoning into me—yet I want it even faster, so I squeeze his muscled ass and pull him deeper.

Yes. Fuck, yes. Moans escape my lips at twenty-nine and thirty-one, and as though through some kismet, he grunts something along the lines "you feel so fucking good" at thirty-seven.

At forty-one, the thrusts turn punishingly hard and are almost too fast to count—and I love every one of them.

By fifty-three, I'm counting the sound of flesh slapping against flesh instead of the thrusts themselves because everything is a blur of pleasure with no discernable start or end.

Eighty-three. I'm close, but I can't come yet. Nor at the non-prime eighty-four, eighty-five, eighty-six, eighty-seven, or eighty-eight.

Here is eighty-nine and it's a prime, but I'm not there yet, though I'm so close I can taste it.

Can I hold off until ninety-seven?

Slap, slap, slap, slap, slap, slap, slap, slap.

My nails dig into his buttocks on ninety-seven as I come undone with a scream.

A satisfied, purely male smile curves his lips as he keeps thrusting.

And thrusting.

Counting is harder now.

Was that one hundred and forty-nine?

Another orgasm starts to build, this one of tsunami strength.

By one hundred and ninety-seven, I don't care if I come on a prime or not. I just want the sweet release.

By two hundred and twenty-three, my throat is hoarse from screaming in pleasure.

Three hundred and seven. I'm *so* fucking close.

"Me too," he grunts.

Fuck. Did I say that out loud?

Doesn't matter.

We're at three-hundred and seventeen, and the black of his pupils nearly overtake the cerulean—and I'm about to explode.

Must hold off just a little bit.

Just a few more.

The release builds and builds.

And then, at three hundred and thirty-one, a prime, Alex grunts in pleasure, his eyes closing as Optimus Prime jerks inside me.

Fuck, yeah. My own orgasm storm makes landfall. All my muscles contract as one as I scream in ecstasy.

Dimly, I'm aware that Alex is hugging and kissing me, but I'm still riding the pleasure wave—one infinitely more intense than all my dildo sessions combined.

By the time I've recovered enough to think again, he's cleaning me with a warm, wet towel.

"That's nice," I mutter, then yawn.

He moves me until we're in a spooning position, with me as the small spoon.

As I lie there, surrounded by his warmth, I feel incredibly content—and in that hazy land between wakefulness and sleep, a thought comes to me.

Whatever this is between us might actually work. He's not the Devil I thought he was when we first met. I like him. Really like him. Way more than I ever did Beau.

The biggest obstacle is our joint workplace. But maybe no one will judge me for sleeping with the boss. Maybe being with him won't be as big of a mess as I feared, and maybe I'll be able to deal with the messy aspects of his life.

On that pleasant thought, I sail away into the land of dreams.

Chapter Forty

I wake up from a wet tongue licking my face.

Memories of last night rush in.

Is this Alex's way of initiating more?

If so, yes, please.

Hmm. His tongue feels long. I don't remember it being that long last night. Only his cock was extraordinarily long. And thick and—

I open my eyes.

Golden eyes stare at me from a koala-like face.

Eeew.

The tongue doesn't belong to Alex.

With a doggy grin, Beelzebub gives my face one more lick.

"Shoo!" I push him away with a giggle.

If you got to first base with a puppy, would it be more pedophilia or bestiality?

His insane enthusiasm undiminished by my rejection, Beelzebub simply switches his licking attentions to Alex's face—and who can blame him.

"Holly?" Alex murmurs sleepily.

"Nope."

He opens his eyes, chuckles, and pushes the puppy away while telling him that waking us like that is a "bad dog thing to do."

"Hi," I say when he's done with his lecture.

Even with dog drool on his face, Alex looks delicious. He grins at me. "Hi, yourself."

"What time is it?" I glance at the sun pouring through the window.

"Fuck. Time." Alex leaps to his feet, gloriously naked.

Grabbing his phone, he barks a few words in Russian.

"I'm running late," he explains at my questioning look. "Forgot to set an alarm. Here." He hands me a robe five sizes too big and begins to dress.

When his glorious nakedness is sadly covered, I slip on the robe and, at his prompting, follow him to the bathroom. Beelzebub scrambles after us and starts slurping water from the toilet bowl.

"No!" Alex says sternly and closes the lid. "That's a bad dog thing to do also."

Beelzebub gives him a contrite look, tail wagging apologetically.

Ooh. I like bossy Alex. Maybe we could play puppy and owner one of these days?

Alex hands me a still-sealed toothbrush that has a

dentist ad on it, and then we perform our morning routines side by side, the domesticity of it all tugging at something in my chest.

Meanwhile, the pup is over his contrition. He's running circles around us, sneaking between our legs like a cat, and in general acting like he might've overdosed on cocaine and amphetamines.

"I've got to run." Alex pulls out his phone. "What do you like for breakfast?"

"Oat porridge."

He makes a few swipes and clicks. "One should arrive in a bit." He grins at Beelzebub, who's just jumped into the bathtub and is attempting to chew on shampoo. Shooing him away from the bottle, he glances at me. "You mind taking him for a walk?"

I give the little devil a dubious look but bravely say, "No problem. After that, can I use your computer? I was going to bring my laptop to catch up on some work, but as you might recall, I didn't get to go home last night."

His grin is directed at me now. "You remember that it's Sunday, right?"

I shrug. "Some folks on my team said they'll be working this weekend, so I feel obligated to do the same—solidarity and all that."

"Suit yourself." He leads me to his office, where he gives me access as a guest user. "You can remotely log into your work computer. That way, you'll have everything set up the way you like it."

"Go to your thing," I say with a smile. "I'll figure things out."

Alex doesn't seem to want to leave. He leashes Beelzebub—even though I could've done it—and sets up a snack inside the toy, explaining that I should use it when I want a break from my furry charge.

"You're late," I say with mock chastisement.

"Give me a kiss, and I'll go."

I'm happy to oblige. This goodbye kiss is as hot as the one from last night—and suddenly, I don't want him to leave. And if his longing stare is anything to go by, he'd rather stay and shag me as well.

Are we both turning into sex fiends like my parents?

"I'll see you later," he says reluctantly.

"Later," I say, trying not to drool as I watch him walk to the elevator.

Beelzebub cocks his head and whines as the doors slide closed behind his master.

I pat his big, fluffy head. "I know how you feel, bud. Now let me get dressed so I can take you out for a walk."

Chapter Forty-One

*I*t's official.

The best way to fall head over heels for a puppy is to take one on a walk.

Fueled by seemingly endless energy, Beelzebub sniffs every inch of our way to the park and barks at things I didn't realize anyone would want to bark at, like blooming dandelion flowers and an empty cardboard box.

Once we get to the area in the park where he can be unleashed, he runs full speed at some mirage only he can see, then jumps at whatever he's imagining. Afterward, he locates a stick and brings it to me with clear intent: "Let's play fetch."

I toss the stick until my arm is tired, but he doesn't seem remotely out of breath.

Well, no help for it. I leash him again, and we resume walking until he finally does his business on a nearby lawn, at which point I learn that when it comes to collecting dog poo in a bag—Gia's worst nightmare—it's not as gross as one would imagine, though this could be a "love is blind" situation at this point.

When we get home, Beelzebub runs after me through the apartment like a duckling imprinted on his mama, even when I need to use the bathroom.

It's so cute I forget to be annoyed.

Still, as soon as I come out, I set up his food and water in the hopes that a food coma will calm him down a bit, and he enthusiastically digs in.

As I watch him eat, the door buzzer goes off.

It's a delivery person with my porridge.

Finally. I was about to try dog food myself.

Pouring the plain porridge into a bowl, I get comfy in the kitchen and devour my meal while browsing the news on my phone. It's not until I'm done with my food that I realize something's off.

Beelzebub is no longer in the kitchen with me.

With a sinking feeling, I go seek the little beast.

Bloody hell.

All the toys I'd collected neatly into the basket are all over the floor again.

I grab the box and begin putting them away—that is, until Beelzebub jumps on me and causes me to drop the box. Barking excitedly, he begins tossing the toys throughout the apartment once more.

Maybe I should simply let this mess be.

I can do that.

Sometimes.

I mean, I do survive Gia's place with my sanity intact.

I hold out for a solid thirty seconds. Then, driven by an irresistible compulsion, I collect the toys again.

Beelzebub immediately recreates the mess. He must see this as a fun game.

I'm beginning to feel overwhelmed, and unlike with Euclid, I can't just take off a VR headset when I tire of dealing with this kind of pet.

Then I recall the hidden treat toy Alex set up.

Aha.

I'm able to clean up the mess once again, and Beelzebub couldn't care less. All his attention is on the treat-hiding toy.

Jolly good. Maybe I could do a little work while I'm at it.

I go into Alex's office, and as I log in, my thoughts drift to the events of last night. Immediately, questions such as, "What did it mean?" and "What would my coworkers think if they found out?" sprout their unwelcome heads.

Maybe Beelzebub did me a favor when he kept me chasing after him.

Deciding to distract myself with work, I remotely log into my office computer and work on Euclid's code—something I haven't gotten a chance to do in a while. When I'm done, I open my inbox so I can ask Alison to test my work, but an email from her is already waiting there, a message she sent last Friday.

The subject is ominous: "I heard a rumor about you."

I open the email and my stomach freezes.

According to Alison, the whispers at the water-cooler are all about one thing: Alex and I are sleeping together.

I stare at the screen blankly, then reply with:

Who started this rubbish rumor?

After I click send, it really hits me.

How could someone from the office know? Is there a spy cam in Alex's bedroom?

No, that's ridiculous. And even if there were, Alison's email is from Friday, *before* we slept together.

Someone lied when they started this rumor, but now it's not a lie.

I grasp my suddenly aching head.

What was I thinking last night?

I wasn't. I just unleashed my hormones. We both did, and now my work life is becoming as big of a mess as this apartment—and it's too much for me to handle.

My phone rings.

It's Alex.

Does he know already? Is he about to say how much he regrets what we did?

Taking in a deep breath, I pick up. *"Privet."*

"Privet." There's a smile in his voice. "Just wanted to see how the day is going so far, and give you an update."

So he doesn't know.

Do I tell him?

No. He's got his father to worry about.

"The day went well, and Beelzebub is doing great," I say. "How did the intervention go?"

He sighs. "As well as such a thing can. Dad offered us a compromise. He'll drink beer instead of vodka."

I gape at my phone. Has stress robbed me of ability to understand, or is this alleged compromise totally wonky?

"Last I checked, beer has alcohol," I say cautiously. "Isn't that what you wanted him to give up?"

"Yes, but this is a step in the right direction. If he sticks to beer, he won't have enough room in his stomach to reach the blood alcohol levels of vodka."

"I guess…"

"It's a decent result, trust me. Dad's generation of Russians scoff at things like the twelve-step program."

Okay, do I tell him about the rumor now?

"All right," he says before I can work up the courage. "I'm heading back. See you."

He hangs up before I can say anything.

Fine. It's fate.

I hurry back to my inbox to see if Alison replied.

Nope, and why would she? It's still Sunday.

Just as I'm about to exit the email dashboard, an email from Alison arrives after all.

I was hoping you'd be on this weekend, it starts. Only instead of naming names, Alison proceeds to say that she'll have to carefully ask around to find out who started the rumor.

Bugger. What's really telling is that she doesn't ask me if the rumor is true. Does that mean she doesn't believe it, or that she thinks I *am* sleeping with our boss?

Sleeping with the bloody boss.

How did I become such a messy, improper cliché?

I pace the room, then sort all of Alex's pens in order of length.

When I run out of physical messes to fix, I look for some more code to work on—and settle on an easy bug from the integration queue list.

As soon as I start, I realize I miss having Alex at my side.

Seriously? Has our pair programming ruined my ability to code independently?

What a bloody disaster.

Before long, I find myself unable to concentrate on fixing the bug, so I type out a command to reverse any changes I just made.

Wait, did I type that in correctly?

Before I can check, my phone rings.

It's Dr. Piper.

I grab my phone. "Hello!"

"Hi," Dr. Piper says, and he doesn't sound like his usual cheerful self. "I fear I have some bad news."

Chapter Forty-Two

$\mathcal{M}$y heartbeat shoots up to one hundred and thirty-seven beats per minute. "Did something happen to Jacob?"

"Sorry, no. Not that kind of bad news."

I exhale loudly. "Thank goodness. What did you mean then?"

He sighs. "Do you remember that consultant I mentioned?"

I almost ask, "The evil one?" but go with a simple "yes" instead.

With everything that's been going on, I'd actually forgotten all about the Evil Consultant.

"Well, he emailed me," Dr. Piper says. "He told me what kind of products Morpheus Group is about to launch."

What?

Oh, no.

No. No. No.

How did the Evil Consultant even find out about the porn? And why bloody tell them?

This doesn't fall into a consultant's purview.

Dr. Piper sighs again. "I was hoping you'd say it was a bunch of lies."

I shake my head, then realize he can't see me. "I can't deny it," I say reluctantly.

A louder sigh. "I'm sorry, dear, but this is a problem then. I mean, not for me personally, but for the rest of my team. They'll want to cut ties when I tell them tomorrow—and I have to tell them. I'm sorry."

I stupidly shake my head at the phone yet again.

"I'm going to give the folks at 1000 Devils a heads up," he says. "Again, sorry about this, but my hands are tied."

"I understand," I manage to squeeze out and hang up.

Tears prickle at the backs of my eyes, and the walls of the office feel like they're pressing in on me.

This is bad. So, so bad. What am I going to do? How do I fix this enormous mess? How do I—

There's the sound of the elevator doors sliding open, followed by enthusiastic barking.

I stagger out of the room toward the commotion, nearly tripping over the dog toys twice.

Beelzebub must've taken a break from the treat to make a mess again—creating a metaphor for my bloody life.

"Bad dog," Alex is saying sternly when I reach them.

Beelzebub's ears are drooping.

I follow Alex's gaze.

Of course. My fuck-me pumps have been ripped into tiny shreds—just like my dreams.

"I'm so sorry," Alex says, looking over at me. "You can wear my sister's slippers when you go home. And I'll get you new shoes."

My hands ball at my sides. "I don't bloody care about the bloody shoes."

He winces. "You've spoken to Dr. Piper, haven't you?"

So Alex is the "folks at 1000 Devils" that Dr. Piper said he'd get in touch with.

I nod, not trusting myself to speak.

"It's a fucked-up situation," Alex says, scrubbing his hand over his face.

I feel the urge to get out of here before I scream or do something else to make him think I'm insane—or scare the poor puppy.

I head toward the door, but Alex blocks my way.

"Where are you going?"

"Home." I try to squeeze past him, but he's like a concrete wall.

"There's something else I wanted to talk to you about," he says as I take a step back, and I could swear there's a look of disappointment on his face.

He dares to be upset with me?

I narrow my eyes at him. "What is it? Did you also

lose your contract with the hospital over the stuff you claim isn't porn?"

He sighs. "Morpheus Group is a different company from 1000 Devils. We talked about this."

Yeah. I remember. It was when he said what just happened wouldn't happen.

My anger is intensifying by the second.

I get that life can be unfair, but this is ridiculous. He sleeps with me, but only *my* reputation is in tatters. We both get caught working on porn, but only *my* project is sacked.

He frowns. "I saw the emails from the people writing code today."

My jaw drops. "You want to talk shop in the middle of all this? Is suit integration the only thing you care about?"

His face is stormy now, reminding me of the day he caught me breaking and entering into his office. "I told you it's important to Bella, remember? You said you wouldn't sabotage it again. Remember that part?"

I back away at the anger in *his* voice. "What are you talking about?"

He advances on me. "Look, I get this was a stressful day for you, but that doesn't mean you can—"

"Stressful?" My emotions boil out of control, all the pent-up stress and frustration releasing at the same time. I know I'm shouting, but I don't care. "Stressful doesn't cut it. This is the worst day of my life!"

"And I sympathize, but——"

"Are you going to get out of my bloody way?" I sound so hysterical at this point that Beelzebub whines —which is exactly what I wanted to avoid.

Jaw hardening, Alex moves out of the way. "Go, if you must."

I rush into the elevator and stab my finger at every prime-numbered floor. As the elevator shoots down, I yell my lungs out between each of the stops.

Ignoring Alex's limo, I grab a cab.

The ride home passes in a haze of tumultuous emotions, and once I get there, I put on *Downton Abbey* and cry until I pass out on the couch.

Chapter Forty-Three

I wake up with a stiff back and pounding head. Pushing up to a sitting position, I rub my gritty eyes, and as the world comes into focus, the events of Sunday morning rush back. My stomach knots, a vise squeezing my chest as I recall everything.

I lost the hospital contract I've worked so hard for.

My VR pet project is as good as dead.

And, to add the cream cheese on top of this cucumber shit sandwich, all my coworkers know I've been sleeping with the boss.

Speaking of which, why was Alex acting so weirdly last night?

I'm the one who should've been upset, not him.

Also, what was that bit about some email? Why was he talking about sabotage?

I jump to my feet and look for my phone, but to no avail.

Bugger. Now that I think about it, I might've left it on the table in Alex's office.

I open my laptop to check the time.

Wow. It's Monday morning. No wonder my back is stiff—I slept all night on a tiny couch.

Okay, back to the email mystery.

I remotely log into my work computer and look in my inbox for messages from Sunday.

Bloody hell. People are panicking because a year of work seems to be missing from the code repository.

Did I do that again?

I frantically pull up the window where I tried to undo my coding efforts from yesterday, and sure enough, I really messed up that command. I even felt like I might've and was going to double-check, but the call from Dr. Piper distracted me.

No wonder my coworkers are freaking out.

The good news is I know how to fix it, since I made this kind of mistake once before.

It takes me a few minutes, but everything is copacetic once I'm done.

Whew.

I reply to one of the panic emails and explain that the issue is now fixed. As I click "send," I notice Alex's name in the address field and recall his accusation.

Oh, fuck.

Now I understand why he looked disappointed.

He must've thought the bad news from Dr. Piper had driven me to mess up the code on purpose—and I didn't deny it or explain what really happened.

I fire off an email asking him if we can talk, then rush to the bathroom to wash my face and brush my teeth.

When I'm done with my morning routine, I check if Alex replied.

Nope.

I eat my oat porridge and check again.

Nada.

It's official.

Alex hates me now. For all I know, he's blocked my email address so I go right into spam—or maybe I've been fired, and my emails no longer reach anyone in the company.

I set my empty bowl into the sink with such force it shatters.

My heart hammers sickly, and the knot in my stomach grows until the oats threaten to come up.

I screwed up.

Alex and I might be over.

If I were rational, I'd be happy about this fact. Assuming I still have a job, us being over means we go back to the employer and employee relationship, which is the proper arrangement. The one that's less messy. The one where people can't talk about me shagging the boss behind my back.

I should be glad, but instead, my heart resembles that poor, shattered bowl.

My interactions with Alex play out in my mind's view. The pair coding... us dancing at his dad's birth-day... the kiss... Sunday's orgasms... All the time we've spent together has etched Alex into my heart, and knowing that I've lost him is making me realize that fact—or more like, admit it.

Desperate, I check my email once more.

There are thank-you messages from the developers confirming that the code is back, so I'm still in the company email system.

Nothing from Alex, though.

My chest squeezes even tighter, the tears threatening to flood my eyes again, but I beat them back and square my shoulders.

Fuck moping around and crying.

I refuse to let our relationship unravel.

I need to fix this—and if Alex wants to bloody ignore me, he'll have to do it to my bloody face.

Throwing on my clothes, I grab Gia's lockpicks on a hunch and hurry to the office.

It's time my devil and I had some words.

———

In my rush to get to Alex's office, I nearly knock over Alison.

"Hey," she says. "I'm getting to the bottom of the source of the rumor. Just give me a few more hours."

"Cheers," I pant. "Email me what you know. I don't have my phone today."

She nods, and I resume my sprint—only to find Alex's office locked when I get there.

I knock.

He doesn't open.

Is he ignoring me?

Wait, no, that doesn't make sense. This could be someone else knocking.

Unless he can see me through a security camera?

The idea infuriates me. Then again, I must've suspected this could happen on some level, since I did bring those lockpicks.

I look around.

No one is paying attention to me, but it's still insane that I'm about to do this in broad daylight.

Well, if Alex is watching, he can stop me by opening the door.

I knock for the last time.

Silence.

I make short work of the lock with the lockpicks.

Heart in my throat, I push open the door.

Empty.

Where the bloody hell is he?

Then again, if he's not at work, maybe he's not ignoring my emails after all. Maybe he's simply taken a day off.

Shutting the door, I rush to Bella's office.

She's not there either.

I hurry to my desk and check my email for any messages from either of the Chortsky siblings.

Nothing.

Since Alex is incommunicado, I write to Bella:

Wanted to chat. Don't have my phone. Can we Skype? My username is PalindromicPrime1035301.

I wait for a few minutes, but Bella doesn't reply or video conference me.

Fine. Since I know where Alex lives, I'll just pay him a visit.

———

Running into Alex's building, I smash into the chest of a security guard.

"Can I help you?" he growls, steadying me when I stumble back.

Bugger. He's not the one I saw on Sunday, so I must look like a complete stranger to him.

"I'm here to visit Alex Chortsky," I say breathlessly, stepping back. "On the 107th floor."

The guard walks over to his desk and checks something in his computer as I reflect on how fortuitous it is that Alex lives on a prime-numbered floor.

If that's not a sign that he belongs with me, I don't know what is.

"Sorry," the guard says, not sounding the least bit apologetic. "Mr. Chortsky left."

Damn it. "When?"

He looks up from the screen. "It doesn't say, but it must've been after I started my shift."

Is this true, or is it an excuse Alex gave in case I showed up?

Then again, the guard didn't even ask my name.

I could be Bella. No, he probably knows Bella.

I dart a glance at the elevator.

Would the guard tackle me if I just went for it?

Even if he did, I think I could make it.

I make a mad dash.

The guard isn't chasing me. At least I can't hear him doing so.

Panting, I reach my destination and frantically jab at the button.

Nothing seems to happen for a year.

"You need the card for the elevator to open," the guard says from his seat in an exasperated tone. "I take it you don't have one?"

Cursing under my breath, I turn to face him. "Can't you press something on your end to let me in?"

"Sure I can. But I most definitely won't."

Why, that bloody… I stop that line of thinking, as you catch more annoying flies with honey. Returning to the front desk, I make puppy eyes at the guy. "Please. Alex said I can visit even if he's not there."

"Can I see your ID?" The guard extends his hand.

When I give it to him, he types something into his computer and shakes his head. "You're not on the guest list."

"He didn't get the chance to put me there," I say.

The guard's expression hardens. "Look, lady, you're lucky I'm not calling the cops. And I'm only doing you that courtesy on the off chance you really *do* know Mr. Chortsky."

"I swear I do."

"Then have him put you on the list, or come back with him, or have him give you his card."

I hate it when people use proper logic against me.

With a huff, I turn on my heel and step outside to get a cab.

There's one more place Alex could be.

A place I'm not keen on visiting again, if I'm honest.

A place that reminds me of a circle of hell, which is fitting because it's called 1000 Devils.

Then again, Alex is worth it.

I rattle out the address to the driver and mentally prepare for the trial to come.

A bloody Nerf gun assault.

Chapter Forty-Four

*W*hen the security guard in *this* building asks me whom I've come to see, I give Robert Jellyheim's name instead of Alex's.

They call Robert, and he tells them to let me in. A quick elevator ride later, I step onto the 1000 Devils' floor and dive into the armory closet.

It's time for the big guns, literally.

I search for the biggest weapon and end up choosing a shotgun-looking thing.

Feeling like a badass, I fish out my earbuds, jam them into my ears, and launch the *Downton Abbey* soundtrack on full blast.

Yeah. The bodies are about to hit the floor.

I sprint out, and as soon as my foes spot me, a dart flies at my face.

I sidestep it.

Boom.

At least that's the sound I assume my shotgun

makes when I unload it, sending a cloud of darts flying at the forty-something red-headed bloke I recall from the last gunfight.

That'll show him.

A new attacker jumps up from her desk.

I unleash another cloud of darts at her chest.

How do these people work here? The desks are still haphazard, gun ammo is caking the floor, and the worst part is that no one has fixed the "four chairs next to some desks" situation.

A lady I previously shot in the crotch and boob joins the fray, looking eager for revenge.

I squeeze the trigger of my shotgun.

Nothing happens.

Why?

Oh, right. I should've known. Shotguns aren't exactly known for large ammo capacity.

The lady shoots.

I dodge her dart.

More attackers join in.

A swarm of darts is about to turn me into an orange porcupine.

I duck behind a familiar desk.

A throat clears above me once, twice.

Yep. I made this exact mistake the last time too.

I look up.

Indeed. I'm face to crotch with Buckley once again.

It's the second bloody time I haven't noticed him in the heat of the battle.

"Sorry about that." As I take out the earbuds from my ears and stand up, I catch a glimpse of his monitor—he's reading an email.

The "To" field looks familiar, but before I can fully process it, Buckley minimizes the window.

"Hello," he says, then clears his throat three times.

Wait. That email. Was it—

A dart smashes into my temple, and another one hits me in the bum.

Huh. These don't hurt as much as I feared. Or at all, really.

"That's enough shooting, guys," Robert calls from his desk nearby.

I turn to face him.

He's no less messy than the last time I saw him.

"Thanks for letting me in," I say, wiping the sweat from my brow. "I'm actually here for Alex."

Robert frowns. "He isn't here today."

Did Alex tell him to say that?

No. They wouldn't let me up here if that were so.

I walk up to his desk. "Do you know where he is?"

Robert shakes his head.

Damn it. "Can I use your computer to check my email?" I ask, beginning to feel defeated.

"Sure, but please make it quick."

He gives me access, and I remotely log into my work machine and check my emails.

Nothing from Alex still, but there is a reply from Bella:

Hey, hon. Just tried to conference with you, but you didn't pick up.

Bugger. I want to videocall her back, but this is Robert's computer, and I'm supposed to make it quick.

I'm about to sign out when I see an email from Alison.

Another moment shouldn't hurt.

I click on it.

Alison says she's triangulated the origin of the rumor and has a name for me.

I read the name, rub my eyes, and read it again.

Yep.

Still Buckley.

Then it hits me.

The "To" in the message I just saw on his screen —I'm pretty sure it was Dr. Piper's email. Or if not, definitely someone with an @nyulangone.org address.

But why would he email them? Unless…

I storm over to Buckley's desk.

"You're the Evil Consultant?" The question comes out much louder than I planned.

Buckley clears his throat. "What?"

"No more games," I growl. "You spread lies about me at the office, *and* you torpedoed my project?"

His next two throat clears sound angry. "What lies?"

"That I slept with Alex," I hiss under my breath.

He rolls his eyes. "And you didn't? I saw how he looked at you when you were here the last time.

'Sexual harassment' was practically written on his forehead."

I'm the most anti-violent person I know, yet I have to fight the urge to punch him. Hard.

"Why would you do something like this to me?" I ask instead, though I already suspect the answer.

"Why?" He clears his throat twice more. "Office romances aren't proper," he says with a British accent that I think is supposed to be a parody of my speech. "I guess that's only when it doesn't help your career, right?"

Twat. He *is* mad about my rejection of his advances.

Since I'm too busy seething in anger to reply, he clears his throat four more bloody times—as though he knows how painful that is for me to hear. "*I* should have been the CTO," he says, his tone dripping with bitterness. "Not you."

So it's not just the rejection. He *is* sour that I got promoted to CTO over him.

"That project at the hospital was extremely important," I say. "Not just to me, to little kids too."

He shrugs, a nasty expression on his face. "You're not my boss anymore, so there isn't much you can do about it."

"No," Robert says. "But *I* can."

Blinking, Buckley turns to face his new boss—who I now realize must've been there through the whole exchange.

Buckley looks like he's just choked on a throat clear. "I didn't do anything wrong."

Robert crosses his arms over his chest. "Didn't you just admit to making libelous claims about the owner of this very company?"

Buckley's next set of throat clears sounds frightened. "You can't fire me over something like that."

Robert's eyes narrow. "Oh, I can. I could fire you even if you weren't on the probationary period. But since you are, it won't even require that much paperwork."

Buckley glares at me. "I hope you're happy."

"Ignore him," Robert says.

I give Buckley a look designed to shrivel his manhood for at least a year. "Oh, don't worry. He doesn't exist as far as I'm concerned."

Turning, I hurry back to the elevator.

———

As soon as I'm home, I grab my laptop and video conference Bella.

The dial music rings and rings.

"Please pick up," I say to the empty screen.

The app keeps ringing. Just as I'm about to hang up, Bella's face shows up and grins at me. "Hi, Holly. Sorry, I'm all over the place today. My other company is dealing with an emergency: Woody Harrelson is suing us for using his likeness for our line of butt plugs."

"Hi," I say breathlessly. "Do you know where Alex is?"

As though in reply, a bark sounds in the background.

It's a strangely familiar bark, one that makes my chest ache.

"Beelzebub," Bella says sternly.

Wait, why is he there?

The puppy barks again.

Bella glares at someone outside the camera—presumably, the adorable koala-dog hybrid. "I bet this is why Alex wants you in doggy school."

Doggy school?

"Where is Alex?" I ask again.

She looks back at the camera. "He didn't tell me. Just dropped off the little demon and asked about the school where Boner learned to be so well-mannered." She frowns. "Now that you mention it, he did seem very stressed. Is everything okay?"

"Bloody hell," I mutter. "I looked for him at our offices, at his home, and then even at 1000 Devils. Where is he?"

Her frown deepens. "What happened?"

What can I say? There's no way to explain everything without coming clean about the sabotage—and if I do, I'll lose her, just as I've lost Alex.

But I can't *not* tell her. She has the right to know.

"It's a long story," I say, and taking a deep breath, I launch into it, starting at the beginning.

To my shock, when I get to the part about sabotage, she just sits there calmly, looking almost bored.

"You're not upset?" I ask her when I finish.

She cocks her head. "About which part? If it were up to me to decide who my brother sleeps with, I would choose you, hands down."

I lean closer to the screen. "But I almost sabotaged your venture."

She shakes her head. "Alex told me about your break-in the day we went for that dog walk. He also told me why you did it, and that made me like you even more. In my experience, driven people are rare."

I tap the screen so it zooms in on her face. "So you knew?"

She nods.

I suck in a giddy breath. "And you still want to be friends?"

She grins. "Hells yeah. And before you ask—I'll be your friend even if my brother ends up being stupid enough to let you slip through his fingers."

That brings me right back to earth. I draw back from the screen. "So you really have no idea where he is?"

She shakes her head. "Let me text him."

I watch her do it and wait. And wait.

"Hmm. Let me try calling." After a minute, she mouths "voicemail" to me and rattles out something in Russian. Then she hangs up and says, "Why don't you chillax for now? When I hear from him, I'll let you know."

"Thank you. Just please tell him that the code mess from Sunday wasn't another sabotage. It was an honest mistake that I've already fixed."

"Will do."

"Okay," I say dejectedly. "Talk to you later."

"Yep, and we'll arrange a brunch then too."

I nod and hang up.

Even the prospect of brunch with Bella can't cheer me up right now.

Getting to my feet, I begin to pace.

An hour passes.

Then two.

No more videocalls from Bella.

Did Alex not call or text her back? Or maybe he did but asked her not to tell me?

Could it be that he doesn't believe the mistake story? Or is he just pissed that I stormed out of his apartment the way I did?

More importantly, where is he?

A completely unsubstantiated idea sneaks into my brain—and makes my knees go weak.

What if Alex got hurt on the way to work?

He *has* been missing for a while.

But no. Surely, his family would be notified—and Bella would tell me if that were the case.

Wait. Something Bella said earlier triggers a memory.

He seemed stressed, she said. And I remember Alex telling Jacob that when he's stressed, he turns off his phone and plays *War of Sword*... for hours.

I exhale a relieved breath.

Can the answer be that simple?

If not for that unpleasant encounter with the security guard, I'd rush back to Alex's apartment and demand to go up again. As is, I grab a VR headset.

As I download *War of Sword*, I do my best to banish the memories from the last time I played this game. Between the violence and the four-fingered limbs, this will be as fun as getting punched in the stomach... four or six times.

Still, since this is the fastest way to banish the specter of Alex in an accident, this is what I will do.

Yeah.

Brimming with determination, I click the game icon.

Four-fingered creatures, I will be your doom.

Chapter Forty-Five

*A*ppearing in the medieval village, I do my best to ignore my elfin hands with their abominable finger count.

If Alex is playing, I should be able to reach him the way I did the last time.

Taking out the special yarn he gave me for this purpose, I give it a shake.

Whoosh.

I show up in a dank underground hall littered with body parts.

Unsheathing my sword, I scan the battle raging all around me and fight my gag reflex.

All manner of creatures are fighting to the death here, and the violence once again feels nauseatingly real.

Still, I will not quit this time. Not until I find what I came for.

Tightening my grip on my sword, I look for Alex's avatar amid the chaos.

With a sudden battle cry, a dwarf jumps at me, holding an ax bigger than his head is in his lets-not-count-how-many-fingered hands.

I sidestep the ax swing and behead the dwarf, fighting the urge to vomit at the digital gore.

Then my heart leaps with joy.

There's a minotaur with Alex's features a few feet away.

He's not in the hospital or someplace worse. As I hoped, he's simply playing his game to destress.

I wonder if I'm the cause of that stress—and where he is in the real world. Was he home when I came by his building but chose to avoid me? Or did he not even realize I was there?

Before I can think up more questions, I spot an orc rushing at the minotaur at full speed.

Bugger. Alex is currently fighting a female elf. He's going to get slaughtered.

Well, not if I have anything to say about it.

Drawing my bow, I send an arrow into the orc's head.

Squelch.

The arrow pierces the orc's eye, killing him instantly.

At the same time, Alex pierces the elf with his right horn.

Hmm. Do I need to be jealous?

"Holly?" Alex says, spotting my avatar.

I grin in the real world. "*Privet.*" Here, I switch the bow for the sword and disembowel a pink goblin mid-leap.

"Behind you!" Alex yells.

I duck as I turn, and a cyclops's spear misses my shoulder by half an inch.

I swing my sword in a wide arc, cleaving the cyclops in half.

Turning around, I see Alex fighting his way to me.

Great idea. Fighting like a berserker, I kill a golem with my sword and shoot an ogre with my arrows while Alex uses his horns and trident to decimate a group of gnomes and leprechauns.

Soon enough, we're fighting back to back.

"No fair," booms a bigfoot-looking fella. "Collaboration isn't allowed in a free-for-all."

Alex silences him with his trident.

"He was right," hisses a hydra, but I cut her snake body in half.

If only winning arguments were so easy in the real world.

We keep fighting until only the two of us are left.

"What are you doing here?" Alex asks.

I turn to face him, my real-world heart pitter-pattering in my chest. "I didn't sabotage the code. It was a mistake, and I fixed it."

The horned avatar's face doesn't change—the game lacks that technology.

Before I can launch into further explanations, the minotaur speaks. "I know that. I saw your email when

I got home a couple of hours ago. Replied to it too. Then I called you, but you didn't answer."

A huge weight lifts off my neck. He came home a couple of hours ago? That means he didn't ignore me when I came to his building.

And he replied? Bugger. I was so busy waiting for Bella to videocall me, I forgot to check my work email.

"Sorry I didn't take your call," I say. "I think I left my phone in your home office."

"Oh. I didn't hear it ring—must be on vibrate."

I realize I might look confrontational with my sword out and proud, so I drop it. "I'm sorry I ran out on you. I was overwhelmed with the bad news."

He tosses his trident away also. "No. *I'm* sorry. I shouldn't have suspected you'd intentionally mess up the code. In my defense, I didn't at first, but when I saw how you were acting, I—"

I hold up my four-fingered hand. "Don't worry about that. I'm just so glad you're okay."

He cocks his head, a gesture that looks wonky due to his horns. "Why wouldn't I be okay?"

Not caring that I sound like a crazy stalker, I tell him how I couldn't reach him and that I looked for him at both of his offices and his home.

He shakes his horns. "Sorry about that. I only checked Morpheus Group emails when I got home from the hospital."

"The hospital?" Worry tightens my chest again. "Are you okay?"

"Oh, it wasn't a medical visit. I met with Dr. Piper."

My jaw is gaping open in the real world, but I guess he can't see that in VR. "Why?"

"I saved your VR pet project," he says.

"What?" My heart is racing anew. "How?"

He scratches his head, his hand unrealistically going back and forth through his left horn. "Remember the conversation we had the day before we met with the folks at the hospital?"

"The one when you asked me not to mention you were part of Morpheus Group?"

Bugger. That came out bitter.

"That one," he says. "I reassured you, but later that day, I spoke to Bella about it, and we decided to take a precautionary step in case I was wrong—and I'm glad we did."

I readjust my headset. "Bella didn't mention any of this when we spoke."

The minotaur shrugs. "Maybe the subject didn't come up?"

I resist the urge to shake the information out of him. "So what was the precaution?"

"We started a new limited liability company. Due to all the red tape, the registration only went through this weekend—and just in time. The new company is called Pet VR LLC, and you'll be the CEO while Bella is just the silent investor—and through Dragomir's company, just in case. This way, there should be no porn association, ever."

I'm on the verge of tackling him in joy, but I don't yet. If I've misunderstood something, I'll be crushed. "But Dr. Piper already knows about the porn."

The minotaur's head bobs. "That's why I went to talk to him first thing this morning, before he told the others. I convinced him to keep it between us. As far as they're concerned, they've had a change of vendor, that's all."

I want to believe this so badly. "And he agreed, just like that?"

The minotaur shrugs his broad, hairy shoulders. "I did have to promise him some favorable terms for when the 1000 Devils contract is renegotiated. He's a practical man, and he doesn't really care what Morpheus Group does—only his colleagues would have."

I walk up to the minotaur and try to kiss him, but the game doesn't support such a thing, so my intention is translated into a head butt.

"I don't know how to thank you," I say, cringing at the sight of blood pouring from the wound I just inflicted.

"Meet me face to face," Alex says, his voice roughening. "I'll think of a way you can thank me then."

My pulse leaps and my ovaries perform a series of cartwheels. "Yes, please. My place?"

"On my way," he says and disappears.

Brimming with excitement, I take off the VR gear.

There's so much to process.

My project is saved, and Alex wasn't ignoring me today. He was busy helping me—even though he thought I sabotaged his company for the second time.

I can't believe I even jokingly called him the Devil.

He's more like a guardian angel and a saint rolled into one.

Rushing into the bedroom, I set up some candles while the implications of what's happened continue to race through my brain.

Alex is not my boss anymore. Not with the way the new venture is set up.

That means I'm free to date him—and date him I shall.

Actually, I think I would've done that even if he'd remained my boss, mess or no mess. In general, I think I'm more comfortable with chaos as of late. I managed to stay in that violent game until the end, I survived the Nerf massacre, and I even held my own with Beelzebub.

Speaking of which, Bella mentioned Alex inquiring about doggy school for the pup. Is that to make *my* life easier?

Knowing his thoughtfulness, probably.

I smooth out all the creases in the pillows, fold the blanket into a pentagram, and am counting the candles around the bed to make sure there are nineteen when I hear the video conferencing tune in the distance.

And there's Bella, grinning at me. "Alex just called."

"I know," I say. "He told me everything."

Her grin turns lascivious. "Let me guess. You guys are about to consummate the new venture."

"When a lady plans to kiss, she doesn't tell."

She laughs. "I'm pretty sure that's not the expression."

My doorbell rings.

"Sorry, I have to run."

She waggles her eyebrows. "Good luck."

I disconnect and hurry to the door.

It's Alex—and he looks so, so much more delicious without the cow parts.

Once again dressed in a bespoke suit, he's slicked his hair back and is clean-shaven. I'm suspecting he's figured out that it's the quickest way to get me randy, and he's ruthlessly using it to full advantage.

Without saying a word, he sweeps me up into a hungry kiss, and I feel like the ground has dissolved under my feet.

We stumble toward my bedroom, lips locked and hands eagerly roaming each other's bodies as our clothes fall off as if by magic. He deepens the kiss, and the next thing I know, it's seven orgasms later— six for me and one for him.

Combined, a perfect prime.

———

"Thank you for coming," I say as I'm lying blissed out in his arms hours later.

"No." He smiles tenderly. "Thank *you*."

I cozy up closer to him. "I've decided to tell you something."

He lifts up onto one elbow and tucks a strand of hair behind my ear, his touch sending a pleasurable shiver down my spine even after all the orgasms. "Me too."

"What?"

His smile turns devilish. "Ladies first."

Fine.

I take in a deep breath to quell the bees fluttering about in my stomach. "I think we fit together really well. Like L and J Tetris blocks."

He chuckles. "Wouldn't that make us two squares?"

"Exactly. Nice and tidy."

He squints at me. "You're more of a T-block."

As in his favorite? The bees in my stomach throw a wild orgy.

"Back to my point," I say, drawing upon all of my courage. "Ever since I learned that a heart has four chambers, I thought it was my least favorite organ—but I don't think that anymore, thanks to you."

He sits up all the way. "As a wise woman said in an awesome show, 'I'm not a romantic, but even I concede that the heart does not exist solely for the purpose of pumping blood.'"

Did he just quote Violet from *Downton Abbey*?

He must've watched it. For me.

Suddenly, what I want to say crystalizes perfectly in my mind.

I sit up also and clasp his hand with both of my palms. "I love you," I say with utmost sincerity. "I love you with all four chambers of my heart."

A slow, wickedly sensual smile blooms across his face. "I love you too, kroshka. With all five vital organs in my body."

Cradling my face between his palms, he kisses me again, and we tumble back onto the mattress in a tangle of limbs, our hearts racing in sync as the kiss leads to so many more orgasms I lose count.

Hopefully twenty-three.

As I lie in his arms afterward, I feel like I've reached Heaven—and all I had to do to get there was make a deal with my very own, personal, lovable Devil.

Epilogue

ALEX

"*We're* almost there," the limo driver whispers to me.

I change into my livery and slick back my hair with a tea-scented pomade I got for this occasion.

My sweet kroshka is going to love this, but to everyone else, I look like a butler—which I guess works, all things considered.

The limo stops, and I tap her shoulder. "We're here. You can take that off."

She turns, and her soft, full breast brushes against my hand.

Fuck me.

My dick—or Optimus Prime to close friends and family—instantly gets diamond hard, as it does whenever I touch her.

"*Do svidaniya,* Euclid," she says, and I can picture her cute little friend replying in Russian. The VR pet venture has been such a success that she's about to launch it in my motherland—a wonderful thing because many of the Soviet-era hospitals there are drearier than anything imaginable in the US.

As a result of this—and of dating me, of course—her Russian is rapidly improving. Also, as I predicted, her Britishisms are giving way to Russianisms, which isn't a word but should be.

As soon as she removes the VR headset, her intelligent blue eyes zoom in on mine. "Can I finally see the *yobaniy* surprise?" Then her eyes widen at my outfit. "I love it. Now take it off."

"The outfit isn't the whole surprise," I say with mock exasperation.

She levels a meaningful glance at the bulge in my pants. "I'd say."

I laugh. "He's not the surprise either. Not yet anyway."

She folds her lips in the most kissable pout ever. "Well, he and you in that outfit had better be somewhere on the agenda."

"Definitely. But after the real surprise." Someone, give me a medal for restraint.

"Fine." She squints at the blackout windows of the limo. "Reveal whatever it is already."

I readjust Prime, then slide out of the car and hold the door for her.

As soon as she comes out and sees our surroundings, she clutches her chest and greedily drinks it all in, speechless.

My smile is devious. I had to ask her illusionist

twin to help me with planning and misdirection, so I could arrange this surprise. I even bribed the limo driver into breaking the speed limit in order to make the trip duration short—and it would be fair to say that I suggested bringing Bella and Dragomir on this UK trip as part of that same plan. All they like to do is explore London—which is why my kroshka was expecting to see something like Hyde Park or Hampstead Heath right now.

But no. Bella and Dragomir aren't here. It's only us... and a huge group of butlers, maids, and groundskeepers.

"Is that what I think it is?" she finally says.

"Indeed, Lady Hyman," I say in my best British accent. "Highclere Castle, at your service."

The smile she beams at me is as radiant as her bright blue eyes. Reverently, she whispers, "This is the real Downton Abbey."

I nod, keeping my expression as impassive as her favorite butler would.

"What about them?" She gestures at the sharply dressed people waiting for us.

"Actors I hired," I say. "A few are even from the show."

She squeals like a kid, and I tell her what else we have planned for today. Dragomir used his connections to get us a royal treatment that includes multiple tea services, a stay in the best rooms, and—especially for Holly—the chance to tidy any room she wants while wearing a maid's uniform.

She looks around again, as though not believing her eyes. "This is the best surprise ever."

"There's more," I say and ceremoniously hand her a thick package, custom made in the shape of a pentagram. "This is the last surprise of the day, I promise."

There's confusion on her face as she fumbles with it—the problem with that shape is knowing which side is up or down.

I'm slightly nervous about this next bit, so I remind myself of all the reasons why it should work out just fine. She's grown to love Beelzebub as much as I do, and the furry traitor probably loves her more than he does me. More to the point, he's finished his doggy school education, so he doesn't make as many messes as he did when she first met him—and I've been following his example by keeping my place neat and organized... with prime numbers whenever possible, of course.

Oh, and it goes without saying that we love each other, and she's been spending most of her time at my place without complaint. Still, I can't take her for granted. For all I know, she might not be interested in my proposal.

"What is this?" She holds a metal key in one of her delicate hands and a plastic card in the other.

Must not think about those hands on Prime— makes it hard to walk. I mean, *difficult* to walk.

She looks at me expectantly.

I point at the metal key. "That's for the door to

our room in the Castle. And *that*"—I point at the plastic card—"is the second surprise." I wait a moment to build up the drama—another tip from her twin. "That's a key to my apartment. Your permanent key."

Her eyes widen.

I give her my best butlery bow, then ask in the most formal manner possible, "Lady Hyman, would you do me the honor of moving in with me?"

With a squeal, she tackle-hugs me—a great sign, as is the passionate, Prime-engorging kiss that follows.

"Yes," she says when we finally pull apart. "It would be my pleasure to move in with you, Lord Chortsky."

It would be unseemly to pump my fist in the air in this outfit, so I settle for another kiss.

Now that this is out of the way, I'm much more hopeful about the success of my next proposal. The challenge there will be to somehow top today's surprise.

Maybe I'll discover a new prime number for her?

Or buy some prime real estate and build a replica of this castle?

No, that's not good enough. But I'll figure it out when the time comes. For now, all I need to know is that she's my future—and that means the future will be everything I want.

Sneak Peeks

Thank you for reading *Hard Byte*! If you enjoyed Holly and Alex's story, please consider leaving a review.

Can't get enough of the Chortsky family? Read Vlad's story in *Hard Code*, and Bella's story in *Hard Ware*! Find both at www.mishabell.com.

Misha Bell is a collaboration between husband-and-wife writing team, Dima Zales and Anna Zaires. When they're not making you bust a gut as Misha, Dima writes sci-fi and fantasy, and Anna writes dark and contemporary romance. Check out *Wall Street Titan* by Anna Zaires for more steamy billionaire hotness!

Turn the page to read previews of *Hard Code* and *Wall Street Titan*!

Excerpt from Hard Code by Misha Bell

My new assignment at work: test out toys. Yup, that kind.

Well, technically, it's to test the app that controls the toys remotely.

One problem? The showgirl who's supposed to test the hardware (as in, the actual toys) joins a nunnery.

Another problem? This project is important to my Russian boss, the broody, mouthwateringly sexy Vlad, a.k.a. The Impaler.

There's only one solution: test both the software and the hardware myself... with his help.

NOTE: This is a standalone, raunchy, slow-burn romantic comedy featuring a quirky, nerdy heroine, her hot, mysterious

Russian boss, and two guinea pigs who may or may not be into each other. If any of the above is not your cup of tea, run far, far away. Otherwise, buckle in for a snort-water-up-the-nose-funny, feel-good ride.

———

"Me?" Eyes widening, he steps back.

I'm committed now, so I barrel ahead. "It makes sense. I presume you trust yourself not to toss me into the Harbor. The privacy of the project isn't compromised. And, well"—I blush horribly—"you have the right parts for it."

Unbidden, my eyes drop to said parts, then I quickly look up.

The elevator doors open.

"Let's continue this in the car," he says, his expression turning unreadable.

Crap, crap, crap. Is he hating the idea? Hating me for even suggesting it? Ugh, how awkward is it going to be if he says no?

Am I about to get fired for coming on to my boss's boss?

We get into the limo again, sitting opposite each other this time.

He makes the partition go up. "Just to clarify: I test the male batch, acting as both giver and receiver, right? I actually already tested one of the pieces on myself after I wrote the app, so I could in theory do the same with the rest of them."

Yes! He's actually considering it. I want to jump up and down, even as the blush that had slightly receded on the walk from the elevator returns in all its glory. "That wouldn't be good end-to-end testing, and you know it. You wrote the code; that makes you biased."

His nostrils flare. "Then how?"

Even my feet are blushing at this point. "You just act as the receiver. I act as the giver, and record the testing data. It's the proper way these things are done."

His eyebrows lift. "That's stretching the definition of the word 'proper' way outside its comfort zone."

"Look." I try to mime his accent as best I can. "If you want to quit, I understand."

A slow, sensuous smile curves his lips. "I don't shy away from a challenge."

Can my panties really melt, or is that just a saying?

———

Go to www.mishabell.com to order your copy of *Hard Code* today!

Excerpt from Wall Street Titan

A billionaire who wants a perfect wife...

At thirty-five, Marcus Carelli has it all: wealth, power, and the kind of looks that leave women breathless. A self-made billionaire, he heads one of the largest hedge funds on Wall Street and can take down major corporations with a single word. The only thing he's missing? A wife who'd be as big of an achievement as the billions in his bank account.

A cat lady who needs a date...

Twenty-six-year-old bookstore clerk Emma Walsh has it on good authority that she's a cat lady. She doesn't necessarily agree with that assessment, but it's hard to argue with the facts. Raggedy clothes covered with cat hair? Check. Last professional haircut? Over a year ago. Oh, and three cats in a tiny Brooklyn studio? Yep, she's got those.

And yes, fine, she hasn't had a date since... well, she can't recall. But that part is fixable. Isn't that what the dating sites are for?

A case of mistaken identity...

One high-end matchmaker, one dating app, one mix-up that changes everything... Opposites may attract, but can this last?

———

I'm all but bouncing with excitement as I approach Sweet Rush Café, where I'm supposed to meet Mark for dinner. This is the craziest thing I've done in a while. Between my evening shift at the bookstore and his class schedule, we haven't had a chance to do more than exchange a few text messages, so all I have to go on are those couple of blurry pictures. Still, I have a good feeling about this.

I feel like Mark and I might really connect.

I'm a few minutes early, so I stop by the door and take a moment to brush cat hair off my woolen coat. The coat is beige, which is better than black, but white hair is visible on anything that's not pure white. I figure Mark won't mind too much—he knows how much Persians shed—but I still want to look presentable for our first date. It took me about an hour, but I got my curls to semi-behave, and I'm even wearing a little makeup—something that happens with the frequency of a tsunami in a lake.

Taking a deep breath, I enter the café and look around to see if Mark might already be there.

The place is small and cozy, with booth-style seats arranged in a semicircle around a coffee bar. The smell of roasted coffee beans and baked goods is mouthwatering, making my stomach rumble with hunger. I was planning to stick to coffee only, but I decide to get a croissant too; my budget should stretch to that.

Only a few of the booths are occupied, likely because it's a Tuesday. I scan them, looking for anyone who could be Mark, and notice a man sitting by himself at the farthest table. He's facing away from me, so all I can see is the back of his head, but his hair is short and dark brown.

It could be him.

Gathering my courage, I approach the booth. "Excuse me," I say. "Are you Mark?"

The man turns to face me, and my pulse shoots into the stratosphere.

The person in front of me is nothing like the pictures on the app. His hair is brown, and his eyes are blue, but that's the only similarity. There's nothing rounded and shy about the man's hard features. From the steely jaw to the hawk-like nose, his face is boldly masculine, stamped with a self-assurance that borders on arrogance. A hint of five o'clock shadow darkens his lean cheeks, making his high cheekbones stand out even more, and his eyebrows are thick dark slashes above his piercingly pale eyes. Even sitting behind the table, he looks tall and powerfully built. His shoulders are a mile wide in his sharply tailored suit, and his hands are twice the size of my own.

There's no way this is Mark from the app, unless he's put in some serious gym time since those pictures were taken. Is it possible? Could a person change so much? He didn't indicate his height in the profile, but I'd assumed the omission meant he was vertically challenged, like me.

The man I'm looking at is not challenged in any way, and he's certainly not wearing glasses.

"I'm… I'm Emma," I stutter as the man continues staring at me, his face hard and inscrutable. I'm almost certain I have the wrong guy, but I still force myself to ask, "Are you Mark, by any chance?"

"I prefer to be called Marcus," he shocks me by answering. His voice is a deep masculine rumble that tugs at something primitively female inside me. My heart beats even faster, and my palms begin to sweat as he rises to his feet and says bluntly, "You're not what I expected."

"Me?" *What the hell?* A surge of anger crowds out all other emotions as I gape at the rude giant in front of me. The asshole is so tall I have to crane my neck to look up at him. "What about you? You look nothing like your pictures!"

"I guess we've both been misled," he says, his jaw tight. Before I can respond, he gestures toward the booth. "You might as well sit down and have a meal with me, Emmeline. I didn't come all the way here for nothing."

"It's *Emma*," I correct, fuming. "And no, thank you. I'll just be on my way."

His nostrils flare, and he steps to the right to block my path. "Sit down, *Emma*." He makes my name sound like an insult. "I'll have a talk with Victoria, but for now, I don't see why we can't share a meal like two civilized adults."

The tips of my ears burn with fury, but I slide into the booth rather than make a scene. My grandmother instilled politeness in me from an early age, and even as an adult living on my own, I find it hard to go against her teachings.

She wouldn't approve of me kneeing this jerk in the balls and telling him to fuck off.

"Thank you," he says, sliding into the seat across from me. His eyes glint icy blue as he picks up the menu. "That wasn't so hard, was it?"

"I don't know, *Marcus*," I say, putting special emphasis on the formal name. "I've only been around you for two minutes, and I'm already feeling homicidal." I deliver the insult with a ladylike, Grandma-approved smile, and dumping my purse in the corner of my booth seat, I pick up the menu without bothering to take off my coat.

The sooner we eat, the sooner I can get out of here.

A deep chuckle startles me into looking up. To my shock, the jerk is grinning, his teeth flashing white in his lightly bronzed face. No freckles for him, I note with jealousy; his skin is perfectly even-toned, without so much as an extra mole on his cheek. He's not classically handsome—his features are too bold to be described that way—but he's shockingly good-looking, in a potent, purely masculine way.

To my dismay, a curl of heat licks at my core, making my inner muscles clench.

No. No way. This asshole is *not* turning me on. I can barely stand to sit across the table from him.

Gritting my teeth, I look down at my menu, noting with relief that the prices in this place are actually reasonable. I always insist on paying for my own food on dates, and now that I've met Mark—excuse me, *Marcus*—I wouldn't put it past him to drag me to some ritzy place where a glass of tap water costs more than a shot of Patrón. How could I have been so wrong about the guy? Clearly, he'd lied about working in a bookstore and being a student. To what end, I don't know, but everything about the man in front of me screams wealth and power. His pinstriped suit hugs his broad-shouldered frame like it was tailor-made for him, his blue shirt is crisply starched, and I'm pretty sure his subtly checkered tie is some designer brand that makes Chanel seem like a Walmart label.

As all of these details register, a new suspicion occurs to me. Could someone be playing a joke on me? Kendall, perhaps? Or Janie? They both know my taste in guys. Maybe one of them decided to lure me on a date this way—though why they'd set me up with *him*, and he'd agree to it, is a huge mystery.

Frowning, I look up from the menu and study the man in front of me. He's stopped grinning and is perusing the menu, his forehead creased in a frown that makes him look older than the twenty-seven years listed on his profile.

That part must've also been a lie.

My anger intensifies. "So, *Marcus*, why did you write to me?" Dropping the menu on the table, I glare at him. "Do you even own cats?"

He looks up, his frown deepening. "Cats? No, of course not."

The derision in his tone makes me want to forget all about Grandma's disapproval and slap him straight across his lean, hard face. "Is this some kind of a prank for you? Who put you up to this?"

"Excuse me?" His thick eyebrows rise in an arrogant arch.

"Oh, stop playing innocent. You lied in your message to me, and you have the gall to say *I'm* not what you expected?" I can practically feel the steam coming out of my ears. "*You* messaged *me*, and I was entirely truthful on my profile. How old are you? Thirty-two? Thirty-three?"

"I'm thirty-five," he says slowly, his frown returning. "Emma, what are you talking—"

"That's it." Grabbing my purse by one strap, I slide out of the booth and jump to my feet. Grandma's teachings or not, I'm not going to have a meal with a jerk who's admitted to deceiving me. I have no idea what would make a guy like that want to toy with me, but I'm not going to be the butt of some joke.

"Enjoy your meal," I snarl, spinning around, and stride to the exit before he can block my way again.

I'm in such a rush to leave I almost knock over a tall, slender brunette approaching the café and the short, pudgy guy following her.

———

Go to www.annazaires.com to order your copy of *Wall Street Titan* today!

About the Author

I love writing humor (often the inappropriate kind), happy endings (both kinds), and characters quirky enough to be called oddballs (because… balls). If you love your romance heavy on the comedy and feel-good vibes, visit www.mishabell.com and sign up for my newsletter.